PENNIE$

DOLLAR SERIE$

by

New York Times Bestseller
Pepper Winters

Pennies (Dollar Series #1)
Copyright © 2016 PEPPER WINTERS
Published by Pepper Winters

Published: Pepper Winters 2016: **pepperwinters@gmail.com**
Cover Design: by Kellie at Book Cover by Design
Editing by: Editing 4 Indies (Jenny Sims)

OTHER WORK BY PEPPER WINTERS

Pepper Winters is a multiple New York Times, Wall Street Journal, and USA Today International Bestseller.

Her Dark Romance books include:

New York Times Bestseller 'Monsters in the Dark' Trilogy

"Voted Best Dark Romance, Best Dark Hero, #1 Erotic Romance"

Tears of Tess (Monsters in the Dark #1)
Quintessentially Q (Monsters in the Dark #2)
Twisted Together (Monsters in the Dark #3)
Je Suis a Toi (Monsters in the Dark #4)

Multiple New York Times Bestseller 'Indebted' Series
"Voted Vintagely Dark & Delicious. A true twist on Romeo & Juliet"

Debt Inheritance (Indebted #1)
First Debt (Indebted Series #2)
Second Debt (Indebted Series #3)
Third Debt (Indebted Series #4)
Fourth Debt (Indebted Series #5)
Final Debt (Indebted Series #6)
Indebted Epilogue (Indebted Series #7)

Grey Romance books include:
USA Today Bestseller Destroyed
"Voted Best Tear-Jerker, #1 Romantic Suspense"

Survival Contemporary Romance include:
USA Today Bestseller Unseen Messages
"Voted Best Epic Survival Romance 2016, Castaway meets The Notebook"

Multiple USA Today Bestseller 'Motorcycle Duology' include:
"Sinful & Suspenseful, an Amnesia Tale full of Alphas and Heart"
Ruin & Rule (Pure Corruption #1)
Sin & Suffer (Pure Corruption #2)

AUDIO LOVERS
Tears of Tess / Quintessentially Q / Ruin & Rule / Sin & Suffer / Debt Inheritance / First Debt / Second Debt are available now on iTunes, Amazon & Audible.

Upcoming releases are:

Pre-order DOLLAR SERIES on All Platforms

2016: Dollars
2016: Hundreds
2016: Thousands
2017: Millions
TBA: The Argument
TBA: Indebted Beginnings (Indebted Series Prequel)

Thank you to those who started this journey with me, for every review, every message, every glimpse into your soul. It won't make a difference if this is my tenth book or my hundredth, I will still love every reader, every smile, and value every wonderful thing that has come into my life because of writing.

WORD OF WARNING

Pennies (Dollars #1) is a DARK ROMANCE. This means there will be hard to read scenes, graphic language, and sexual content (both implied and explicitly written). Please do not read if falling in love with a man who dresses in monster robes rather than knightly armour offends you. This is *not* a fairy-tale. This is a black abyss that must be climbed blind before deserving the light. Along with literary darkness, this is book one of a five book series. Each subsequent novel will be released every few months (so your fingernails don't tire holding onto the cliff-hanger), and each is full-length. Please also remember not all answers are given and not every character is as they seem. There are beasts adorned in angel clothing and angels hiding in beast's fur.

Remember that.

You have been warned.

Don't say you weren't told.

Read at your own peril.

Fall in love with Elder Prest at your own risk.

Are you ready?

You sure?

You really, *really* sure?

Okay then…enter the world of pennies and dollars.

FREEDOM.

Such a modest word.

It carried very little importance for those who had it. But for those who didn't, it was the most precious, prized, and promised hope of all.

I supposed I was lucky to know what freedom felt like.

For eighteen years, I'd been free. Free to learn what I wanted, befriend who I liked, and flirt with boys who passed my rigorous criteria.

I was a simple girl with ideals and dreams, encouraged by society to believe nothing could hurt me, that I should strive for an excellent career, and no one could stop me. Rules would keep me safe, police would keep the monsters away, and I could remain innocent and naïve to the darkness of the world.

Freedom.

I had it.

But then, I lost it.

Murdered, resuscitated, and sold.

I lost my freedom for so many years.

Until the day *he* entered my cage.

Him, with the black eyes and blacker soul.

The man who challenged my owner.

And set my imprisonment on an entirely different path.

Tasmin

DEAR DIARY,

No, that didn't sound right. Far too light-hearted for my tale.

Dear Universe,

Scratch that. Too grandiose.

To The Person Reading This.

Too vague.

To The Person I Wish Would Help Me.

That would get me in trouble. And I refused to sound weak. Not if these words were the only thing a stranger would remember me by.

To...

Tapping the broken pencil against my temple, I did my best to focus. For weeks, I'd been confined like a zoo animal being acclimatised to its new cage. I'd been fed, washed, and given medical attention from my rough arrival. I had a bed with sheets, a flushing toilet, and shampoo in the shower. I had the basics that all human and nonhuman life required.

But I wasn't living.

I was dying.

They just couldn't see it.

Wait...I know.

Inspiration struck as I came up with the perfect name to address this sad letter to. The title was the only right in this wrong, wrong new world.

To No One.

The moment I pressed those three words onto my parchment, I couldn't stop the memories unfolding. My left hand shook as I kept the toilet tissue flat while my right flew, slowly transcribing my past.

I WAS EIGHTEEN when I died.

I remember that day better than any other in my short life. And I know you're rolling your eyes, saying it only happened three weeks ago, but believe me, I will never forget it. I know some people say certain events imprint on their psyche forever, and up until now, I haven't had anything stick in such a way. You see, No One, I guess you could've called me a brat. Some might even say I deserve this. No, that's a lie. No one would wish this on their worst enemy. But the fact remains, only you know I'm not dead. I'm alive and in this cell about to be sold. I've been hurt, touched, violated in every sense but rape, and stripped of everything I used to be.

But to my mother? I'm dead. I died. Who knows if she'll ever truly find out what happened to me.

The scribbling of my pencil stopped. I sucked in a ragged breath, trembling hard as I relived what I'd been through.

My will to stay breathing had vanished. It'd taken them a

while to break me, but they had. And now that they'd achieved their goal, I was nothing more than cargo waiting for the transaction to line their pockets.

For days, all I'd had for entertainment were my chaotic thoughts, awful memories, and overwhelming panic of what lay ahead. But that was before I found the chewed up, snapped in half pencil beneath the bed.

The find had been better than food or freedom; better because my traffickers minutely controlled both those things. I had no power to sway the regimented arrival of breakfast and dinner nor the ability to halt the fact I was being sold like meat to the highest bidder.

I had no control over being alone in a tiny room that had once been a hotel suite before its premises were bought for more unsavoury stays. The towels were threadbare with the sigil of some decade-ago establishment, and the carpet swirled with golds and bronze, hinting the décor hadn't been updated since the seventies.

Was that how long the pencil had lurked beneath my bed? Were the bite marks on the wood given by a rowdy toddler waiting for its parents to stop fussing so they could explore a new city? Or had a maid lost it while tucking starched white sheets with military precision?

I'd never know.

But I liked to make up fantasies because I had nothing else to do. I spent my achingly boring days going over every nook and cranny of my jail. They'd broken my spirit, washed away my fight, but they couldn't stop the determined urge inside me. The instinct everyone had—or at least, I *thought* everyone had.

I'd been alone for so long now I didn't know what the other girls processed with me would do. Did they lie star-spread on the bed and wait for their future? Did they huddle in the corner and beg for their fathers to stop this nightmare? Or did they accept, because it was easier to accept than to fight?

Me? I ran my rubbed-raw fingertips over every wall, every crack, every painted and locked window frame. I crawled on my hands and knees, searching for something to help me. And by helping me, I didn't know if I meant as a weapon to fight my way out or something to end my struggle before it truly began.

It'd taken me days to go over every square inch. But all I'd found was this half-mangled pencil. A gift. A treasure. The nub was almost down to the wood, and I wouldn't have long before I had to find a way to sharpen my precious possession, but I'd worry about that another day. Just like I'd become a master at shoving aside my worries about everything else.

The one thing I didn't find was any paper. Not in the drawers of the weathered desk or in the cupboard beneath the non-functioning television. The only apparatus I could write on was toilet paper, and the pencil wasn't too keen on that idea, tearing the soft tissue rather than imprinting its silvery lines.

Nevertheless, I was determined to leave some sort of note behind. Some piece of me that these bastards hadn't taken and never would.

Taking another deep breath, I shoved aside my current conditions and clutched the pencil harder. Glancing at the door to make sure I was alone, I spread out my square of toilet tissue, making it tight and writable, and continued with my note.

I wish I could say a monster killed me. That a terrible accident caused this. And I can say that…to a degree.

However, the real reason I'm dead and a new toy about to be sold is mainly because of my upbringing.

That poise and confidence my mother drilled into me? It didn't grant me in good stead for a profitable career or handsome husband. It pissed people off. I came across as stuck-up, a know-it-all, and vain.

It made me a target.

I don't know if anyone will ever see this but you, No One, but if they do, I hope they forget what I'm about to admit. I'm an only daughter to a single parent. I love my mother. I do.

But if I ever survive what's about to happen to me, and by some miracle, I find freedom again, I'll keep this next part to myself when I recount my time in purgatory.

I love my mother, but I hate her.
I miss my mother, but I never want to see her again.
I obeyed my mother, but I want to curse her for eternity.
She's the only one I can blame.
The one responsible for me becoming nothing more than a whore.

Tasmin

TWO DAYS passed.

In the world I'd been stolen from, two days was nothing. Two alarm clocks, two lessons at university, two evenings of talking on the phone to my friends, and two nights of wonderfully protected sleep where I stupidly believed no one could harm me.

In this new world?

Two days was enough for me to scratch at non-existent itches just to feel something. Two days meant I wore down my pencil then slowly picked at the wood to reveal more lead so I had something to occupy my time.

Two days meant I continued writing my toilet paper novel, all the while not knowing that at the end of forty-eight hours, my brief stay in limbo was over.

My processing was over.

My sale date complete.

They came for me at dinnertime. Instead of the usual bland rice and chicken or watery stew shoved through the hole in the wall, the door opened.

The door *opened*!

For the first time in weeks.

I'd been so alone with only grimy mirrors reflecting my slowly sallowing complexion for company that the visit clutched my heart. When I'd first been taken, I'd been curvy with adolescent softness, perky breasts, and rounded tummy. My brown hair curled and dyed a rich chocolate thanks to an appointment with my personal groomer at my mother's demands to look my best for her charity function.

The same function I'd been stolen from.

Before, my thoughts had been superficial, wondering how to lose my puppy fat and apply my makeup like models on YouTube. Despite my prissy appearance, I was smart and had just enrolled at a prestigious university to study psychology—just like my mother wanted. Following in her footsteps like she'd arranged all my life.

Now, my appearance and thoughts were of an entirely different girl. No longer a teenager, but a woman. My hair had faded back to its normal dark treacle brown. My frame had lost its curves thanks to the low-calorie infrequent menu I enjoyed.

I supposed I would've been happy if I still had my freedom. I got what I wanted. I was a little skinnier and no longer cared about hair dyes and fashion. Instead, I hated my transformation because it added another chain to the proverbial collar webbing around my throat.

"Come." The man clicked his fingers.

Seeing another human ought to have filled me with some sort of relief. Something intrinsic inside me needed company—even if that company was my doom. But I couldn't see his eyes or mouth or nose. He was a phantom, a caricature, hidden behind the Venetian face mask of a black and white joker with tears dotting his cheek.

Were the tears for me? Or just a mockery?

I took a step toward him, hating the obedient cower they'd instilled in me the first few days of my imprisonment. The bruises had faded, but the lessons had not.

But then, I stopped, looking back at the toilet tissue sheets of letters.

Letters telling my story.

A story that would forever change the moment I left this

room.

I had nothing of value anymore. The rags I wore from so many previous trafficked women weren't mine. The pillows I cried myself to sleep on weren't mine. My life wasn't even mine anymore. The desire to keep my scribbled thoughts was nonsensical, but I refused to leave yet another piece of me behind.

If I must face this new trial, I would do it with my past fisted in my palm like a talisman reminding me if I could breathe it, I could write it, and when I wrote it, I would find freedom from it.

"Now, girl!" The man stalked into the room, his mountainous posture ready to hurt.

Before he could grab me, I scurried to the desk and scooped up the flimsy pieces of my life. Clutching them tight, I ducked around his large girth and vanished out the door.

Out the door!

I'm out of the room.

The familiarity of my imprinted space was gone as I padded barefoot down the corridor graced with the same gold and bronze carpet. The heavy footfalls of my captor thundered behind me.

He didn't grab me or force me to slow. He knew as well as I did there was no escape. I'd been blindfolded when I'd been driven here, but they'd let me have my sight back once inside the building.

As we moved past locked rooms like any normal hotel, I forced myself to stand taller and brace myself for whatever came next.

You can get through this.

They wanted me alive, not dead.

For some reason, that thought didn't give the intended comfort…if anything, it made my fear escalate.

"Get in the elevator. We're going down." The man's voice boomed in the claustrophobic space.

Turning left, I entered the open foyer where four silver

doors sat two by two. I cursed the slight shake in my hand as I pressed the button summoning one of them to open.

The chime sounded immediately, the elevator groaning wide, welcoming me into a dingy mirrored box.

I couldn't look at my reflection as I stepped inside and turned to face the closing exit. My legs peeked beneath the faded yellow shorts I'd been given. My skinny arms held the last remnants of my juvenile age in the baggy moth-eaten grey t-shirt. I didn't care to look at myself because the outward body didn't portray the inward soul.

Yes, I looked broken.

Yes, I obeyed implicitly.

But inside, I'd somehow glued the parts they'd shattered into something I treasured. I was stronger now than when I'd first arrived. I was no longer the wailing girl who'd been stripped, rough-washed with angry paws, and catalogued with other women. I kept my screams inside because there, no one could hear me.

No one could use them against me. Silence was a weapon I could wield better than panic. And if it meant I never uttered another word until I found freedom, then so be it.

The man crowded beside me, pressing level four.

Judging from the numbers on the hotel room doors we'd passed, I deduced they'd stored me on level twelve. How many girls were locked behind those barricades? How many floors held prisoners just waiting to be sold?

The descent swooped a little too fast, gravity clutching my tummy. I held my breath as the elevator opened again, revealing an identical landing platform.

The man nudged me between my shoulder blades.

I shot forward. No stumbling. No begging. Not one question or plea.

There was no point.

I rubbed my cheek where I'd been punched within hours of my arrival all those weeks ago. I'd demanded all sorts of things. I'd promised them pain once my mother found them.

I'd believed I was a princess with a regiment of knights who would chase after me.

I'd learned quickly with their boots in my stomach and fists in my face that everything I trusted was a lie.

"Down here." The man pointed at the left corridor.

Padding in the chosen direction, I shivered as the softness of the carpet did its best to comfort me. The hotel was the perfect backdrop of nothingness. The temperature hovered at comfortable, so I never shivered or sweated. The lights shone an even illumination, so I never squinted or strained. Every sense controlled until I forgot what the wind felt like on my skin and the sun's rays upon my face.

Would I be allowed outside now?

Where is he taking me?

The man paced in front of me, pushing open a door to the old gym. The hotel must've been a four-star establishment, once upon a time, before it'd been bought and shot to ruin.

Entering the female changing room, where ivory tiles had turned grimy and ancient hairdryers hung like gas masks, I stopped for further instruction. Hanging on the wall was a garment bag, zipped but translucent, showing a white dress. Even from here, the pearled bodice and diamante scarf draped on the hanger spoke of finery not welcome in such a downtrodden place.

The man behind his Venetian mask muttered, "Shower, do your hair, and get dressed. I'll collect you in one hour."

One hour of primping?

For what?

He leaned in close, smelling of fried food and beer. "Don't get any thoughts of running." Cocking his head, he stepped back as two other girls entered the space. "Ah, company."

The recent arrivals' shepherd pointed at matching garment bags on the opposite wall. Their dresses were black and grey. "Get ready, both of you."

Just like every facet of sensation was stolen by regimented air, heat, and approved stimuli, so too were our wardrobes.

White, black, and grey. Monotones with no spectrum of colour.

My handler nodded at his lion-masked colleague. "You stand guard. I'll tell the boss we're almost ready."

The girls glanced at me. I glanced at them. We all glanced at the men who held our fate in their dirty clutches. The urge to ask what would happen burned my tongue. But I didn't. Not because I daren't or lacked the courage, but because I already knew the answer: the cold laughter, the mocking undertones, and the cryptic reply meant to terrify rather than console.

No, I wouldn't ask.

But my conclusion didn't reach the girl closest to me wearing a tatty pink sun-dress with tangled blonde hair. "Why are you doing this? What's going to happen to us?"

Venetian Mask looked at Lion. Together, they advanced on her, backing her against the tiled wall. They let the force of their aura batter her rather than physically maul, leaving me to think they'd hurt us to control us at the beginning, but now, we were worth more unmarred.

After all, what good was merchandise if it was ugly and bruised?

"I told you already. You're going to be sold, pretty angel." Lion stroked her cheek. "You're going to be chosen and transacted, and when that sweet, sweet money lands in our hands, you'll be gone. Bye-bye. No longer our concern."

The other girl with lacklustre red hair tripped backward, her mouth parting in a silent wail.

As if they didn't know? As if they'd spent the same amount of time as I had locked and alone and didn't see something like this coming. Perhaps, I'd read too many dark books or watched too many crime shows on television. Either way, I wasn't stupid, and I definitely wasn't naïve anymore.

Just like I would never go to university to finish my psychology degree, these girls would never return to their lives. Unlike me, who blamed her mother for her mess, they might blame a bad boyfriend or idiotic decision of drinking too much and trusting the wrong person.

No matter what led us here, we were on the same journey. Just with different destinations, determined by whoever bought us.

Turning away from the tears and laughing captors, I stripped from my shorts and t-shirt, placed my precious toilet paper words on the counter, and walked straight into a shower. There were no blinds or screens. My nakedness remained on display as I turned on body temperature water and squirted unscented shampoo into my hair.

Being nude in front of strangers would've petrified me a month ago.

Now, I no longer put stock in such things because I had no control over who looked or touched or ultimately raped and destroyed.

Don't think about that.

Gritting my teeth, I lathered shampoo into bubbles. No aroma or comfort came from the soap. I missed my watermelon body scrub and raspberry lip-gloss. I hankered for fizzy drinks and a soft fleece blanket after a long day of studying.

What I wouldn't give to smell again. Hear again. *Feel* again.

While the other girls mourned their lives and feared their future, I welcomed relief. I was glad this stage was over. Another hour in that room would've driven me completely mad. At least this way, I had something to do, someone to challenge, someplace else to go.

And who knows, maybe I'll find a way to escape.

The noise of the shower as I held my head under its stream blocked all sounds. I kept my eyes closed while lathering my hair and didn't turn until I'd washed, used the razor provided to shave, and wrapped yet another threadbare towel around myself.

The men and their masks had gone, and the women had copied me, each taking a stall and dutifully but tearfully washing.

This wasn't a simple cleansing or preparation.

This was a baptism into Hell.

TO NO ONE,

My mother always told me that bullies are people, too.

She warned me never to judge first impressions or be superficial like others. She said it wasn't my place to critique—not knowing if they were hurting or living a terrible life while picking on others.

Well, I would disagree based on my current predicament, but then again, these men aren't bullies, they're monsters. So I guess my mother's rule is safe.

Don't judge. Listen.

She promised me it would keep me in good stead, and I'd make friends, not enemies. What she didn't tell me was nobody liked to be watched like a specimen, and everyone hated a compassionate know-it-all.

And that was why I was targeted.

Or at least…I believe it was.

You see, No One, it all started as a normal evening. I dressed in my bedroom opposite my mother's. I slipped into the low heels she'd chosen, into the off-the-shoulder gown she'd selected, and hopped into the taxi she'd arranged.

I was thankful to be included because normally I wasn't.

I was proud of my mother. Respectful, wary…but not adoring. She loved me but didn't have time for silly children, even if that silly child was her own. She made sure I was old and wise so I could fend for myself while she dealt with adult bullies on a daily basis. She sold her services to the State to ease the burdens of psychopaths and paedophiles.

She treated us all like guinea pigs, wanting into our minds—asking why I did something instead of reprimanding. Demanding articulated words rather than messy displays of emotion.

My friends called me crazy for trusting my mother's guidance. But I was a good girl, a kind daughter, a child guided by a woman who earned her living by lifting the veil in which humans hide. She made me believe I had the same magic, and it was my duty to help those without such a gift.

She made me what I was.

I suppose I have to be grateful for that because, without her strict upbringing, I would be like the girls snivelling even now in the corner while we wait to be collected for whatever comes next. I'm thankful to the woman who birthed me for giving me these life skills, but it doesn't mean I'll ever forgive her.

From the hours of 9:00 p.m. to midnight, I was safe. I mingled with suits and entertained in whispers, representing my mother and her business with the poise she demanded.

Only, around that witching hour when rules relax and tiredness creeps beneath fun obscurity, I met a man. While my mother intoxicated benefactors with her wit and hard-edged charm, earning generous donations for her charity for the mental well-being of people on death row (why anyone would want to donate, I had no idea), a mystery man called Mr. Kewet flirted with me.

He laughed at my teenage jokes. He indulged my childish whims. And I fell for every goddamn trick in his dastardly arsenal.

While others skirted this man, instinctually noticing something evil, I made it my mission to make him feel welcome. I didn't let the voice inside my head warn me away; instead, I believed in the firm and fast rule of 'Don't judge. Listen.'

My mother taught me wrong.

She made me sympathise rather than fear.

She made me believe in good rather than recognise the bad.

I danced with my murderer.

I smiled when he corralled me outside.

I tried to soothe while he threatened.

And when his hands went around my throat and strangled me, I still believed I could redeem him.

He killed me on the balcony of the ballroom only metres away from my mother.

And the entire time he did it, I still thought he was the one who needed saving, not me.

"Time's up. You'd better be ready to go."

My pencil stopped hacking at my toilet vellum. I needed to write what happened after I fell unconscious into Mr. Kewet's killer embrace. How he'd brought me back to life in a world I no longer recognised. How everything I'd known and everything that'd made sense was suddenly scrambled and utterly foreign.

But Venetian Mask had returned, crossing his arms over his huge untoned bulk. Even his voice was nondescript with no accent or hint. Without facial features or racial clues, I had no idea where I'd been transported and what country I would belong.

Scrunching up my handful of pencil-scribbled paragraphs, I stuffed the tissue down my pearl-beaded bodice. My fingers trailed up the decorative dress to whisper over my throat. Even now, the shadows of finger-bruises marked me. Being strangled was a painful death. And one that left remnants in both aches and contusions, always there to remind when glimpsed in a mirror.

He'd killed me. I hadn't been able to stop him.

So why couldn't he have left me dead?

Why couldn't this have been over rather than just beginning?

Because you're worth far more alive.

I straightened my back.

I'd blow-dried my hair and applied the mascara and lipstick provided. I didn't know why I bothered. However, prettiness might be a curse that could grant me a kinder fate. In my unsettling rationale, I figured the more someone paid for me, the better my overall treatment might be.

Unless that backfires and a psychotic billionaire buys me for marksman practice.

My throat closed as my heart did its best to find a stepladder and climb its way out of my chest. I swallowed it down again. As much as I didn't want to face this, I needed my heart beating if I stood any chance of surviving.

Clipping over the tiles, I smoothed my white gown as if being presented to the prime minster. The quaint buttons on the back had been secured thanks to the help of the redhead. The satin kissed my body with no underwear to protect the sensitive skin of my nipples and core and whispered over the floor a millimetre from being too long. The measurements were exact, right down to the size five white heels on my feet.

I'd never been a fan of white. I much preferred to wear black—because it gave the image of authority (according to my mother)—or pastels and colours depending on my mood at class.

White was too high maintenance. It got dirty with life stains within moments of putting it on. But it also granted an innocence that I understood why my traffickers had dressed me in it. My hair seemed glossier; my green eyes bigger, my complexion prettier.

The girl gowned in black looked harsh and older while the redhead in grey seemed washed out and already begging for a grave.

If we were about to enter a wolf's den, I didn't want to smell of blood before the fight. Keeping my shoulders back, I strode past the guard and fell into step with Lion Mask.

Silently, I followed our shepherds and led the sad train of slaves down the corridor, into the elevators, and down to level two.

There, commotion welcomed with sounds of conversation, masculine laughter, and a softly played piano.

It'd been so long since I'd heard music or felt the warm buffet of bodies that I lost myself. Forgetting my need to remain aloof and untouched, I slammed to a stop. My forgetfulness earned me a swat to the side of my head as Lion Mask shoved me forward.

I stumbled for the first time since I'd answered back during the first beating I'd endured and suffered through the lesson all over again.

Eyes locked onto me from all corners of the room.

Hungry eyes.

Mad eyes.

Lust-filled, terrible eyes.

All peering from behind a treasure trove of paper mache and plaster of paris masks.

A spotlight moved from the glittering silver ball drenching the space with twinkling lights directly on us. The piano stopped playing as the two girls and I made our way to the centre of what used to be a dance floor under the guidance of Venetian and Lion.

Now, it was a market pen. Complete with podium for inspection and auctioneer with his gavel. The two girls I'd showered with sobbed quietly as they were lined up in a procession of other women. Women who'd lived in this hotel with me, but I'd never seen. Women of all ages and ethnicities, all stolen from their rightful place and treated like livestock.

My friends wouldn't really miss me because they didn't understand me. I had no boyfriend to mourn me, no father to come search for me. As far as connections and family went, I was lacking.

I supposed it made it easier for me to switch off the desire to love and be loved, knowing I would never feel such a thing again. But it also hurt more because, at least, if I'd had those things, I could say I'd lived briefly; that I hadn't taken my freedom for granted.

Now, all I would know was captivity.

As a man in a perfectly pressed tux and black executioner's mask strode around the room holding a microphone to his hidden lips, the atmosphere hushed in expectation.

"Welcome, gentlemen, to the QMB, also known as Quarterly Market of Beauties." Sweeping his hand down the line of merchandise, he said, "As you can see, we have quite a turn-out for you tonight."

One by one, he pointed at us.

We were the only ones bare faced and on display.

One by one, we shrank into ourselves.

Twelve counted before me.

I was lucky thirteen.

Or was that *unlucky* thirteen? All I needed was a black cat, a fallen down ladder, and a witch's superstition to well and truly curse me.

The man strode proudly as if he'd personally created each and every one of us. If he was in charge of stripping us of everything and rebuilding us into nothing, then perhaps he had. Maybe he *did* own us and had full right to sell something I no longer recognised.

"As usual, we have a range of beauties available for your pleasure. You've all had time to peruse their files and photos we supplied."

Wait, what photos and files?

Had our rooms had cameras? Were we secretly catalogued and investigated? My chest rose and fell, pressing against the words I'd scribbled on the stolen toilet paper. Did they know about my tentative writing? Would they take it away from me?

My questions kept me occupied while the man cut over the dance floor and grabbed the first girl in the lineup. Dragging her forward, he forced her onto the podium, holding her until she caught her balance.

The spotlight showed her every stress line, every terror, every tear. She couldn't hide anything beneath such an invasive glare. Her facial nakedness was made worse as no humanity stared back. Only animal masks and robot masks and all manner of creations.

I don't want to look like her.

I wouldn't let these assholes see my horror. If they refused to let us see them, I refused to let them see me. I didn't have feathers or diamantes to hide my true self, but I did have willpower.

It took four girls to school my features into a rigid, unfeeling shell. Another four girls for me to delete emotion from my gaze and grab what was left to stuff into a newly formed suitcase inside (or should I say soulcase) and slam the lid closed. It took the final four girls to find a way to lock that soulcase, banish all my secrets, hopes, and aspirations, and toss away the key.

My name was Tasmin Blythe, but as my turn rolled around and I was forced to stand proud and prideful on the podium, they gave me a new name. A name forever reminding me of where I came from but stripping me of everything else at the same time.

Pimlico.

After the London suburb where my mother's function was held.

No longer Tasmin. Pimlico...*Pim*.

I'm glad.

I no longer had to fake being strong and aloof; Pimlico *was* strong and aloof. Tasmin was locked deep, deep inside and forgotten as I blinked in the bright lights and heard the most damning thing of all.

"I'll pay one hundred thousand."

"I'll go two hundred."

"I'll outbid you all and double it." The room sucked in a gasp as a silhouette of a tall, slender man stepped onto the dance floor. "Four hundred thousand dollars for the girl in white."

My heart once again tried to build a parachute and escape. That was the highest bid of the evening.

It *disgusted* me.

How dare they decide my worth? What my fellow slaves were worth. No price tag existed on a human life.

My life.

I hadn't said a word since the third day of my incarceration. I hadn't answered their questions about my age or sexual history. I refused to share any number of invasive requests.

I'd taken that small power even though they no doubt knew everything they needed thanks to my driver's license and social media.

But now...here, on the eve of my sale, I had something to say.

Balling my hands, I glared at the indistinct man who wished to own me. My voice rang out, soft but pure, the only feminine sound in a nest of men.

"I bid one million. Let me buy myself, sir, and I will forget any of this ever happened."

The bought girls, already ushered and clung to by new masters, gasped. My audacity could shorten my life or prolong it. Either way, it was a gamble I willingly and knowingly chose.

I didn't have a million. My mother might if she sold our two-bedroom flat in London. But just like I pushed other worries to be solved on a later day, I pushed this one aside, too.

Money was just money.

Pennies added to dollars and dollars added to hundreds.

In the end, the prettily printed paper was worthless because inflation stole its numerical profit, unable to keep those who owned it happy.

My life, on the other hand, would increase in value, growing wiser and richer in experience the longer I survived. I was an investment, not a liability. And I would invest everything I had into giving myself a future.

The man stepped forward, cutting through the glare so his silhouette turned into physical mass. His dirty blond hair was the only thing visible behind the princely mask of some English Lord. "You're bidding on yourself?" His voice sounded foreign, but I couldn't place the accent. Mediterranean, perhaps?

Tipping my chin, the podium put me higher than him as I

looked down as if he were my subject and I was his queen.

I would rule him. I would never bow.

"That is correct. I am too expensive for you. One million pounds, not dollars. I bid well over your pathetic amount."

The auctioneer fumbled, clearly uncertain what to do with this change of events. His business was in the money-making game. Selling women was high profit, but if he could earn more by selling me to myself, what did he care if certain corporate rules were broken?

He got paid either way.

Ignoring the man in his English Lord mask, I faced the executioner, begging his gavel to fall on my offer. "One million, sir, and I walk away and never mention this again."

What about the other girls?

My mother would curse me for the shame and guilt I suffered at the thought of leaving the sold women. But she'd also be proud because I'd chosen a path with decisiveness and conviction. Something she said I'd always lacked.

Happy now, Mother?

The room erupted in murmurs of deliberation while I stood in the sea of ebbing voices.

For a moment, I stupidly believed I'd won. That I'd played my hand at the perfect time and earned my freedom. But I hadn't learned my final lesson.

Pride goeth before the fall.

And I was about to plummet.

"I see your offer and raise you," Lord Mask murmured. "One million, five hundred thousand *pounds*, not dollars. What say you?"

Before I could reply—before I could increase my bid and change my circumstances, the dreaded gavel fell.

"Sold!" the auctioneer yelled. "To Mr. Lord for one million, five hundred thousand pounds."

* * * * *

To No One,

That was the last time I spoke. The last time I lost. The last time I knew what it was like not to live every day in pain.

From that day onward, I was Pimlico the Mute, the Voiceless Woman in White.

No matter what that man did to me, I didn't break.

No matter the beating he gave or the sexual punishment he delivered, I remained speechless and strong.

I'd like to say I found a way to escape. That I ran. That I'm writing this to you from a quaint coffee shop in London with a handsome boyfriend on my left and a best friend on my right.

But I've never been good at lying.

This toilet paper novel was never going to be fiction.

This is my autobiography so that one day, when my worth has been used, and every penny my master paid for me has been cashed, someone might recall the wordless slave who endured so much.

Maybe then, I'll be free.

Pimlico

INSTEAD OF COUNTING what I'd lost and would never see again, I preferred to count what I *did* have.

It kept me occupied as the transaction for my sale went through, the room emptied as successful bidders took their new possessions home, and my arms wrenched behind me for coarse twine to wrap around my wrists like some sort of twisted wedding ring.

I didn't say a word as a blindfold settled over my eyes with a blackening shroud nor did I make a peep as dominating hands guided me from the warmth and piano-note filled ballroom, down corridors I couldn't see, and through a foyer I hadn't witnessed.

Soft voices were exchanged as I was pushed like a fugitive inside the back of a car, my white dress and scarf still decorating me as a prized toy fresh off the rack.

I didn't know if a beaten up Honda or an expensive Maybach transported me from *Hotel de Sex Traffic* to a private airstrip. I wasn't permitted to see or touch or move without the aid of the two hands that'd purchased me.

He didn't speak to me. I didn't speak to him. And the staff around us didn't need to speak because they had their orders and obeyed them explicitly.

Ducking past the fuselage of what I guessed was a private

jet, gentle pushes guided me up the gangway before directing me to perch on an unseen seat. At least, away from that dreadful no-sensory cell, I had what I needed.

Snippets and sensations of life surrounded me. The city air on my face, the sounds of civilisation as we'd driven down streets, past unsuspecting parents and lovers out for a stroll, and now...sitting on the softest leather imaginable with my back locked, wrists bound, and no vision.

It heightened the senses I did have. Tart scents of liquor, full-bodied whiffs of cinnamon and caviar, and a deeper, headier note of a man's aftershave.

Throughout my imprisonment, I hadn't tried to free myself by being stupid. I never answered back (not after the first welcome beating) and not once refused the meals I'd been served. All such ridiculous notions of starving myself and fighting with words were removed within the first few hours of arrival.

In these new circumstances, I wouldn't stop being wise. I wouldn't scream or cry or try to befriend my jailer. Instead, I would remain quiet and strong and never be idiotic by refusing whatever sustenance this man wanted to give me.

I needed all the health and determination I could cling to.

Icy bubbles of champagne were held to my lips.

I hadn't tasted anything so sharp in a very long time. My mouth opened, and I sipped.

The flute was removed after precisely two swallows. Private jet engines whined into power, someone pushed me deeper into the chair to fasten a seat-belt over my lap, and the crackle of an unknown pilot announced we were ready to take-off.

I wanted to know where we were flying.

I wanted to know who this new adversary was.

I wanted to know how long I could last before the mask I'd plastered in place on the podium would shatter. Paper mache only lasted so long before the elements dampened and destroyed it. What about a guise made of sheer stubbornness and rebellion? How long did those prevail?

But wanting was different from receiving, and I had no choice but to sit back in my chair as we careened down the runway and shot into the sky. My ears popped with steep ascent, and no one muttered a word for a long time. No one moved to untie me or give me back the gift of sight, either.

Minutes switched to hours, and I stopped waiting for the man to speak. I relaxed as much as I could and turned inward, keeping myself sane by mentally preparing for the next step.

I'd known this would happen ever since the bastard who'd strangled me revived me thanks to mouth-to-mouth CPR. I had no one to rely on anymore. No one to tell me what to do and how to act. It was entirely on me. Whatever pain or mistreatment may or may not be in my future, I had to hold my own hand, wipe away my tears, and find comfort in my arms no matter how bloody.

Terror existed in that acknowledgement but encouragement too. Because I only had to look out for myself. I could be selfish by being alone. I could lock myself tight from emotion and turn my heart as mute as my mouth.

The other sold girls would be forgotten, so I didn't worry about their existence. My mother would be ignored, so I'd become my own person rather than her protégé.

It was the only way I would survive.

As more minutes passed, and the plane cruised long enough for two air-hostesses to serve the man who'd bought me and the pilot to announce we had another one hour of flying time, my nerves fought a losing battle.

For all my positive thinking, I couldn't stop the tick-tocking inside, counting down to the next event I'd have to overcome.

I tried to remain calm—to keep my rioting mind quiet from questions. But all I wanted was to know who I would have to endure while planning my escape.

Who was this bastard who'd exchanged money for a life?
What did he expect from me?

And how often had he escaped with such a transaction?

"Let's get the necessary introductions out of the way, shall we?"

I froze as the man's voice broke the stagnant silence. His timing sent shivers down my spine, almost as if he'd heard my thoughts.

Did he expect me to talk without seeing him? Without watching his body language and picking up so much more information than I would if he kept me blind?

I'd promised not to speak again. Ever. But in this instance, it would be beneficial for me, not for him. I'd permit myself three words. A meagre diet of syllables before I went back to starvation.

"Untie me first."

For a long moment, he didn't reply. Then the slight rustle of his suit as he leaned forward and pushed my shoulders off the seat. My skin prickled beneath his touch, bristling with hatred.

Doing my best to move away, I wriggled to the edge of the plush leather, holding my wrists out to make it easier. With a quick saw, the stringed devils around my skin fell away, their teeth muzzled for another day.

The blindfold relaxed over my eyes, granting a smidgen of relief from the headache caused by its tightness.

The moment I was freed, the man reclined in his chair.

I blinked, fighting the glare of finally having vision again. He sat directly opposite me rather than across the aisle as I'd thought. He'd removed his mask, and the second I met his gaze, I wanted to slam the blindfold back on and have every sense forgotten.

I didn't want to see, hear, touch, or heaven forbid, ever taste this man.

The English Lord mask he'd worn had been far too kind for the monster beneath.

Struggling to keep my face tight and unreadable, I tilted my chin. The urge to blurt plea bargains and terrifying questions formed a gag around my throat.

I was thankful.

He deserved no more words from me. He deserved nothing but a firing squad and my footsteps dancing on his grave.

Back when life was safe and my only concern was what TV show to view when I couldn't sleep, I'd binge-watched police shows, forensic documentaries, and crime investigations. I loved working out the suspect before the presenter got to the real perpetrator, drinking in the DNA testing and glaring at each potential murderer on the screen.

A lot of the time, the person who'd killed looked like any other neighbour or family friend. Old or young, rich or poor, they were just a person.

A person with darkness inside.

However, when the camera zoomed on their features as the show's conclusion revealed their comeuppance, one thing always linked them together.

Their eyes.

Something about their eyes revealed the truth, just like this man's did.

Something was missing. I didn't want to say a soul because I didn't know entirely what that was. But it could also be something so much worse. An imposter. Not human enough to feel compassion and empathy. People who killed and raped were cold-hearted, pain-thirsting demons.

I'd been sold to that demon.

He smiled, showing square white teeth in a tanned face. His dirty blond hair pegged him as Swedish or maybe Norwegian. He had the same bone structure of the lanky Europeans with a long nose, pronounced cheekbones, and piercing blue eyes.

I guessed his age would be late thirties. An age where he could've been my father if he'd had children young.

Wait…

Did he have kids? A wife? A family?

We stared at each other, neither saying a word. It felt like a contest, battling for domination, but I knew better. He wanted me to walk into his trap. I already had by requesting he untie me. I'd done my part. The rest was up to him.

He grinned coldly. "Now that you can see me, let's begin."

Leaning forward, he dug pinching fingers into my kneecaps. No one had ever grabbed me there before, but as his fingernails sank swiftly into the satin of my dress and curled around the pieces of bone protecting my joints, I suddenly understood how vulnerable knees were. How easy to pop off and rip away.

I gasped, turning ice-cold in my chair.

"My name is Alrik Åsbjörn. To you, I'm Master A. Do you understand?" His fingers dug harder.

My lips glued together, refusing to speak. I had power over speech, but I didn't over my eyes. They glassed with pain as he continued to hurt me.

"Don't have anything to reply?" His jaw clenched as he dug deeper into my kneecaps. "What happened to the girl who bid one million for herself? I rather like that bitch."

Agonising discomfort flared down my legs, but I didn't break. I couldn't. If he won this battle, then I'd lost the war. I couldn't do that to myself so soon.

"Gone shy on me? Fine." Removing his threat, he sat back. "You'll talk. You'll see."

The relief around my bones throbbed with every heartbeat.

I'll do my best that you'll never hear my voice again.

"I see we'll have some breaking in to do, but don't underestimate me, girl. You don't want to mess with me." Pulling a black file that I hadn't seen wedged beside him, he unzipped the leather shell and pulled out a sheaf of paper. Waving it in my face, he smiled. "This is you. The sum of your life. Your friends on social media. Your family photos. Your personal messages. Every silly thought and ugly reminder of your past."

His soft voice stupidly lulled me until he exploded in a violent outburst, throwing the paperwork across the wood and silver-trimmed cabin. "Gone! All of it. You are no longer that slut. You're *my* slut. You've been given the name Pimlico, and from now on, that's all you are. Got it? You're name-less, family-less, and mine."

His hand raised, and the lessons the traffickers had taught kept me subservient. I cowered before his strike, already giving him the control he so desired. He whacked me around the ear, causing a sharp ringing inside my skull.

I bit my lip, holding back any cry or tear, bowing forward to send a wave of brown hair to hide my face.

I needed to vanish. To disappear.

He didn't seem to care that I didn't scream or beg. Rubbing his hands together, he grew calm again.

Too calm.

He acted as if we were on a business date, discussing a transaction beneficial to both of us.

I wanted to teach him what was beneficial: his balls in my left hand and an arrest warrant in my right.

Alrik—as if I'd ever call him Master A? (the sadist prick)—ran a palm over his clean-shaven jaw. "It's only fair I tell you something about me, seeing as I know everything there is to know about you." Buffing his nails on his shirt, he sighed as if this entire thing was boring him. "I'm taking you to my home in Crete. There, you will do what I want, when I want. You will not refuse unless you enjoy agony." His eyes hollowed with no mercy. "Then again, perhaps you like pain. Do you, Pimlico? Answer me; don't be coy. Do you secretly enjoy being hurt?"

I stiffened as he stroked my knee again, threatening with reminder of what he'd already done. "Whatever empowerment you hope being silent gives you...think again." His hand gathered my dress, bunching it up my thighs.

No. Please, no.

I squeezed my eyes, waiting for his gruesome fingers to

climb between my legs. But he stopped. Hovering on my delicate skin, he grunted, "You *will* talk to me. Eventually. But don't worry, if you only learn to scream, I can work with that."

Reclining backward, his vile touch gave me a reprieve as he picked up his glass. Taking three long sips, he twirled the breakable flute with a lingering smirk. "Forget everything about your past and only remember this. You are my toy; my most prized possession. Don't forget how much I paid for you and what I expect in return."

His words fell to the plane's floor like loaded grenades.

I waited for them to detonate and destroy me, but whatever freedom I'd found by locking myself away prevailed.

The silence stretched like a dirty pause, but I didn't care. If I was to remain true to my voiceless future, I had to befriend silence and find sanctuary in whatever awkwardness it created.

However, Alrik wasn't prepared to do such things. His eyes narrowed as he leaned into me. "Are you not going to ask what you can expect in return?"

Every instinct commanded me to shake my head. To reply in some way. But I fought that, too. Verbal and nonverbal communication were now forever forbidden. Just as I'd locked away who I was, I would banish all memory of companionable connection.

He growled beneath his breath. "The more you defy me, the more you'll pay when we arrive."

Arrive.

Away from my home and mother. Away from everything I'd been.

I could control my outward response, but I couldn't control my heart bucking suicidal in my chest.

Alrik sighed heavily, snapping his fingers for another glass of champagne. Instantly, a dew-covered flute with sparkling liquor was delivered directly into his outstretched paw.

Enjoying a sip, he said, "Seeing as you won't ask, I won't tell. But just so you know, by the time the week is through, you'll be on your knees wishing you'd been smarter. You'll chant yourself to sleep begging to know what comes next."

He painted a horrible picture. A future I wanted nothing to do with.

A few heartbeats thundered past, my chest rising and falling, tickling my nipples against the toilet paper words stuffed in my bodice.

My note to No One.

I was stupid to find comfort in those silver-scribbled scraps. But I did. My back straightened, and my fingers linked demurely in my lap.

This bastard was just a man.

Scum.

Yes, he could hurt me. Yes, he could make me beg for death. But we were the same species. Same adversaries.

And one day soon, I would figure out a way to win and be free of him.

Alrik toasted me with his champagne, not offering me a drink or dinner. His gaze travelled over every inch of me as the plane banked to the left. "We're almost home. I can't wait to show you around."

He chuckled, enjoying being the joke creator and punch line to the new narration of my life. "Once we get there, you'll realise how much you wasted my openness to talk. Poor Pimlico...you really should've asked.

"And now...it's too late."

Pimlico

"THIS IS YOUR room."

Alrik shoved me over the threshold, barring the doorway with his body. My white heels clipped on the sparkling silver tiles, sinking deep into a sheepskin rug as I stumbled from his push.

I wanted to rub my skin where he'd touched me. I wanted to wash and wash and wash.

We'd arrived a little while ago, soaring from clouds to land, concluding our journey at a private airstrip. A chauffeur-driven car delivered us from there to here, and the resplendent home of my captor did nothing to make my stay more welcoming.

The moment he'd dragged me inside, he tore me through the space, past the dining room, kitchen, lounge, and up a flight of steps that branched off in two directions. He took the left, wrapping his fingers tightly around my wrist as if I'd run away any second.

There's nowhere to run.

I had no idea where I was. No hope of escape.

I lost count of how many rooms existed off the corridor until he opened a white-lacquered door and tossed me inside.

Either Alrik had a fascination with white, or he had no inspiration when it came to decoration. The walls were white, the bed white, even the dressing table, bedside units, and armoire. White, white, white.

My eyes dropped to my dress.

Was that why he'd bought me? Because I'd been prepped for sale in snow?

I backed away toward the alabaster curtains, hiding a view of a country I'd never visited, hidden in the lateness of night.

His hands spread like shackles as he marched toward me. "Time to welcome you to your new home, don't you think?" Grabbing the front of my dress, he yanked. Hard.

The pretty pearls and intricate stitching did its best to withstand such torture, but the pieces tore with a loud shriek.

My arms came up automatically. Not to protect my decency—that luxury had been beaten out of me back at the trafficking hotel—but to hide my toilet paper novel.

Too late.

The scribbled pieces scattered onto the carpet like tiny squares of misery. My bitten pencil bounced free like a splinter from my heart. I wanted to scoop them up, but there was no point. He'd seen, and no matter if I picked them up or left them, he'd steal them from me.

That was what men like him did.

I'd been bought to share his perverted life in whatever way he saw fit. I wouldn't cry over my revealed words, and I wouldn't beg him to leave them alone.

His eyes latched onto the mess on the floor, a sinister smile twitching his lips. "Well, well, what do we have here?"

I sucked in a breath, glowering with all the force I had left.

He raised an eyebrow as he squatted to pick up a piece. Reading the scribbles, he looked up. The fact he bowed before me didn't escape my knowledge. However, I wasn't silly enough to believe the position put him below me. He could cause just as much pain down there as he could with me scrunched up and crying on his toes.

"What exactly is this?"

I broke eye contact, glaring at the white painted wall. No

artwork. No personality—a blank void of nothingness.

"Not replying to me is getting very old, very quick." Alrik straightened, shoving a handful of my pages in my face. "Don't want to tell me? Fine. In that case, you don't need them anymore."

Snatching up every last sheet, he stomped to the door. "I suggest you get some sleep, Pimlico, because tomorrow, your true welcome begins."

To No One,

He's gone. He's taken my previous confessions to you but not my pencil. I'll hide whatever I transcribe now, so he'll never have these new pages. It's late, very late, but I don't have a clock in this emotionless tomb. Tomorrow, my life will change, and I may or may not be able to write to you about what I live through.

Just knowing you're there to listen is enough. Having your acceptance and no judgement will keep me going.

My mother would be proud of me. I've lasted this long with my dignity intact.

Can I tell you a secret, No One? Whatever Alrik does to me tomorrow—sexually—will be the first thing anyone has done to me. I'm eighteen and a virgin. Laughable, right? But that's what happens when you live in my world. My mother forced me to choose books over boys and studies over sex. I mean, if I'd found a guy I liked enough to last a few dates and sloppy kisses with, her rules wouldn't have stopped me. But I didn't find him. And now, I never will because that choice has been taken from me.

Is it stupid not to be afraid of his fists or boots or chains? Is it ridiculous that I don't fear sticks and whips and torture equipment? All I truly fear is him. His...penis.

Will it hurt?

Will I bleed?

Who will be there to talk to me when it's over and I feel different? When he forces me from girl to woman? Teen to slave? Free to broken?

You, I guess. Only you.

Until tomorrow, No One.

Sleep well because I won't.

Pimlico

TO NO ONE,

I—I thought I could do this. But I can't. I thought I could tell you what he did. But I won't. All I can say is…his idea of welcome included things I never want to experience again. It hurt. So, so much. I can barely sit without wanting to scream in agony while writing this to you.

He took my virginity.

Multiple times.

He made me wish sex was never invented.

God, it hurt so much, No One.

But he didn't kill me.

So I'll focus on that.

And do my best to figure out how to survive.

Pimlico

TO NO ONE,

How long have I lived here? I've forgotten. Is it two weeks or three? Ten weeks or twelve?

Alrik deliberately keeps calendars out of the house, and every technology device he owns is password protected. I know because I've tried. I've stood in the dark trying to hack his encryption. I've pretended to sleep, chained in the corner of his bedroom, all while fumbling with the number lock on his cell-phone.

The only way I can judge passing months is the regular contraceptive injection he gives me.

Oh, No One, if you could see me? God, I'm so glad you can't see me.

How was I ever so vain to think I was pretty? Why did I ever want to lose the puppy fat that gave me curves? I can honestly say if my mother saw me now, she'd walk right past me. She wouldn't recognise me. I don't recognise me.

Alrik cut my hair three nights ago. Or was it six? I don't know. All I know was his fists on my skin and his boots in my belly weren't enough for him. He had to slice away the hair I used to shield my face from his. He took away my protection with four snips of the kitchen scissors.

He left me with a mismatched jaw-length massacre. That doesn't bother me. The hacked strands can't weaken me, but the fact he didn't tidy up his awful hack job damaged my belief that I could endure what my *future holds.*

By leaving me this way, he's shown how much he doesn't care.

He called me his prized possession.

I'm not.

I'm his trophy to be tarnished and dented and then put back on a mantel to fade from gold to dirty bronze before being shoved in a box and forgotten about. How long before I'm in the box, No One?

Do I even want to know?

POSSESSION OF ALRIK:
SIX MONTHS

To No One,

I talk to you every day (if I can steal the time), but have you noticed I'm not writing everything down? Not walking you through my daily horrors or regaling the truth of what I endure?

Do you want to know why?

Because nobody should have to read what has become of me. No one should have to see what that raping bastard does.

I'll spare you.

And I'll spare myself by not recalling it.

POSSESSION OF ALRIK:
ONE YEAR

Dear No One,

Today, Alrik told me I've been with him for a year. A year! One disgusting, awful, crippling year.

A year...

That's far too long to contemplate.

I did everything I could to escape—you know that. I hid from him, I fought him—I even tried to kill him.

And I paid for my attempts.

You're the only thing I have, No One. Only you know the true facts. Only you understand what I've done to survive. How I gave up a piece of myself to protect what I have left. How he can hurt my body but he can no longer hurt my soul.

I've learned to manipulate him. He still beats me—my God, he finds new ways every day—but after all this time, he promised he would've broken me by now.

The opposite is true.

I'm stronger now than I've ever been.

I'm older now.

I'm wiser now.

And I finally understand what my mother tried to teach me.

There is power in listening, watching, observing. Alrik is a snivelling cesspool of evil, but he has me trapped. While I look for ways to kill him, I control him...little by little. Inch by inch, I win an extra meal for being polite. I undermine his abuse by being obedient.

He hasn't broken me.

He will never break me.

And soon, I will be free.

POSSESSION OF ALRIK: ONE & A HALF YEARS

Dear No One,

A year and a half…

My mother…she'll have moved on by now. My friends will be halfway through their degrees at university. Their lives progressed while mine has regressed.

Am I even a girl anymore? I don't know. All I know is pain. I was strong for so long. I set up home deep, deep inside me. I had safe sanctuary to flee to when he came for me.

But yesterday…he broached my inner kingdom and invited his friends to break me.

They didn't succeed.

But they did succeed in something else.

It kills me to admit this to you, No One…but I…I've been as brave as I can. I've held on for so long.

I'm tired.

When does living become the wrong choice and death the right one? When does taking your own life become wiser than letting someone else destroy it?

I don't want to die because I'm weak.

I want to die because it's the last thing I can do to win.

He wouldn't have me anymore. I would take away his power.

Suicide could be the final rebellion and one act he couldn't prevent.

Do you think taking my life would be weak? Do you believe I've withstood enough? Have I endured enough broken bones to prove my desire to keep living?

I'm a slave, No One.

A slave to his whims even while I curse his very creation.

He's scarred me, ruined me, and now, he's sharing me as if I'm worth nothing.

I'm worth everything.
And I've finally had enough.

POSSESSION OF MASTER A:
TWO YEARS

DEAR NO ONE,

You've been there for me through every cut and concussion. You've listened to my nightmares, and held my hand while that bastard made me bleed.

So many times you've listened and hugged and been there. But did you ever think you'd have to listen for two years?

Two.

Years.

I've been with this awful monster two years.

I have nothing else to say. Nothing else to give.

Six months ago, I reached my limit. I shut down whatever was left inside and decided on death or delirium. Death if I could cheat his fun at hurting me. Delirium if couldn't run to my grave.

But somehow…he knew.

One day, the knives in the kitchen were in the butcher block like always, tempting me closer and closer; the next, they'd vanished.

The curtain cords, the household tools, electrical appliances—anything that could've aided in my suicide magically disappeared.

He did it to keep me weak.

But it didn't work. He reminded me that I've lasted this long. I can last longer. Why should I die? He's the one who deserves to meet his maker and pay for all that he's done.

And he will pay.

I'll make sure of it.

It's taken a long time but he doesn't suspect me of treason anymore. I stopped outwardly fighting, I...obeyed. But not because he broke me.

Oh, no.

I obeyed because I'm smarter than him. I'm patient enough to bide the perfect time.

It doesn't matter that I've become a master of sleeping while chained, breathing while bound, and living while beaten.

I've done things I'm proud of. I've done things I'm not proud of. But ultimately, none of it matters.

I felt things before, No One. I still believed in fantasies like hope and home and happiness. Now, all I believe in is numbness, the clinical assessment I manipulate my master with, and the ticking time bomb inside me that could detonate at any moment.

Gone is the vain teenager who thought she would rule the world. My bones do their best to tiptoe from my skinny flesh. My eyes vacant and cold. The hair-cut he gave me has grown back tattered as a rag doll.

I don't care that he's taken everything. There's still one thing he'll never have.

Two years without a word.

My voice is his holy grail and my ultimate fuck you. He will never earn it. Not that he'll stop trying.

Nine months ago, Master A broke my leg just to hear me scream. He earned that one. I couldn't stop it. And yes, you heard that right. I stopped calling him Alrik when he...you know what? It doesn't matter.

All that matters is today is our anniversary.

Two years.

It will be our last anniversary.

That I promise you.

* * * * *

"GET ON YOUR fucking knees, Pim."

My bruises bellowed, but I wouldn't give him another reason to hit me. My kneecaps popped as I gingerly did as I was told.

Living in this house with him? It was perpetual purgatory.

I hated every damn second, but I hated waking up the most. At least asleep, I had some freedom. Free to be outside again. Laugh again. Run far, *far* away again.

He was a bored asshole with nothing better to do than torment me. He didn't go to work. He didn't have staff apart from a cleaning crew that came once a week and a chef delivery service at six p.m. every day. His funds were unlimited. He had the power to get away with everything.

In the beginning, I had no idea what made him tick or why he treated me so terribly. But two years was a long time, and I'd learned quickly. Every strike, every lash, every horrendous night spent beneath him gave me clues on how to survive.

Answering back was not an option. Running, screaming, disobeying—they all earned me more pain than I could stand.

But observation.

That was my arsenal.

At first, knowing his gait changed from smooth to choppy meant he'd rather whip me than fuck me didn't help in the slightest. I couldn't avoid whatever he had planned. It didn't matter if his voice told me his mood or what torture recipes he plotted.

But as time crept onward, it forewarned me. I fortified myself better, numbed my body, and won just by breathing. I began to understand who he was past the whips and chains and found him incredibly lacking. He was the epitome of a disgusting, spineless coward who kept me in line with violence.

I'd entered his home believing I could remain strong.

That was before the first rape.

The first beating.

The first kick and punch and whipping.

My disobedience lasted longer than I thought, but it all screeched to a stop when he showed me the photos of what happened to his last girl.

Dead.

He killed her.

However, as he wrapped yet another rope around my body to hold me down, he murmured that I wouldn't end up the same as her. He'd paid quadruple for me what he'd paid for her. I truly was his most expensive toy, and even though he wanted to destroy my spirit and shackle me to his soul, he wouldn't kill me.

I was worth more alive than dead.

It was a horrifying conclusion. And my defiance quickly switched from blatant to hidden. When I averted my eyes in submission, I really denied him the right to read me. When I pre-empted him by dropping to my knees, I refused him the chance to beat me.

And while he made me do tasks completely naked, my mind wrapped itself in clothing full of retribution and revenge.

I'd have one shot at killing him. Just one.

And even if I did succeed, I had no guarantee I could escape without being smart. Everything in this house was on an electronic system. If I killed him without learning that code, I would die here. I refused to share a crypt with this rapist.

"We have something to celebrate. Don't you agree?" He stalked around me with his narrow chin held high. "Two years, my dear. I can imagine at your tender age that's the longest relationship you've ever had."

This isn't a relationship, you pig.

My upper lip twitched in disgust as I dropped my gaze to the sheepskin rug.

Unfortunately, he'd seen my facial slur.

His fist struck the side of my head. "Don't fucking give me attitude, Pim! Not on our anniversary."

I tumbled sideways, shaking away throbbing stars, forcing

my body back onto my knees before he kicked me to regain my pose. Ignoring the sudden headache, I catalogued his mood. Everything spoke to me these days—not just his demeanour but his chosen wardrobe, selected watch, even the way he styled his hair. Each was a clue to his disposition.

As he strolled around me, prattling about how his drive into the city was good and whatever business he concluded went in his favour, I looked at his shoes (black loafers meant he was carefree and confident). I glanced at his trousers (light denim indicated his visit to town wasn't entirely work related). My eyes trailed to his wrist and the gaudy gold Rolex (he wanted to show off today and flash his superiority). Finally, I snuck a look at the baby blue long-sleeved shirt (relaxed but preppy). However, the unbuttoned linen jacket was not part of his usual repertoire (he wanted to impress but still show indifference).

To who?

I didn't like things I couldn't understand.

Had he dressed up for our 'anniversary,' or did he have guests coming tonight?

My heart curled into its shell at the thought. When he'd first given me to his friends, Darryl, Tony, and Monty, I'd thrown up not only from the horror at being used by four men, but also from the repeated blows to my belly.

Ever since then, the sharing was often. I didn't have a choice. But at least his arrogance and those of his friends gave me a shelter in which to shut down and hide in. They could have my body, but while I floated in a world, not quite here and not quite there, I was able to keep my soul intact, and my voice forever denied to them.

He yanked a hand through his spiky blond hair. "Were you a good girl while I was gone?"

You know the answer to that, you bastard.

I glowered at the wall.

For some reason, whenever he left on errands, he was so sure I'd never find a way out, he didn't bind me like he did at night. The first few instances he'd left me alone, I'd commandeered the knives in the kitchen, even scurried a few blades away with hope of killing him in his sleep.

But when he'd returned, he'd known exactly what I'd done. Fisting my hair, he'd dragged me through the house, collecting the three butcher knives I'd tucked in secret places. After rounding up my arsenal, he'd carted me to a private security room in the garage hidden behind a piece of drywall and revealed how he'd known.

Every inch of his property was recorded.

How had I not seen any cameras?

Not one blind spot or unreported room.

At the time, my heart had grabbed a spade and dug a hole so deep and cavernous inside, I feared I'd never climb back out.

But I had. Because I had no choice.

"Ah now, Pim, don't be like that. I've been gone for three hours...surely, you must've missed me."

Like I'd miss ebola.

I narrowed my gaze, risking a look at him.

The moment we made eye contact, he smirked. "Still refusing to speak, I see. You can clamp your lips together, hell, you can rip out your tongue, but I hear you screaming at me. I hear your retorts even if you don't say them aloud."

I hate you.

I hate you.

I hate you.

I hoped he'd heard those; the decibels vibrated through my body for any deaf or blind person to feel.

He chuckled, ducking to my level on my knees. His fingertip traced the line of my jaw, deliberately pressing the bruise he'd left there last night. "You know...if you'd just spoken to me from the beginning, I might've been a little nicer to you."

Bullshit.

I wrenched my face away from his touch.

He sucked in an angry breath. His hand dropped to my

naked chest, pinching my nipple. "I might've given you clothes, at least."

I don't believe you.

He wouldn't. He had no compassion and only lived to hurt.

The morning of my welcome, he'd stripped me of my white dress and never given it back. Once stolen, I had nothing. No clothes existed for me in any of the wardrobes of his twelve-bedroom estate. When I'd tried to commandeer one of his t-shirts, he'd beaten me so black, I avoided all the bathroom mirrors for weeks. Feeling him abuse me was one thing. Seeing the ownership and betrayal on my skin was entirely another.

After that first initiation, I'd gone crazy. I'd flown around his house like a psychotic bird trapped in a cage. I'd rattled every door, clawed every window—I'd searched and searched for a chink in the house's fortress, looking for something, *anything* to free me.

I'd failed.

However, my fight hadn't faded.

He'd tried to make me talk. He'd become…inventive with persuasion.

But I hadn't faltered.

If he spoke to me, I stared at a wall. If he took me to bed, I shut down my mind. If he threw things or beat me, I curled tight around my soulcase and held on until it was over.

And each time, I got back up.

One step in front of the other…until one day, I would stop.

But that day wasn't today.

Or tomorrow.

"Do you know what special thing I have planned tonight?"

Is it your death? That's the only gift I want from you.

"It's gonna be a doubly awesome night for me." Patting my head, he grinned. "First, I have a very important visitor who I expect you to entertain if requested."

I froze.

"Second, once he's gone...we'll have our own celebration to mark two years." He smirked. "Oh, while I was out, I went shopping. I picked up a new gag and fresh rope. I'm so generous when it comes to you, Pim."

The ladder and spade and parachute my heart had tried to escape with clattered against my ribs as the damn organ grew legs to sprint far, far away.

He could keep his barbaric generosity.

Heading to the small fridge beside the dressing table, where he kept a stock of beer to stay hydrated while spending hours making me wish I was dead, he twisted the top off his favourite brand and drank deep. "One thing you should know about tonight, Pim, is this bastard doesn't know how unique our love is. It's special; do you understand?"

It took everything I had not to roll my eyes.

You're deluded. Insane!

Love? Bah!

His ownership of me was the very definition of fucked up.

"You'll be on your best behaviour because I have something else to give you."

My shoulders rolled, protecting myself from a wallop or painful kiss from whatever new item he'd purchased. My ability to read him had scrambled as if sudden inference switched his usual agenda.

If you can't predict him, you've failed Psychology 101.

My mother wouldn't be proud.

My thoughts didn't often go to her, but when they did, I wondered if she ever mingled with the bastard who'd taken me. Smiling at him, thinking he was there for her business all while he smirked with the secret of stealing me for profit.

How much of the one point five million did he get for me?

What would he get for me now? Now I was skinny and beaten and blue?

Master A turned to face me.

My flesh prickled with foreboding.

All I wanted to do was shoot him and walk away. I needed good news to tell No One. Even though I shared my life with my imaginary pen friend, I couldn't write most confessions.

He'd hurt me worse than I wanted to immortalize in graphite. He could defile me, abuse me, and even cajole me to speak, but I would never give him what he wanted most.

My voice.

Sometimes, he brought me to the brink of speech through throttling or cutting me, hovering me on the precipice of saying one word to make him stop. But, as if sensing that if he made me talk, I would be worthless, he pulled back at the last excruciating moment.

After such an incident, I used my remaining strength to barricade the door with my dresser—blocking him from hurting me further.

He'd gone berserk, grabbing an axe from the garage, hacking through the immaculate furniture.

And what he'd done when he got through...

I shuddered, unable to relive it. But it didn't stop my fingers trailing to my foot where every metacarpal had been broken as he stomped and brutalised me.

"Stand up. I have a surprise for you."

Surprise?

I hated surprises.

Surprise meant being strangled.

Surprise meant being sold.

My lips clamped together as I stood.

He vanished from the room only to return a second later with a bag. "Go on. Have a look at my gift. Don't be an ungrateful bitch."

If I hadn't taken a vow of soundlessness, I would've cursed his rotten soul. I would've screamed for him to die multiple times over.

Taking a hesitant step, I accepted the bag and peeked inside.

Clothes.

Why the hell is he giving me clothes now...after all this time?

Was he somehow hoping I'd forgive him for what he'd done? Cotton and silk couldn't do that. Nothing could. Not that he'd ever be human enough to seek forgiveness or even sane enough to realise how sick he was.

Not waiting for me to pull the clothing free, he yanked the bag from my fingers, and tossed the white garments on the floor. They merged with the tiles and sheepskin below. "Yours. I expect you to wear them."

When I didn't move, he came up behind me, rubbing his erection into the crack of my ass. "Fuck, you piss me off not talking." He slapped my thigh. "You think you're so strong, but you're not *that* strong. You don't want to talk to me? I don't *need* you to talk."

Biting my earlobe hard enough to draw blood, he laughed as I flinched. "One day, you'll break, and when you do, I'll fucking celebrate by listening to your screams."

Grabbing my nape, he marched me forward until I crashed against the dressing table. "Carry on not talking to me. I don't need your girlish voice when I know you like to write."

My flesh rippled with indignation as a droplet of crimson from my bitten ear landed on my shoulder.

He rolled his hips, digging his cock into my back. "Remember those notes I stole from you when you first arrived...they were entertaining reading. I want some more. I want to know what you feel when I take you. I want to know everything you keep locked inside that mute little brain."

I forced myself not to look over my shoulder at my hiding place. Sheets and sheets of notes to No One hidden so damn close to where we stood. I'd have nothing left if he found them.

I couldn't breathe as he slammed my face against a large book resting on the edge of the table. "This is another gift because I'm feeling like Santa fucking Claus tonight." Pressing my cheek on the ornate bound diary, he hissed, "Scribble away, my dear. Let's see what else you have to say about me."

The new Mont Blanc pen beside the new pages begged me to use it as a harpoon. To stab it in his eye and dance in his blindness.

Do it.

Kill him.

Now!

My fingers crawled to the pen, but he swiped it into his fist. "On second thoughts...this is too good for you." Licking my ear, he smeared my blood. "I see your plans, Pim. Shame on you for thinking about using my gift for other activities."

Damn you.

Screw you!

Let me go!

Hot, angry tears blurred my vision.

And then nothing else mattered as he threw me to the floor and planted his foot into my stomach. "Such an ungrateful bitch. The things I do for you!"

Kick.

Kick.

Kick.

Instinct curled me tight, but discipline made me unravel and accept. I'd long since learned trying to avoid his tirade only brought another and another.

"You think you're better than me. You're not!"

Kick.

Kick.

My ribs screamed. My lungs suffocated. I hurt.

I'm strong enough to obey.

The doorbell rang with perfect punctuation of his damning abuse. The cheery chime sent blades slicing down my spine.

Breathing hard, he reached down and almost ripped a handful of my hair as he dragged me to my wobbly feet. "Ah, he's here. Time to play."

I bit back a hate-filled breath, existing in fire-searing agony.

He let me go, straightening his shirt. "Now that you've seen the length of my generosity, it's time for you to do the same by being the perfect whore for my guest tonight. Get fucking dressed. And come downstairs."

* * * * *

To No One,

I'm sitting here fingering these strange new clothes, and I don't want to wear them. Does that make me odd? I don't want to be confined. I don't want whatever strands weave this creation to strangle me.

Can you see them—the white monstrosity? No, of course, you can't because you don't have eyes or ears or a heart.

He said he has a guest coming tonight. A different one from the usual animals he shares me with.

I don't know what that means. I don't like not knowing.

Can I crawl inside your soft squares and hide behind your pencil lines until it's over?

...

...

I got dressed, No One.

I slipped into the skirt and polo neck and stared so damn long in the mirror. I'm confused why he's making me wear this. It isn't sexy. The material hangs off me, hiding my gaunt frame and all the bruises and scars he's given me.

But why would he do that?

Why hide the accomplishments he's marked me with? He likes them. He calls them my jewellery. Tells me how generous he is to give me yet another strangled necklace or rope-granted bracelet.

Oh no, he's calling me.

I don't want to go.

I have no choice but to go.

ELDER

THERE WERE MULTIPLE versions of Hell.

Most were cliché-filled and nothing more than a nuisance—overdramatised and the topic of conversation for attention wannabes. However, some versions warranted the name.

One version visited for a brief moment, tore apart a life, and left the ruins for whoever was brave enough to pick up the bloody pieces. Another version appeared especially for bastards, delivering payback for whatever atrocities they'd committed. A third acted as a hurricane, bringing destruction to all those in its path—deserving or not.

And then, there was this.

The lying, cheating form of Hell where every twitch, every vowel had to be carefully chosen and meticulously delivered, because if care wasn't given, death wasn't the worst punishment available.

I was in that Hell.

I'd willingly walked into a demon den, and for what?

Why the fuck am I here?

The answer dangled like a worm inside my mind. But if there was a worm inside my thoughts that meant the core of me was bad. A rotten apple slowly devoured by filth.

And it was.

For many years that was exactly what I was.

But not anymore.

Where the worm had tunnelled through my humanity and righteousness, something else had filled the holes. Something that thirsted for power, even though I already had endless amounts. Something that craved wealth, even though I already had oceans. Something that demanded I never forgot who I was at the beginning.

And who I was at the beginning wasn't a worthwhile citizen. I was shadows and gore and screams. I'd lost my honour, my family, everything that made me human.

Losing everything meant that when I'd gained everything, the luck bestowed on me didn't make the darkness inside me better…it made it worse.

So goddamn worse.

Not that my new host knew that.

My lips twitched as I climbed from my car and nodded at Selix. "I won't need your services tonight."

My bodyguard, driver, and all-a-round minion narrowed his gaze. His dark hair in a bun on top of his head sucked up the light of the early evening, his jaw clean-shaven and sharp. "Are you sure? You know what this man is. You did the research. I would advise rethinking your—"

"I would advise you stop trying to give me advice."

We'd met in the days before I was someone. An enemy who struggled the same toils I had. When my luck had changed, I'd hauled him from the gutter with me.

After all, there was no better person to employ than an enemy.

If I could buy his loyalty and earn his friendship after we tried to kill each other, nothing could break us apart. We'd built a foundation on something so much stronger than light and happiness. We were forged from the same despicableness.

There's weakness in that as well as strength.

And because of that, I wouldn't stop reminding him that I might trust him with my life, but he wasn't my conscience. Not before, not now, not ever.

I doubt I even have a conscience anymore.

According to my heritage, I was a no one. Not worthy to be called a man.

I'm fine with that.

Selix snapped his lips together. "I'll be around the block if you need me."

Doing up my blazer button, I nodded. "You'll know if I do." Dismissing him, I strolled toward the front door of the large white mansion.

White.

I sneered.

The biggest lie of all.

It gave a visitor the impression of innocence and purity. But the opposite was true. White was the colour with multiple faces. It lied about its identity, hiding its pigment while smothering others. The final blank thought before death.

My new host believed I was what I said I was. If he'd researched me as I'd researched him, he would know nothing true about me. Only the carefully laid crumbs of worthless knowledge.

He wouldn't know my background.

He wouldn't know my skills.

And he wouldn't know my end agenda.

But soon, he would.

And then, my task in Hell would be complete.

Pimlico

TONIGHT WAS DIFFERENT.

I didn't like different.

My stomach hurt from where he'd kicked me. My head swam from his punch. My ear stung from his teeth. And that was him being gentle.

My mother's lessons on how to read bullies had become a full-time occupation. I knew now what made men like my master tick. I stole pieces of him every moment he looked my way or touched me.

I was the sponge to his evilness, soaking everything I could for my benefit. However, no matter the small victories I enjoyed, the tragedies far outweighed my triumphs.

Tonight wouldn't be a triumph.

I could sense it.

What's going to happen?

I shivered as awful answers unspooled, each one worse than the last. The house felt dangerous and strange, poised for something I couldn't prepare for.

Leaving my doorless bedroom, I made my way downstairs. My bare feet couldn't camouflage the black and blue shadows from him breaking my bones, nor hide the malnourished pigment of my skin. But the white skirt, as it fluttered around my legs, covered my nakedness and scars for the first time since

I'd arrived in Crete.

If that was even where I was.

The colourless polo neck gripped my throat with cotton fingers, making me fidget and pull at the obstruction.

Lately, he'd had a tendency to use collars and ropes, keeping me bound in awful positions. Normally, that position ended up strangling me as he finished. It terrified me while it was happening, but it'd also stained the times when he wasn't. Whenever he touched my neck now, tears instantly brimmed. No matter how strong I was, he'd turned that part of my body into a trigger for terror.

And now, he'd dressed me in clothes that suffocated me on his behalf.

Gulping my rising panic, I stopped midway down the steps.

I can't do this.

Turning around, I bolted back up.

You don't have a choice.

I paused on the landing with my face in my hands, sobs threatening to undo every rib. I hated my sudden fear. Unknowns did this—they rattled my fragile strength—ready to unleash the detonation building inside me.

Over the past two years, I'd developed a security system that ensured I breathed another day even when some days I wanted to die. Others, I wanted to scream. Most, I wanted to slaughter him.

It was thoughts of slaughtering him that kept me going.

And I evolved.

Before, he'd force me to kneel, and I would stand to disobey. He'd crunch my face into the floor, and I'd spring up in defiance. For my troubles, I was hurt over and over.

Now, I bowed because it made him believe I respected him, all while my heart sharpened the daggers I wanted to plunge. I kneeled because it gave him power, and when he had power, he didn't assert it as often.

He was a coward with a vicious, sadistic drive. But I

played him the best I could. I got into his head. I couldn't avoid his daily ferocity, but I could avoid utter excruciation by being smart.

However, being smart and subservient came with a price. My actions of survival made me live and breathe the existence of a slave, and occasionally, just occasionally, my constant fear and unhappiness won.

As it was winning now.

The sobs swelled until my skin begged for relief from the tight clothing. I wanted to strip and disappear.

You're running out of time.

Move.

If I didn't go willingly, he'd come for me. He'd hurt me. I'd been hurt enough today.

I'm strong enough to obey.

That sentence had become a war cry, a lullaby, a prayer. I reminded myself constantly that it was true. It didn't matter if some days it was a lie...I was still here. In a strange way, I'd *won*.

Sucking back tears, I did my best to straighten a spine that'd long since bowed beneath domination and pain and trudged down the steps.

Slowly.

So slowly.

But not slowly enough.

My toes reached the bottom floor before I'd had time to wipe away the droplet on my cheek. My throat constricted as I inched around the corridor to the lounge. The polo latching on my neck clung tight, turning my fear into something thick and cloying.

I was two seconds from tearing off the offending items when I saw Master A's guest for the first time.

My first thought was...*run.*

His eyes matched those of the men surrounding him.

The eyes of a killer, pain-deliverer, and user.

But my second thought was...*run to him.*

He didn't know me.

Master A didn't rule him. He could finally be the one to set me free.

Or kill me.

Either conclusion would do because for the first time in such a long time, I remembered what it was like to see a stranger. To feel hope instead of forcing myself to remain strong.

My knees wobbled as his attention remained on the usual gang of assholes who took advantage of me at Master A's discretion.

He hadn't seen me, hovering ghost-quiet against the wall.

The interloper sat tightly wound like a sword waiting to leap from its sheath, glaring at the three men on the opposite couch.

Master A had never fully introduced me to the animals who'd abused me, but I knew their names. I knew their barbarous tastes. And I knew they were as bad as the rest.

Darryl, Monty, and Tony all discounted me the second they sneered in my direction. I was nothing to them. Just like the crystal chandelier above the dining room table was nothing or the vase on the sideboard in the entrance hall.

They saw me, might even appreciate me for a brief moment, but then I was unimportant.

I just wished I were unimportant enough not to entice sexual interest when alcohol flowed, and Master A gave the order to do whatever the hell they wanted.

The sick prick got off on his friends hurting me three at a time. He sat there masturbating while they—

Stop!

I stuffed each awful memory deep, deep inside. It was the only way I could endure more on top of a mountain already scaled.

Besides, it doesn't matter.

I was far more interested in this foreigner in my nightmare midst.

Who is he?

My fingers twined in the ugly skirt, seeking refuge from their cold fragility. It'd been so long since I'd been dressed; I'd forgotten how comforting a simple covering could be.

Not that it protected my body.

Every part of me was still visible, just…shadowed. The white material didn't hide my nipples through the tightness, and the skirt hinted at secret, violated places between my legs.

I vaguely remembered my mother saying sometimes clothes were more provocative than downright nakedness. Maybe that was what this was? A tease? A reverse strip show?

Master A noticed me, striding from the kitchen with a glass of champagne. He didn't drink it often, and I almost backed away in surprise as he passed the delicate stemmed flute to me.

Kissing my cheek, he looked at the stranger before hissing in my ear. "Our guest isn't aware of our little games okay, my sweet Pim? And if you know what's good for you, you won't give him any reason to find out."

Facing away from his guest, he subtly drew a line over his throat in a threat.

I didn't know if that meant he'd kill the newcomer or me.

Stealing the champagne from my fingers without a single drop splashing my tongue, he wrapped an arm around me and carted me toward the man.

The closer we drew, the more intrigued I became.

Unlike Master A and his similar blond counterparts, this man was a black stain in the middle of European fair complexions.

His hair was blacker than black, looking like an ink spill on the death of a perfect night. His gaze matched the coal depths, hiding so much but taking everything in.

I guessed he'd given up adolescence a while ago and bordered late twenties, early thirties. He was what my mother used to call 'confused ethnicity.' He wasn't like me, who could track her roots back to Anglo-Saxons and Vikings. He was a mismatch of origins—enticingly exotic.

He was handsome and staring right at me.

Staring as if he didn't expect a girl to be here; a slave who'd well and truly forgotten the outside world.

I dropped my gaze, encouraging a sheet of hair to obscure the remnants of bruising on my cheekbone.

I hadn't been anywhere or seen anything new in two years. Until this man.

Stopping before the stranger as he stood stiffly from the couch, Master A grunted, "I thought I'd add one more to our dinner arrangement if you don't mind." Digging his fingernails into my elbow, he smiled cordially. "This is my girlfriend, Pimlico."

The man raised an eyebrow, drawing my attention from his hair and eyes to the rest of his symmetrically masculine face. His nose held just enough authority without being too big. His chin was square enough to expose every clench of his teeth, and his throat powerful enough to reveal every swallow, rippling with sinew and muscle.

My eyes followed his neck, following the contours of his flawless skin until it disappeared beneath a dark grey shirt with the collar unbuttoned. He wore a casual black blazer as if he'd shrugged into it at the last minute while shopping at Armani or Gucci, and his long legs put him half a head taller than Master A, who already towered over my shorter frame.

Only, where Master A made me feel small and defenceless, this new man...didn't.

I couldn't describe it.

I'd often heard my high school friends mentioning some sort of kismet reaction when they met their boyfriends, but I'd never felt it.

My heart turned traitor as the man tilted his head, his eyes never leaving mine. He moved like liquid as if he held the power to drown everyone with a mere drop or eradicate entire landscapes with a tsunami.

I couldn't breathe as he bent forward in a slight bow,

holding out his hand. Every motion was oiled and perfected, sex appeal surrounding him like a fine mist.

I flinched.

Why did he look at me as if I was worth something? Couldn't he see he'd get me into trouble if Master A deemed I'd received gifts I wasn't due?

My shoulders rolled as I glanced at the white tiles beneath my feet.

Master A crushed me to his side with a warning squeeze. "Shake Mr. Prest's hand, Pim."

Shake it?

I'd forgotten such social niceties. For two years, an outstretched palm meant incoming pain, not a common introduction.

What the hell is going on?

If I hadn't played Master A's games for so long, I might've bowed to his wishes, hoping that tonight would have a happier outcome than other times. But I couldn't deny I'd been his for too many years and no longer believed in hope.

I couldn't avoid pain.

No matter what I did.

So why should I do anything at all? He might want me to shake so he could scream at me for touching another man against his wishes. Or he could berate me for not obeying.

Either way, the consequences were the same.

I won't do it.

Cocking my head, I locked eyes with Mr. Prest.

And crossed my arms.

Darryl, Monty, and Tony snickered on the couch, knowing what I did—that I would be hurt. Badly. Once this interloper had left.

Tony cackled. "Aww, shit, you're gonna get—"

"Enough!" Master A snapped, silencing their potential slip. His face blanched, matching the blond strands on his head.

Interesting.

It wasn't a charade; he truly didn't want this man to know.

My heart did its best to shrug off its death shroud and find hope once again. For so long, it'd packed up its stepladder and parachute, settling in for guerrilla warfare as I stayed alive by following fucked-up rules. But now, it shook off dust and battle debris, glowing with tentative crimson.

If I remembered how to use my voice, I might've informed this mysterious Mr. Prest that he'd just walked into a sex prison. He willingly made friends with these animals who shared and hurt and gave no thought to the soul screaming silently inside me.

But two years was a long time.

And a blurted word was as foreign to me as being free.

Dropping his unshaken hand, Mr. Prest scowled. His gaze danced over me, his face hiding his thoughts but unable to thwart his questions.

Just like I wanted to know who he was, he wanted to know me.

I fought the urge to drop my eyes, but the fierce intensity in which he studied me granted courage rather than stripped it. I never looked away as his black gaze switched from my closed-off posture, lingered on my nipples visible through the white polo, and skated to Master A's arm clutching me tightly.

His lips thinned as a dark conclusion dawned on his face.

I wanted to applaud him. Give him a damn award for noticing that not everything was as it seemed.

But then, whatever realisation he'd come to vanished as he grinned just as cold, just as evil, just as nastily as Master A and his associates. "Hello, Pim."

Pim.

Just like that, he shortened my name as if he knew me.

My crossed arms tightened.

You don't know me. You will never know me.

His gaze drifted to my shoulders where my muscles twitched. Not that I had much muscle anymore. I'd wasted away thanks to one meal a day—and only if I earned it.

I hadn't seen the sun in two years, unless it was through

the window.

I hadn't felt a breeze in two years, unless it was from an air-conditioning unit.

The craving I'd had in the trafficking hotel for outdoors was just as insistent here where marble had replaced seventies carpet, and Egyptian cotton sheets had switched overly starched white.

The black despair living permanently beneath my strength threatened to throttle me. My heart kicked my other organs as if trying to wake me up or kill me. Forcing a reaction that I'd long since ordered to remain hidden.

This stranger might be the only one I'd ever see before I died. I'd never again inhale a flower's fragrance or taste a raindrop on my tongue.

I gasped as an impending panic attack swirled. For a year and a half, I'd been able to control my hysteria. But a few months ago, I'd suffered such a vast void of horror and despair, Master A was forced to call a private doctor (who didn't ask questions) to ensure I wasn't dying of heart failure. I'd been diagnosed as severely depressed with panic tendencies.

I was grateful for a diagnosis but full of hatred that the strong teenager I'd been was now nothing more than an emotional, wrung-out wreck—no matter how brave I forced myself to be.

Master A clutched me harder, hissing in my ear. "Get it together, Pim. You will *not* have an attack while company is present."

If I could control it, I'd obey. There was nothing good about revealing just how deep my fear went.

But once the crashing, smashing breathlessness gripped me, I was swept away.

Gulping, I clawed at the tight cotton around my throat.
I can't breathe.
I need air.
I need to run and run and run.
His weapon-like fingers dragged me to the side. "Calm

down!"

I can't.

I can't.

Memories of inky, sleepy death corrupted me. I recalled what it was like to see the last thing I'd ever see and feel the last thing I'd ever feel. Suppressed recollections of being strangled and waking up in this sex-trafficked nightmare swarmed.

Stop!

Make it stop!

My choking turned to open-mouth gasping.

Master A manhandled me across the lounge to stuff me somewhere where I wouldn't embarrass him.

Mr. Prest followed in our wake.

As I stumbled through the doorway to the corridor, a cold voice demanded, "Let her go."

Master A froze, looking over his shoulder. With angry hands, he spun me to face the stranger. "This is of no concern of yours."

I can't breathe.

Clutching my chest, I rode out the confused double-beats of my heart. According to the doctor, I had the power to stop the attack by reminding myself that my current situation wouldn't change, no matter how I felt about it. I had no reason to stress when I couldn't reverse the circumstance.

He had the audacity to say that.

To *me*.

The mute slave girl who was beaten, raped, and starved on a daily basis.

I was fully justified in my terror. I was just surprised the attacks only started a few months ago and not the day I'd been sold.

Oh, God.

Two years.

Two long, long years.

I folded in half, holding my chest, doing my best to keep my soul from jackhammering free. While trapped in the middle of an episode, my head roared, my heart hopscotched, and all I wanted to do was die. Stopping the horror and becoming calm again seemed like an impossibility.

I can't handle two more years.

I can't even handle two more days.

Mr. Prest cocked his head, running a hand over his shadowy jaw. Everything about him boycotted the white starkness of Master A's mansion, bringing blackness into its corridors.

"If you want to do business, Alrik, consider this my concern." His eyes trailed over me. He wasn't sympathetic toward my suffering, merely cold and mildly annoyed.

His eyebrow rose with an aristocratic arch as my lips cooled to blue and my gasping turned haggard. He watched me as if I were a circus freak putting on a performance just for him.

A performance he didn't like.

Ignoring Master A, still struggling to keep me upright and not kneeling on the floor as I wanted, Mr. Prest murmured harshly, "Stop it."

I wanted to scream. To shout. To speak. To show him I was human and not something he could command. But I shrivelled beneath his heavy glare, slouching in the biting fingers of my owner.

Being reprimanded wasn't new. The only conversation I endured was snide comments, snapped orders, and putrid curses. So it didn't shock me that this stranger was the same as them. No kind word or commiseration. No empathy or ability to see past the lies and understand the truth.

Even if he could…why should he care?

I was nothing to him.

Just a rebellious toy swiftly becoming tiresome and ready for replacement.

Master A shook me, hissing in my ear. "You heard our guest. Stop it." Yanking me closer, he added so only I would hear. "You think this behaviour will go unpunished? Silly, silly,

Pim. Tonight, your back will be shredded. Scars on top of scars."

I convulsed, breaking his tight fingers and slithering to the floor.

No. No. No.

Get it together.

Breathe!

My entire body shook as I tore at the cotton around my throat. My broken fingernails scratched painful slices over my skin as I finally managed to grab the offending clothing, rejoicing in the crack of ripping material.

The clinging neckline opened as I shredded and slashed.

I didn't stop until the white top hung open and gaping, revealing the whip lacerations, painful scabs, and silver scars on my chest from belonging to a troll like Master A.

Mr. Prest stiffened.

I daren't look up, but his thighs locked into steel tree trunks, tightening his black trousers. The soft rustle of his blazer hinted he no longer watched as a bystander but as a witness to my ruin.

Once upon a time, I would've hidden my bare chest, tried to cover my nipples—be demure and shy.

Now…I didn't care.

After so long with no clothing, I was more comfortable naked. I couldn't stand anyone or anything touching me.

Touch, just like speaking, had become taboo. It only brought pain. Not pleasure.

Master A yanked me upright, his hands fierce and unyielding beneath my arms. "What the fuck did you do?" His temper built like a blizzard, swirling with hail and sleet.

I shivered, waiting for the arctic freeze.

But Mr. Prest stepped forward. Shrugging out of his blazer, he ignored my master as he draped the material over my half-naked form. I flinched, dreading the slightest touch.

But nothing came.

He gave me his jacket, still warm and smelling richly of

heady incense and something exotically spicy, but he did it all without a single finger graze.

I froze.

I drowned.

The act of kindness threatened to send me into another panic attack.

I slouched beneath the weight, so unused to heavy heat smothering me.

One heartbeat demanded, *Get it off!*

The next remembered what my flesh had forgotten. It recalled how nice it was to be protected. *Don't...don't take it away.*

"Get that off her, Mr. Prest," Master A growled. "She'll run upstairs and dress in her own things, won't you, Pim?"

With what?

I had no other clothes.

But Mr. Prest didn't know that, and I waited with eyes downcast, my heart burning at the thought of having the one element of comfort I'd been given in so long taken away.

All I wanted to do was slip my arms into the wide, beckoning sleeves, fall to the floor, and hug myself. I wanted to curl into a chrysalis, protected by my blazer armour, and re-emerge so much braver and bolder than before with paper wings and powder beauty able to soar me far, far away.

At least the shock of Mr. Prest sharing his wardrobe interrupted my nerves. Adrenaline stopped crackling through my veins; I did my best to breathe rather than asphyxiate.

Mr. Prest crossed his arms, his dark grey shirt pushed up to his elbows, revealing ropy muscles and a tattooed bracelet with Japanese characters around his wrist. "She can keep it."

Master A glowered, digging his fingernails into my shoulder as he directed me toward the staircase. "No. She can't."

"Why?" Mr. Prest slouched against the doorjamb, never taking his black eyes from me.

"Because I said so." Master A shoved me toward the

bottom step. "She'll be back down as soon as she's changed."

I stumbled, the loose jacket fluttering like clouds behind me.

Mr. Prest lowered his jaw, watching from shadowed features. "I want to hear it from her."

Master A froze. "What?"

Mr. Prest pointed in my direction. His liquidity and grace came across as bored and uninterested, but a vein of lethalness simmered beneath. "Her. I want to hear it from her."

I spun to face the man, soaking up the wrongful whiteness around him. We made eye contact before I remembered my place and stared at the ground.

Master A dragged stiff fingers through his blond hair. "You don't understand, Elder. She doesn't speak."

Mr. Prest snapped into stealthy power. "*Don't* think we're on first name basis, Alrik. And certainly don't take liberties not given to you."

My back bunched. No one spoke to Master A like that and got away with it.

But the unthinkable happened.

Master A swallowed his curse-filled retort, nodding respectfully. "Of course. My apologies." Moving toward Mr. Prest, he waved over his guest's shoulder. "Perhaps, we should begin the evening again. We have a nice meal planned. Let's eat…shall we?"

"No." Mr. Prest didn't budge from the doorway. "I want to know what the fuck is going on."

Master A's eyes bugged.

If I weren't so afraid of the man being disciplined, I would've enjoyed this change of events. But I knew I would be the one who ultimately paid once the stranger had left.

"Nothing is going on."

Mr. Prest cocked his head, a cold smile on his lips. "Lies. I don't do business with liars."

"I'm not lying."

"Then let her speak." Mr. Prest's eyes latched onto mine

again. "Pimlico...tell me yourself. Do you want to keep my jacket or would you prefer to wear your own clothes?" His gaze drifted to the nasty white skirt I wore, barely hiding anything. "You have odd taste in fashion, but I won't judge. You may wear what you wish. Not that it's my place to direct you." His glower landed on Master A. "But then again, neither is it the place of your *boyfriend* to order you how to dress."

His accent teased at the corners of my mind, reminding me of wealthy travellers and foreign places. The way he said 'boyfriend' made me stiffen.

I was right.

He did understand. He saw through the bullshit and knew what I was.

My heart jumped into an ocean of tears. Why did that hurt me so much? To be seen as what I was? For this stranger to never know me as happy, confident Tasmin but as beaten, ugly Pimlico?

"Answer me," Mr. Prest said. "My jacket or your own?"

The question didn't prompt me to reply. After two years of muteness, a query no longer held such power. My larynx didn't prepare to speak. My lungs didn't inflate to talk.

I had no urge to vocalise.

My body stiffened as I focused on Mr. Prest's powerful jaw and throat. I'd guess he had foreign blood in him somewhere in his lineage. It wasn't a strong part of his features, but his eyes were too beautifully almond to be strictly European.

The three of us stood in tense silence.

Mr. Prest slowly exhaled, his temper overshadowing Master A's, turning the white blizzard into a dark typhoon. "Speak."

Master A chuckled. "I tried to tell you."

"Tell me what?"

"She doesn't talk." Master A waved in my direction as if I were faulty goods and only good for the torture he put me through. "She's mute."

"Through choice or medical condition?"

Whoa…what?

The personal question hacked through the silence like a machete.

Master A grinned, slowly gaining control of the situation now attention was back on him. "Ever since we got together, she's been mute. You see, when I found her, she was so broken, she didn't know how to act normally. I thought it endearing, and I've done my best to help heal her." He ran his hand over my scalp, petting me with false affection. "But of course, these things take time and a lot of patience."

What a load of utter bull—

"Bullshit," Mr. Prest barked.

The fact he'd stolen the word from my mind and delivered it with as much contempt and disbelief as I would have made my heart hop with a pink skipping rope.

Laughing coldly, Mr. Prest added, "*Heal?* Those scars and cuts on her skin aren't old." Stalking forward, he towered over Master A. "They're recent. Care to lie about how that happened?"

Master A shrugged, doing his best to come across as unruffled. "A number of things are wrong with her. Being mute is only one of them."

Wow, he's claiming I hurt myself now?

I wanted to get angry, but I had nothing but disgusted acceptance left.

Would Mr. Prest believe him if I tore off his blazer and revealed my whipped back, bruised inner thighs, and cigarette burned ass cheeks? Or would it take deeper evidence such as the god-awful internal injuries I'd sustained from non-consensual items being thrust into my body?

Mr. Prest paused, looking me up and down. "I don't believe you. No one would self-harm to that extent." His face blackened. "And believe me, I know."

How does he know?

Was that a veiled hint that *he* self-harmed? Beneath his

expensive tailored clothes, was he as scarred as I was?

Somehow, I doubted it.

However, his hands did hold injuries—both new and old. Overhead lights flickered over silver wounds and knuckle bruising. He used them for business other than introductions with assholes.

Master A's temper gathered ferocity. "Well, you don't have to fucking believe me. She's *my* girlfriend. I figured you might like some female company because I heard you've been at sea for months. But this is fucking ridiculous. I don't need the third degree." Waving his arm, he growled, "She's mine, got it? Not yours. Forget you ever saw her."

Directing his wrath on me, he ordered. "Upstairs, Pim. *Now!*"

The obedience he'd beaten into me kicked in. Turning on the bottom step, I grabbed the banister to climb away.

Only, Mr. Prest snapped, "Stop."

Storming forward, he snatched my wrist and yanked me down the stairs.

No!

I didn't want to be in the middle of whatever power trip this was. I wanted to bolt back to my room and tell No One of how confusing this meeting had been. I wanted to inhale Mr. Prest's blazer in private and give in to the scalding tears left over from my panic attack.

But it didn't matter what I wanted.

It never did.

I became the rope in a nasty tug-of-war.

His fingers were just as cruel as Master A's as he tightened his grip and pulled me close. Too close. Far too close. The mint decadence of his breath smarted my eyes. "Tell me your story. Now."

I looked at the floor.

Master A abducted me from his guest's hold. "What the fuck is your problem? She's mute. I just told you."

Mr. Prest shoved a finger in Master A's face. "My problem

is I don't do business with people I don't understand." His eyes narrowed. "And I don't understand where she fits in."

Master A shoved me against the wall. He did it in a way that spoke of authority and almost protection from an aggressive stranger in our supposed happy home. However, Mr. Prest saw the truth as I wobbled, reaching for something firm for purchase.

Grabbing my free arm as I fought to stay standing, Mr. Prest growled, "You. Start talking."

Master A struggled to hold me, a battle of possession on my flesh. "Let her go."

"If you want to complete our transaction, you'll shut the fuck up." Mr. Prest's voice dropped to a scary whisper. "Think hard, Alrik. Is sharing your girlfriend too much to pay for what you truly want?"

Slowly, a calculating gleam filled Master A's watery blue gaze. "Share?" He chuckled, raising an eyebrow in my direction.

To someone unknown, that look would hint at undecided decisions. To me, who'd been shared every damn day for years, it was a threat. A forgone contract that before the night was over, Elder Prest would have sampled me, used me, and ultimately destroyed me with hate as much as he had with kindness.

"You're right." Master A unlocked his fingers, removing his resistance.

I ricocheted forward, tumbling against Mr. Prest's sculptured body.

The moment I smashed against him, I recoiled.

He wasn't different.

He was the same.

And I had no wish to be close to him or any man.

Master A puffed out his chest, crossing his arms. "Is sharing an official requirement to complete our deal?"

My mismatched hair hung over my face as Mr. Prest manhandled me around his body, placing me behind him. His arm clamped tight, keeping me wedged against his hard back.

"You really are a sick fuck."

Energy and untapped power siphoned down his spine as he chuckled, infecting me with whatever insanity he suffered.

Because he had to be insane.

He protected me from Master A, all while discussing sharing me to complete a business transaction.

Who does that?

No one I wanted to be around.

A year ago, I might've struggled—bit his wrist for the chance to be free. But just like I'd evolved in obedience to survive, I learned that antagonising for no reason wasn't smart.

Master A spread his hands. "Rather offensive thing to say. I'm not judging you. So I'd appreciate it if you don't judge me."

Looking over my shoulder, my skin crawled to find Darryl, Tony, and Monty had repositioned themselves to stand behind Mr. Prest, ready to maim or kill him if he threatened their friend.

I squeezed my eyes, deliberately avoiding what would come next.

However, I'd underestimated Mr. Prest.

Almost as if he sensed the imminent attack, he stepped back, forcing me to move with him until he entered the lounge and spun to face the three men, pinning me against the wall.

He faced them all as Master A stalked to stand with his evil accomplices.

Mr. Prest clenched his jaw, his eyes hooded and dark. "Let's start this again. With the fucking truth." Yanking me from behind his back, he placed me beside him. "She's a whore."

I jolted at the word.

I *hated* that word.

It conjured such sad and broken things. But I wasn't that. I was a daughter, a student, a friend. I was smart. I'd been pretty, once.

I *meant* something.

Master A shared a glance with Tony before smiling. "She's

more than a whore. I bought her. Fair and square."

"So, she's a slave." Mr. Prest didn't phrase it as a question. Somehow, he'd known all along what I was the second he saw me.

I'm his slave; it's true.

But I don't want to be.

Master A stared at his guest for a long moment before his shoulders relaxed and a broad smile split his face. "She's a slave, a whore, a slut. She's whatever you want." Coming forward, he held out his hand a second time. "Meet Pimlico…my possession. And you have full invitation to use her."

No…

My eyes flew to Mr. Prest, hoping like hell the proposition abhorred him. That he'd rather walk out the door than deal with such awful people and take me with him.

But the tense standoff ended as he accepted Master A's handshake, smiling coldly.

"That's more like it." Breaking the introduction, Mr. Prest slung his arm over my blazer-cloaked shoulders. "Why didn't you say that before?"

Don't…

"That makes this evening a *lot* more interesting."

ELDER

THIS PLACE STANK of lies and deceit.

And that said something, seeing as I was the one who usually had the most to hide.

This asshole had cleared most of my vetting channels, but my research hadn't revealed a live-in girlfriend.

Definitely not a *mute* girlfriend.

Yet she's neither of those things.

She was a beaten, broken whore.

A slave.

I'd seen some shit in my past. I'd committed crimes. I'd done my fair share of filth. But I'd never met someone who thought they could own a human soul before.

Part of me wanted to unleash every wrath he had owing. But the other...a stronger part was intrigued.

Distancing myself from Pimlico, I couldn't deny my flesh heated at the fragility of her bones. I couldn't look away from the translucency of her skin with its map of blue veins and red arteries.

Balling my hands, I took another step.

Her breathing fluttered, not as a flirt but in fear.

That was not a good thing.

Not where I was concerned.

Over the years of my dominion, I'd earned a name that'd

paved the gold-brick road into the underbelly of this sick and twisted world.

Kaitou.

Phantom Thief.

First, because I was a pickpocket, robber, and five-fingered master.

Second because, instead of stealing objects, I started stealing lives.

But only those lives owed to me or those too feeble to be of any use.

What category does she fall into?

She was feeble but not useless.

Something about her got under my skin, itching with an intolerable curiosity.

Where did she come from?

How long had she been here?

And just how long had she wanted to die?

The look in her eyes was a classic invitation for death.

I took another step away from the slave girl.

Just in case.

I saw strength in her, but I also tasted the yearning for her end. Once someone enticed thoughts of suicide into their soul, it was there to stay, slowly corrupting them until they found their way back to life or gave in and let demise claim them.

I'd underestimated Alrik Åsbjörn.

He'd kept this woman alive for who the fuck knew how long, even when her wish to die echoed with every heartbeat.

That was impressive.

The sharp thrill knowing I could do anything I wanted to this girl with no repercussions disgusted me. I could hurt her, fuck her, treat her with no bloody respect. And she could only accept it because that was her place. Her bought and sold place.

I could kill her, and she'd probably thank me for setting her free.

Maybe I should.

Perhaps I will.

Depending on how the evening and our transaction went, I might steal her life and keep it as a trinket, a token, for yet another shadowy deal struck with monsters.

"Let's eat." Alrik grinned, strolling toward the eight-seater table positioned beneath a generic chandelier.

His house irritated me. The stark white. The impersonal walls and sterile furniture. I preferred personality in my décor. Why live in a box this soulless? He might as well live in a fucking coffin.

Alrik's friends took their seats, not waiting for the guest of honour—me—to sit first. My lips tightened at the lack of courtesy and respect.

My culture demanded such things.

Even when I lived on the fucking streets as an unwanted rat, I'd remembered what my elders had taught me.

Reverence for those wiser, older, and smarter than you. Appreciation for those kinder, gentler, and nicer than you. And utmost worship for those who could fucking annihilate you without a single thought.

Grasping the back of the chair, I looked over my shoulder at the wraith of a slave as she faded into the background.

Judging by her current well-being, I'd say she'd become a master at accepting pain. She was like me in that respect. And because of that, she earned my interest. She wasn't just a possession, but a puzzle, ready to be deciphered.

Sinking to her knees on the hard white tiles, she bowed her head.

Even with my blazer covering her stark skeleton, her malnourished body imprinted beneath it. My jacket looked five times too big for her. Her hair was a disgusting brown mop with no style. Her green eyes resembled a swamp, and her skin hinted as if she bordered scurvy.

She wasn't healthy.

Why didn't she speak? And why did her defiant thoughts scream so much louder than words? How could she remain so impertinent when she rang the doorbell of death with eager fingers?

Tearing my gaze away, I glared at the unwanted guests around the table. Alrik assured me, when we set up the meeting, that it would just be him and me. Not three other bastards and one silent girl.

I'd put up with it through dinner because I refused to talk business while eating, and never when drinking, but the moment the food was consumed, they had to fuck off.

My back stiffened as precautions filled me.

Could he have poisoned the meal?

Thanks to my tireless research, I knew he didn't cook—that his chef service provided delicacies every night. I had to trust he wouldn't slip ricin into my main course purely because of his ego and what he wanted from me.

If Alrik did, by some imbecile decision, try to dispatch me rather than do business, I was ready.

He wouldn't be the first to try to kill me.

And he wouldn't be the last.

However, the trail of cadavers left in my wake would steadily grow longer as I proved I was invincible.

Sitting down, I readjusted my silverware, running eager digits over the serrated knife. I could murder everyone in this room before one scream was uttered.

Perhaps I should.

Maybe I will.

Before the night was through.

Alrik remained standing, opening bags of gourmet food and serving us with each element: bok choi with oyster sauce, Peking duck, Singapore noodles, and wontons.

The scents replaced the blandness of the monochromatic space with welcome.

Finally, he sat at the top of the table and smiled. "Eat. Enjoy."

As he arranged his napkin, I looked once more at the girl.

She hadn't budged. Her head remained bowed, her eyes locked on a speck in front of her.

Picking up my fork, I pointed at her. "You don't feed your

slave?"

Alrik slurped a mouthful of noodles, no longer trying to hide the truth. "She gets fed when she's behaved. She knows that." He raised his voice so the girl could hear. "And tonight, she didn't. That unsightly episode before is not tolerated." He grinned, stabbing a piece of duck. "She'll eat tomorrow."

I agreed.

A naughty pet ought to be punished.

But she wasn't just a pet.

She was a human being, and I wasn't done inspecting her.

I need her closer.

I ordered, "Invite her to eat with us."

Alrik and his friends froze, food half-chewed or dangling on their forks. "What?"

"Invite her to eat. She's hungry."

"But this is a business dinner. I won't have it sullied by her—"

"This is not business. This is merely a social nicety to feel as if we've bonded before our transaction is concluded. If it were up to me, I would've arrived to find you alone, as per our discussion, and left a few minutes later, rather than this fucking spectacle."

My chin lowered as my temper siphoned through my veins. "*You're* the one who changed the rules. Now, I want to change them for my benefit. Let her eat."

Alrik's fair skin turned puce with anger.

I smiled, just waiting for an outburst, any outburst. I'd happily teach him a lesson that he would never win with me.

Ever.

Slowly, he put down his utensils and looked at his whore. "Pimlico, grab a plate and join us. I've changed my mind. You can eat tonight."

I didn't turn around, but her gasp trickled down my nape, making me shiver. It was too easy. Hunting was a lot of fun. Just like thievery. The trick to pulling off a great heist was to gain the trust of your intended victim first.

Trust me, Pim.

Let me steal your secrets.

Alrik had tried to do that by luring me to dinner with his friends. But he couldn't mask his eager greediness for what I could offer him. Pimlico, on the other hand, bought my sanctuary with every heartbeat, hauling herself into a standing position and shuffling into the kitchen.

I didn't move as the sounds of collected crockery and the clink of knives and forks echoed in the white space. Her footfalls were as quiet as a shadow as she hesitantly approached the table.

I narrowed my eyes as she kept her vision on the floor, holding her plate like a shield.

Alrik's friends snickered, sucking on beer bottles, enjoying her discomfort far too fucking much. I didn't need to ask to know they'd taken from this girl, too. They were responsible for some of the bruises and scars decorating her body.

Alrik sighed heavily, rolling his eyes. "Well, sit, Pim. Fuck, don't just lurk there like a freak."

Instantly, she darted forward and slipped gracefully into the chair beside me.

Either deliberate or subconscious, the fact she'd chosen to sit so close did strange things to my insides. Half of me wanted to stroke her cheek and promise that as long as she wore my jacket, I'd protect her. While the other half wanted to see how pretty her tears would look falling into her dinner.

Tearing my gaze from her sad face, I stole her empty plate and replaced it with my untouched, full one.

She sucked in a breath as I nudged the delicious smelling food closer.

I didn't speak. I didn't need to.

She knew what I offered, and she'd accept—if she knew what was fucking good for her.

Alrik's fork clattered to the tablecloth, smearing garlic sauce and oil. "Wait…she can have a sandwich. There isn't enough for—"

I held up my hand with a sharp glare. "I'm not hungry. She is. Problem solved."

Besides, there was power in not eating when everyone else was. I had the freedom to stare and calculate. I could ask questions and probe all while they swallowed inconvenient mouthfuls, scrambling for lies.

No, this was perfect.

I got to do a good dead—something I was sorely lacking—and I also got to put these men on the back foot.

Let the interrogation begin.

Pimlico

I COULDN'T LOOK up.

Whiffs of delicious food made eternal hunger snarl.

Is this real?

Was I truly sitting on a chair at the table with a plate in front of me? Was it a cruel joke where Master A would snatch away the meal as he sometimes did for spite?

I shuddered, remembering last month how he'd made me crawl after him for miles, up and down the stairs, along tiled corridors, taunting me with my dog bowl full of spaghetti carbonara.

I'd wanted those rich, creamy noodles more than anything and hated what I did when he finally stopped and demanded I suck him in return for my dinner.

The flavour of his cum had ruined the reward.

I never wanted carbonara again.

My fingers shook around the utensil as I forced myself to recall the mechanics. How could I forget something as simple as using a fork? And if I couldn't remember, what would Mr. Prest think of me?

He'll see a whore and a heathen.

An untrained slave with awful table manners.

Why did I suddenly want to be noticed instead of forgotten? Recognised instead of alone? Why did this man make me come more alive than I had in years?

Fighting my tremble, I raised a mouthful to my lips.

The food tasted like cardboard even though I knew from eating scraps off Master A's plate that the ordered menus were five-star gourmet.

My taste buds were in shock.

My mind, my body…everything in tentative anticipation thanks to the stranger beside me.

I couldn't breathe without inhaling Mr. Prest's heady, exotic scent. I couldn't move without brushing against his powerful arm or teasing myself with his warm blazer draped over my shoulders.

I couldn't blink without thinking all of this would disappear, vanish, *poof*. I'd never been allowed at the table before. Never been given a fork or knife or plate. And definitely never been treated as a person by a man who overshadowed Master A in every way.

I was grateful.

I felt alive.

I both hated and thanked Mr. Prest for it.

Every mouthful, I expected Master A to scream and throw something at me. I already felt the kick and the coldness of the floor pressing against my cheek as he held my face down.

The awful games he played. The demeaning tasks he forced me to do. This was just a minor blip of kindness in a world of torture.

The food slid tastelessly into my belly, but the decadent richness made me feel sick. My system wasn't used to such opulence.

But I wouldn't stop eating.

I couldn't.

I would devour every piece, slurp every noodle, and then lick my plate if I could get away with it.

My mouth watered as a faint memory interrupted. Of Japanese sushi and soy sauce; of cheeseburgers and french fries. It seemed so long ago.

Had I truly been allowed to go where I wanted whenever I pleased? Did I really laugh and find happiness?

I was so naïve.

Master A lifted his wine, toasting Mr. Prest. "Cheers to exciting business ventures and new friends."

Ugh, what an ass.

I didn't blink or frown, but inwardly, I stuck out my tongue and gave him the finger. The smarminess, the fake charm. He was a reptile and utterly cold-blooded.

Only, Mr. Prest didn't return the toast; merely tilted his head, leaving Master A hanging and forced to take an awkward sip of alcohol.

Tony cleared his throat as everyone focused intently on their food. The clink of knives and forks was the only noise apart from the classical music raining from overhead speakers.

Master A liked music. Considering just two of us lived here, it was never quiet.

I. *Hated.* It.

My synapses had associated classical notes with torture, and I couldn't listen to a piano or violin without reliving his cock driving inside me or his fist pummelling my skin.

Master A sneered in my direction, slurping a mouthful of noodles. His rage at my position beside his guest hissed down the table.

The fork shook in my hands. I'd lived here for so long, yet I couldn't predict my jailer. My imagination painted countless punishments for defying him, but I'd be surprised. Like always. Master A liked to think outside the box where I was concerned.

"How long has it been since you ate?"

The question wrenched me from my thoughts. I blinked, stupidly forgetting myself and turning my head to the source.

Mr. Prest stared back. His dark eyes didn't budge, doing their best to tear every secret I had left. Pointing at my plate, he said, "You eat like a bird, yet I know you're starving."

My heart breathed into a paper bag with worry. It'd been so long since someone looked at me as a person rather than a doll. But it was too late. With far too many witnesses. I was more possession than anything else these days.

My gaze flickered to Master A. The outrage on his face wasn't because of something I'd done but because I'd attracted the attention of someone he wanted to deny.

"Don't ask things you're not privy answers to." Master A slammed his knife onto the table. "I take care of her. That's all you need to know."

My blood incinerated with hatred for the history between us. For all the monstrous things he'd done.

Took care of me?

What a crock of shit.

Mr. Prest froze, his straight spine vibrating with ruthless energy. "I asked her a question. I don't need you replying for her."

"And I told you before, she will never answer you."

"She answers me just fine."

Wait, what?

My gaze danced between the men.

How had I answered him? And why would he say such things? Couldn't he see my refusal to communicate drove Master A berserk? He'd kill me if he thought I spoke to another and not him.

"Leave what isn't yours alone, Mr. Prest," Master A threatened. "She's mine. Direct your questions to me and only me."

Mr. Prest didn't move. "Why?"

"Why?" Master A spluttered. "Why should I command you to stop talking to *my* slave?" He stood up with his fists on the table. "Because she's mine and whatever answers you think you see are lies."

"You're afraid she'll tell me things about you that will stop this business arrangement."

Wrong. He's afraid I'll tell you that I want you to kill him.

He's afraid I'll give you the final piece of me that I refuse to give to that bastard.

"She will tell you nothing—either good or bad." Forcing himself to relax, Master A slid back into his seat. "But that's beside the point. You're right. I offered Pimlico in friendship, and you have full right to do what you want. Whatever ensures our mutual interest in business." His smile was a shark. "Nothing else matters."

For five achingly long seconds, Mr. Prest didn't accept the olive branch. Testosterone swirled across the table. At least Darryl, Tony, and Monty stayed out of it.

"Sometimes, it isn't what's spoken that is the loudest reply, Mr. Åsbjörn," Mr. Prest muttered. "And I've just learned all I needed without your slave uttering a single syllable."

Master A lost interest in his dinner. "What are you saying?"

Mr. Prest glanced at me, his charcoal eyes looking like hunters in the dark. "I'm not saying anything. Just like Pimlico." With graceful precision, he wrapped strong fingers around my wrist.

I stiffened.

He had more power and danger in his left hand than Master A did in his entire blond body. He hummed with authority that terrified but also encouraged me to move closer hoping he'd use that power to protect me.

Lies.

All of it.

He wouldn't protect me.

I shook my head free from such stupid thoughts.

Mr. Prest suddenly removed his touch, freeing my wrist.

I had the awful sensation he'd been counting my pulse not just holding me for the sake of touching. Could he feel how fast my heart galloped? Could he see the terror and desperation in my gaze?

Never looking away, he placed his hands back into his lap and clasped them tightly together, as if he didn't trust himself to let go of whatever restraint he held. "Eat, Pim. Our conversation is over...for now."

My breathing turned shallow. His lingering touch threatened me. I wasn't stupid not to recognise how dangerous he was, but there was a hidden safety, too.

It whispered that if he hurt me, he'd help me at the same time. I just didn't know how.

He was a contradiction. A conundrum. Something fascinating I couldn't figure out.

Slowly, the atmosphere at the table resumed its tentative calmness; the men returned to their dinner.

I did too. After all, I wouldn't waste good food.

My eyelids fluttered as my taste buds finally worked, signalling to my brain how rich and delicious the piece of duck was as I placed it on my tongue.

Tony, Darryl, and Monty were their usual gross selves with no manners, and Master A remained on his best behaviour. But he couldn't hide the fact he hated my position at the table.

Whatever nutrition I earned would most likely come scalding back up my throat when he kicked me in the guts later.

The thought was almost enough to stop me eating.

But not quite.

Meekly, I dropped my gaze. Boldly, I took another bite.

I couldn't stop what he'd do to me, but I would give my system every inch of vitamins and sustenance as possible.

"I changed my mind," Mr. Prest said quietly, leaning closer. "I want to know about the mute girl called Pimlico."

His voice.

Like molasses and candy; salty crisps and decadent chocolate.

His body scalded me—not because he was hot, but because his proximity set off all sorts of warnings in my blood.

Sneaking a quick glance, I met his gaze as he brazenly stared. Where did he come from? What nationality? What country?

And who named him Elder?

He wasn't old or the leader of some sect. Or he could be, for all I knew.

What the hell is he doing mixing with this riff-raff?

Master A narrowed his eyes in my direction.

I knew that look. He wanted me to reply. For so long, he expected I'd slip and unwittingly speak.

For the first few months, it'd been hard training my ingrained desire to communicate when asked a direct question. To ignore the pull to respond. But over time, it'd gotten easier. But even this handsome, dangerous stranger wouldn't break my silent armour.

Taking another bite, I deliberately dropped my gaze, letting him win the staring contest but losing the battle to make me talk.

The fire burning inside kept me fighting even when I wanted to give up. Only I knew how bad my life had become, but something (oh, my God, was it pride?) hated that Mr. Prest saw a skinny, scarred girl who couldn't escape.

He'd never seen me in a dress with pretty hair or perfect makeup. Never heard me answer professors with wit and intelligence. Never saw me dance and entertain chairmen of charities and probe the psychology of my fellow counterparts just like my mother had taught me.

Who I was never existed for Mr. Prest. He only saw what I was now. He'd leave and forever remember me as a slave, not a free girl.

I scoffed, chewing my final piece of duck.

As if.

He'll forget about you the minute he departs.

Sometimes, my ego could still hurt me, even now.

Not letting my silence deter him, Mr. Prest leaned into my personal space. His large hand vanished into his trouser pocket, followed by the delicate clink of coins.

Catching my eye, he shifted his muscular bulk, depositing a single American penny by my wrist.

My eyes flew to Master A.

Just as I hadn't been allowed at the table for two years, I hadn't handled currency or wealth of any kind.

Master A placed his knife and fork on either side of his plate with eerie calmness. "Mr. Prest, can I ask why the fuck you're giving money to my slave?"

Mr. Prest never tore his eyes from mine. "That's between Pimlico and me."

My heart sank with a two-tonne rusty anchor.

Couldn't he see he'd just ensured my normal beating would be ten times worse? He'd undermined Master A, and no one should ever, *ever* do that.

I fought terror and unhappiness as I kept my gaze locked on the table. However, it didn't stop me noticing Master A from the corner of my eye. An evil smile crooked his lips, promising many more nights where I'd go hungry.

His three friends smirked, understanding yet another punishment would be extracted, and they were invited to partake.

Damn you, Mr. Prest.

Swallowing hard, I didn't give myself permission to look up, but when Mr. Prest pushed the penny closer, my eyes flittered to his.

I froze.

The thickest, longest eyelashes I'd ever seen framed his black pupils. So dense and opaque, they looked like fur. It wasn't fair that a man had such bewitching eyes; it was doubly unfair he'd entered my harsh existence and made it so much worse.

I would remember him always.

He would forget me tomorrow.

Why did I sit next to him?

I should've sat at Master A's feet.

This was my fault.

Stupid.

So stupid.

Lowering his heady voice, Mr. Prest whispered, "A penny for your thoughts, girl."

The old-fashioned phrase echoed in my chest.

He wanted to pay for my muted replies?

He valued my responses enough to bribe me?

Why?

Master A had never offered me kindness to chat. He'd only punished and reinforced my desire to remain quiet.

But this man...

He was treacherous.

Taking a deep breath, I nudged the penny back to him with my pinkie.

The urge to shake my head crept over me. Nonverbal was almost as bad as audible.

I fought the urge, gathering my final mouthful of noodles and doing my best not to hyperventilate as Mr. Prest forced the penny toward me.

He didn't say the phrase again.

He didn't need to. I heard it loudly.

A penny for your thoughts.

Fucking speak.

Master A slammed the table with his palm, making Tony, Darryl, and Monty jump.

But not Mr. Prest.

He moved like the slickness of oil on water, cocking an eyebrow at his host. "Yes?"

Master A bared his teeth, his hand fisted around his knife. "I'm done with whatever games you're playing. Forget about her. She's nothing. Let's talk business." Stabbing the air with his food-soiled blade, he yelled, "Pim, clear the fucking table. You're done. Get out of my sight."

Immediately, I shot to my feet.

Luckily, I'd wolfed down my dinner and didn't mourn the lack of time to finish. My empty plate glowed with reminders that my belly was full, but I hadn't earned it without pain.

Already, my middle cramped with indigestion from eating such rich meat, joining the symphony of all the other kicks and punches I'd endured.

Keeping my eyes down, I dutifully collected the empty

containers and plucked the paper bags under my arms. Mr. Prest's blazer kept getting in the way, but until he stole it from me, I wouldn't take it off.

It was mine.

If only for a little while.

Mr. Prest watched me as I took the packaging to the kitchen, rinsed, and placed them in the recycling bin. Returning, I did my best to stay out of reach of the men's probing hands as I collected soiled plates.

Mr. Prest glowered as Monty slapped my ass and Darryl gathered strands of my hair to sniff dramatically. Master A didn't notice his guest vibrating with rage, and I wouldn't tell him. I'd become invisible again as I did my servantly duties.

Master A leaned back in his chair. "So, we've broken bread together. Let's get down to it."

Mr. Prest placed his hands on the table, his fingers steepled with poise and power. "Before we do, I have conditions."

"What conditions?"

"I don't discuss details in front of others." Cocking his chin at the three rapists, he growled, "I want them gone."

Darryl sniffed. "Hey, loser. We're here for our buddy. We've got his back."

"Yeah. No *us* equals no *deal*." Monty crossed his arms.

I carried my embrace of dirtiness to the kitchen as Mr. Prest stood so fast his chair screeched against the tiles. "Understood."

Stalking from the table, he passed me. His eyes sparked with black violence, glittering harder as he looked me up and down. "Keep the jacket."

My mouth fell open as he stormed toward the exit.

I wanted to scream that he couldn't go.

I wouldn't let him.

With him here, I didn't have to fear Master A nearly as much. I hadn't had enough time to figure out if I could use him for my benefit. Could he help me? Free me?

Don't go…

Master A kept him from vanishing.

Launching from the table, he snapped his fingers. "You lot. Out." Chasing after Mr. Prest, he caught him as he reached the front door. "Don't be like that, Elder. You win. No company. Just you and me."

Mr. Prest paused with his hand on the doorknob. His shoulders remained tight and bunched. I didn't know if he'd accept Master A's offer or just disappear.

I took a gulp of air, the tower of crockery in my arms clinking together.

Finally, Mr. Prest turned around, his hands balling by his sides. "Don't make me remind you about using my first name, Alrik. Last fucking warning. As for our discussion, I want you, me, and her." His smouldering gaze locked onto mine.

Oh, no…

No, no, no.

I didn't want to be privy to their chat. I didn't want Master A to have any more reason to think I valued myself too highly.

Depositing the plates in the sink, I bent over in an awkward bow, backing out of the room toward the corridor and the staircase.

Please, let me get there before he stops me.

Then I could bolt upstairs and write to No One and plug my ears so I never had to know what illegal things Master A was up to.

But of course, that didn't work in my favour.

Nothing ever did.

Mr. Prest was the one to stop me. "Stay, girl. And take your penny. You might not give up your thoughts for so cheap, but you're not leaving until I say so."

My eyes flickered to Master A's, looking for permission.

Mr. Prest might be the top hunter in this pack of animals, but he wasn't the one who'd bought me. He wasn't the one I had to live with after he'd gone.

Master A clenched his teeth, suffering a few goodbye slaps

of his friends as they donned removed clothing and let themselves out.

Anger permeated him, swirling like toxic smog. Raking a hand through blond hair, he grunted. "Fuck, all right. Stay, Pimlico. Get the shot glasses and bourbon.

"Mr. Prest and I have something to discuss."

ELDER

I FUCKING HATED the taste of bourbon.

I preferred sake or gin or even the occasional absinthe. I wasn't a big drinker. I had my reasons. And hadn't touched a drop in almost a year.

But a man like Alrik expected a deal to be done over alcohol because he was still a bloody Neanderthal.

I would indulge him on this one topic, seeing as I'd won every other round.

The slave girl hadn't sat down, flitting around like a fucking hummingbird, gathering shot glasses, straightening white cushions, and placing the dishes in the dishwasher.

Alrik didn't seem to care. She wasn't just his sex slave but house servant, too. He was barely aware of her anymore, happy to let her starve and waste away to nothing.

He deserved something for that.

Something painful.

Over the next few days, I'd get creative and figure out an apt punishment.

The tap ran in the kitchen, heralding my eyes as the girl sprayed herself accidentally with water.

Fuck.

My lips curled in disgust. The sleeves of my jacket were sodden as she rinsed knives and forks before adding them to the dishwasher.

Nursing my shot of bourbon, I snapped, "Enough, girl. Sit."

Alrik shifted on the opposite couch. He'd already tossed back one shot and sniffed his second. If he grew drunk during this discussion, all the better for me. The terms would be heavily in my favour and the clauses I normally snuck into the paperwork, hoping they weren't noticed, would go by unseen.

Fucking idiot.

I had things to say, but I wouldn't start until the girl sat down and stopped fidgeting. I didn't like distractions, and she was a damn distraction.

Something clattered behind me before Alrik bellowed, "For fuck's sake, Pimlico, sit your ass down."

Immediately, she darted into the lounge and kneeled on the white carpet by the coffee table, resuming the same bowed position she'd been in before I'd invited her to eat.

She didn't touch the furniture, almost as if she wasn't permitted. Like a bad dog that'd been slapped too many times for jumping on prized settees.

The more I found out about this bastard, the more I despised him.

Ignoring Pimlico as she huddled on the floor, Alrik toasted me with his shot. "To being alone and able to discuss our new venture."

"Not so fast."

I thought I could drink this shit, but I couldn't.

Why the fuck am I here again?

From the moment I'd met this sleazebag, I'd had the overwhelming urge to wash whenever he looked at me. The way he watched me. The way he laughed and spoke as if I couldn't hear his stinking secrets.

But I could.

And the longer I was in his company, the less I wanted him to breathe. Money was money. Business was business. But when instincts screamed to ignore the deal and walk...I listened.

Only, I didn't want to go.

Not yet.

Because of her.

Pinching the brow of my nose, I glared at the windows behind Alrik where presumably a garden rested in the night.

The second I'd walked into this psychopath's house, I'd been fascinated by her. Not because I could see her tits and shadows between her legs but because of the way she watched me.

She saw everything.

The world had two types of people. The first were the takers. They only noticed those who could help them, offering friendship for false reasons—their egos preventing improvement of their superficial interest.

The second were the givers. Those who knew they were being taken advantage of but couldn't stop it. They'd give and give until they had nothing left. But by giving, they saw things, watching silently in the shadows.

This girl was a giver.

She was soundless judgement, taking everything in while her master and his acquaintances pretended she didn't exist. She was strong inside, but she hadn't found her freedom despite begging for it, which made her lacking.

And I didn't do lacking.

So fucking forget her, finish this, and leave.

Leaning forward, I deposited the crystal glass on the coffee table, lacing my fingers between my legs. "Do you have the funds?"

Alrik smirked. "Seriously? You're gonna ask me that? Even after your invasive background checks?"

Huh.

He'd found out about that. That was interesting and earned a sliver of my respect. My hacking skills weren't as good as some, but normally, I could infiltrate, extract, and patch up my entry without notice.

He huffed. "Look, are we gonna do business or what?"

"Perhaps."

He threw himself onto the soft leather of the couch. "Fuck, I was told you were exhausting. I should've believed them." Tossing back his drink, he clicked his fingers for Pimlico to refill it.

She did so without a peep or eye flicker.

I'd been around others who refused to talk. Taking a vow of silence wasn't all that unusual in my profession (or rather, ex profession) but it didn't ease my mind at all.

Mainly because I wasn't a fucking idiot like Alrik.

His slave girl obeyed him, but she hated him with the death of a thousand shadows. And where I came from...that was not a good death. If my nickname were *Kaitou* for Phantom Thief, hers would be *Mokusatsu*. Kill with Silence.

She absorbed everything, just waiting for her opportunity to end his life.

Good luck to her.

In the brief interaction I'd had with them, she deserved to win over this overly pampered rich dick. She just had to notice her power and commit.

"It's not exhausting to be thorough." I fisted my fingers, holding back my wrath. "It's exhausting to enter into business with untrustworthy people."

Alrik frowned. "Look, you knew the deal when you got here. You were highly recommended. Don't make me regret inviting you into my home."

I laughed. This asshole thought he was better than me. That he could win.

Wrong.

Ignoring him, I once again looked at the slave on the floor. I hated the way she kept drawing me to her. She wasn't acting. She truly was fighting to survive. But the humming vibration of her determined strength was a drug to me.

Patting the couch, I murmured, "Sit here, girl."

Her shoulders rolled as she bowed deeper into the carpet.

Her tattered hair shivered as she glanced at her master.

Alrik tried to slaughter me with his eyes.

If I were any other person, from any other background, I might've second-guessed my decision to play with his possessions.

But he did say I could share.

And I wasn't afraid of him. I was never afraid of pretenders.

Silence fell, clashing with temper from Alrik, terror from Pimlico, and authority from me.

Guess who fucking won?

Alrik threw back his third bourbon. "Go to him, Pim."

Instantly, the girl levered herself from her knees and scurried to my side.

My heart pounded as she perched like a frail bird on the stark white leather, her thighs bunched—ready to fly away if Alrik changed his mind.

Judging by the way she kept her body facing him, I guessed he changed his mind a lot—either to spite or hurt her.

Peering at my ruined jacket with its dripping wet cuffs and slouchy way it hung off her shoulders, I ordered, "Give her permission to obey me without having to go through you." I glanced up, catching Alrik's eye with the command.

Do it.

What the fuck was I doing?

This girl didn't matter. I ran the risk of destroying this business deal. Then again…did I care?

I paused, taking stock of what it would mean if I deliberately sabotaged this transaction. Sure, I'd be out of pocket by millions. But I had more than I could count and it wasn't about the money. Yes, I'd lose the notoriety I'd done my best to earn. Finally cracking open the realm where, up till now, I'd been denied. But I didn't need fucking Alrik to open doors for me. I could kick them down on my own damn accord.

No, this girl interested me more than Alrik ever could. She was worth the price tag if it all fell to shit.

Alrik glowered at his slave before giving me a curt nod. He'd disliked me before. Now, he hated me.

I smiled coldly. "You did say I could share."

The girl shivered, her body sending minor ripples along the couch. I hadn't touched her yet but every nerve ending shot to intensity.

"Pimlico." Alrik sat forward, his hand clutched white-tight around his glass. "Obey Mr. Prest as you obey me. Got it? Do whatever he wants without question."

I fought the thrill running down my spine.

Pimlico glanced at me, before dropping her gaze to the floor. She didn't nod or give any indication of agreement.

But I knew she'd heard, evaluated, and accepted the new terms.

The fact she didn't talk fuelled my interest—not because I wanted her silent secrets but because she challenged me to do what my teacher had taught a decade ago: *'Listen with your entire body, not just your ears. Watch with your entire being, not just your eyes. And judge with your entire soul, not just shallow perception.'*

I hadn't forgotten that lesson. I wasn't a person to educate and then waste that education by letting such valuable knowledge fade. But she was a good refresher.

I wanted to be alone with her. To ask her questions that she wouldn't answer but I would earn her reply anyway. I wanted to steal her so my own disciplinary hand delivered her bruises not this lying asshole's.

Testing her obedience, I patted my thigh. "Come closer."

For a second, she hesitated. Her lips pursed, but her hand crept slowly outward, pulling herself forward.

She didn't come as near as I wanted—her leg still created a chasm between us—but I inhaled, doing my best to smell her.

She smelled of nothing.

No, that wasn't true.

She smelled of fucking desperation.

Wanting to change her opinion of me, to kiddingly prove I wasn't such a bad guy, I rested my hand on her thigh.

She jolted but stayed seated even though her eyes narrowed with fury.

Her skin was ice beneath my touch; her white skirt offered no thermal properties.

Alrik never took his livid glare off me as I stroked her with a gentleness I doubted she'd had in years.

Instead of relaxing, she only stiffened further.

If I were a kind man, I would've removed my hand and allowed her to return to her crouch on the floor where she obviously felt some semblance of safety.

But I wasn't a nice man.

I was a tormentor. A killer. A thief.

And I wanted to steal her courage drop by fucking drop.

Pimlico

WORDS AND VOICES and business.

How long did I sit there? Chained by invisible tethers to a man I had to obey just as absolute as my master.

My eyelids drooped as jargon and empty promises flew around the room.

I had no idea what arrangement Master A entered with Mr. Prest, but whatever it was, it held a price tag of over thirty million dollars and came with uttered phrases such as 'undetectable, irrefutable, and ironclad in both speed and delivery.'

It'd been so long since I'd listened to the ebb and flow of normal conversation that it lulled me into a semi-relaxed state. I wasn't the centre of attention, and a barked command between these two men were their issue, not mine.

Subtly, I rubbed my knees where constant bruises from kneeling marred my flesh. The white skirt irritated me as it clung tight while my ribs and belly ached from their earlier beating.

As nice as this reprieve was—no matter how grateful I was to be sitting on a settee after years of grovelling—it didn't come without consequences.

I'll be shared tonight.

Just like most nights.

Mr. Prest had been given carte blanche to control me, which Tony, Darryl, and Monty were never given. He could ask me to do anything, and I'd have to obey. And once I'd obeyed, Master A would hurt me because he hated others taking liberties he hadn't given.

I'd seen it first-hand when Tony went too far and took something from me he wasn't supposed to take. He hadn't returned for a fortnight because of the wounds Master A had inflicted.

Whoever Mr. Prest was, he must have something of priceless importance for Master A to tolerate me even sitting on his furniture, let alone permitted to listen to such incomprehensible lingo.

Master A sipped another shot. "And you'll install top-of-the-line ghost deflectors?"

"As per your request, yes."

"And the weaponry will be far superior to what they'll use in retaliation?"

Mr. Prest stiffened. "Do you doubt my work ethic and the contract?"

"No. But it is a lot of money and a sensitive arrangement."

"As are all my transactions. Utmost discretion is required from both parties. Not just me." Mr. Prest raised his eyebrow, disregarding Master A's pompous accusation. "Do I have your oath that you'll never mention my name or the origins of the weaponry on board upon delivery of the vessel?"

Huh?

The sleepiness I'd been cursed with snapped into awareness. A crackle of adrenaline flooded my nervous system. What were they discussing? Vessels and weapons?

What is this?

Master A had said something about Mr. Prest being at sea for a few months and in need of female companionship.

Was he in the Navy? Selling State secrets and espionage?

Master A nodded. "Of course. But only if the torpedoes aren't detectable by radar."

"With increasing technology these days, it's not completely guaranteed."

"And you're sure you can't get a nuclear warhead. I'd pay extra."

"I told you I don't deal in those. If you want them, it won't be through me." Mr. Prest's voice dropped to a growl. "But you're already aware of those terms." His eyes flickered to mine, their endless depths sucking light and life from me. "What do you think, Pimlico? Want to be locked on a boat rather than in a mansion? Your master here seems to be going to war."

A boat?

War?

What the hell is he talking about?

I couldn't visualize such a thing. An image of a dinghy with oars for propulsion and wooden sides to prevent drowning came to mind. Why would anyone want to trade a house for that?

Gritting my teeth, I looked over Mr. Prest's shoulder, ignoring the question.

I didn't care that I didn't understand. What I cared about was he'd tried to trip me into replying.

It won't work.

I'd had years of practice.

He chuckled. "Don't worry. I'm sure he won't take you to war." His hand landed possessively on my thigh. "And if he did, at least you might find what you're looking for."

I froze.

What?

What am I looking for?

How would you know what I need?

Even as my questions solidified, I doubted my conviction.

I survived in this world with tiny goals that kept me strong. I took pleasure from avoiding a broken arm by doing tasks before being asked. I was awarded extra hours of sleep or hard-won dinners when I successfully hid my hate.

I did all that because I needed something to reward myself with. If I didn't, whispers of ending it were never far away. If I focused on small things, I could ignore the tug of freedom.

But if I didn't...death.

It was a calculated vindictive seducer, promising an end to pain and suffering. I'd listened once and would've obeyed its commands if the knives hadn't disappeared. I'd thought my momentary weakness was over.

I lied.

The murmurs of taking my own life hid in the panic attacks that lay waiting to pounce when my strength wavered. I was no longer completely whole—parts of me had become an enemy, wanting me to die rather than survive.

He's sniffed suicide on me.

He'd done it the second he'd laid eyes on me; the same way I'd tasted he was more than a businessman and aristocratic bastard.

He was a killer.

And a good one seeing as he was here with us and not caught.

Mr. Prest's fingers drifted down my thigh and dug into my knee—just like Master A's had on the plane ride here. Unlike before, when that little threat had freaked me out, it was nothing compared to what I'd endured. I was trained in touches like those.

I didn't jolt as Mr. Prest squeezed and relaxed, palpitating my joint, forcing my body to pay attention. However, as my muscles locked for abuse and my heart scurried with nervousness, his touch switched from testing to calming.

His breathing turned shallow as he dropped his gaze to where our two bodies met. "I'm not going to hurt you."

Please.

As if I haven't heard that one before.

I wanted to roll my eyes at his empty promise, but I didn't dare. Who knew what Master A would do? He might carve out my eyeballs with a spoon if I showed any more rebellion.

Master A cleared his throat, his focus riveted on where Mr. Prest touched me. He vibrated with loathing and jealousy, even though he was the one who offered me up to sweeten whatever deal they'd concocted.

"Do you get to experience things like fresh air and new places, Pim?" Mr. Prest never stopped stroking. His fingers slowly left my knee, going slightly higher with each stroke.

Just like my taste buds came alive after a few mouthfuls of delicious food, so too did my skin as I received gentle caresses for the first time in so long.

My flesh turned itchy and hot, straining with sensation for more.

Traitor.

I swallowed hard, forcing my gaze to go hazy and not focus on the man touching me, my master, or the things I would be made to do in my future.

"She's not a damn dog, Elder." Master A chuckled. "I don't clip on a leash and take her for a walk to the fucking park. She's a whore. This is her home. She doesn't need to go anywhere."

Yes. Yes, I do.

I need to go somewhere.

Far away from you.

Far away from this cage.

Mr. Prest's fingernails replaced his soft caress, branding my thigh. "Third slip, Mr. Åsbjörn. One more and this fucking deal is off. I don't care if production is arranged and contracts are drawn up." His hand left my skin, flying up in a wedge of severity to point at Master A. "Use my first name once more and you'll never speak again. *Got it?*"

I shivered as the same hand that vibrated with violence fell back onto my body. One moment, vicious and resolute with cruelty, the next, serene and tranquilizing.

Master A poured himself another bourbon and slammed it down. His brittle hatred moved like glass shards in his limbs as he forced himself to remain calm.

Mr. Prest didn't care. His full attention fell to me again, inching closer, pressing his knee against mine.

I sucked in a breath as his head tilted toward my ear, his heady incense and spice aftershave whipping up my nose like a forest fire. It blazed through my lungs and over my tongue, making me inhale and taste him all at once.

"Tell me, Pimlico, do you like being touched gently or are you used to much rougher handling?" His palm splayed over my thigh, gripping hard enough for me to flinch.

Permanent bruises flared. I held my breath, willing pain receptors to quiet and numbness to take over. I'd enlisted that trick multiple times.

Mr. Prest was cruel and harsh and dominant. But beneath that darkness, he couldn't fully erase the strangeness lurking deep inside him. I didn't know if it was a bad strange or good, but he was different from Master A.

That oddity called to me.

Master A flung himself back into the couch, eyeing us with disdain. "I don't know why you're bothering. She doesn't talk. Hit her, hurt her, whisper, or woo her—it's all the fucking same."

Mr. Prest brushed his nose against my earlobe, murmuring so Master A couldn't hear. "You might not use your voice, silent one, but you speak all the same." The tip of his tongue ran over the highly sensitive flesh from my ear to the start of my jaw. "Want to know what you've told me already?" His hand trailed higher up my leg, creeping to the place where I'd been hurt the most.

I'd gone my teenage years with an occasional fumble from an eager boy who'd earned my interest to get close enough to touch. And then, I'd entered womanhood with a brutal rape that'd forever tarnished sex. Everything about men and women coupling was sick and filthy and wrong.

No part of me, under *any* circumstance, wanted to be touched there. Not by Mr. Prest, not by Master A, and certainly not by any of his dastardly friends.

I hated him for taking liberties. I didn't want my skin to be alive. I didn't want my senses to be alive.

I wanted to be numb.

Aloof.

And the audacity of Mr. Prest to make me notice things again, for my heart to beat and my taste buds to fire—it wasn't fair.

But at least, my body was as repulsed by him as any other man.

I didn't feel a quickening in my belly. My pussy didn't clench; my blood didn't heat. My spirit might hold on, refusing to break, but Master A had broken my body.

Sex was revolting.

Sex was *sickening*.

Sex was not something I would ever grow to love.

I was sure of it.

It didn't stop Mr. Prest from brushing his fingertip between my legs. His voice stayed heavy and low. "I'm used to silence, silent one. But you're not very good at hiding your thoughts from your eyes." Pulling away, he brushed my chin with his knuckles. "Want me to prove it? I know that you hate me touching you, and you can't stop the loathing inside you."

His eyes flickered to Master A as his head bowed close again. He gave the impression that we whispered secrets to each other. "He doesn't see you like I do. He doesn't hear you like I do."

Master A shot upright, clearly ready for this meeting to be over. "I think we've covered the finer details. The rest can be done when you drop the contract off for final signature."

Mr. Prest understood the underlying message.

Leave.

Leaning away from me, he grinned. "Want your slave back so soon?" He patted my leg, antagonising him. "I don't think you understand the concept of sharing, Alrik."

I bristled.

I'm not some toy to borrow.

I wasn't a novelty or tatty doll to play with on a whim then dismember when boredom replaced fascination.

I was in two minds. Mr. Prest had kept my heart catapulting like some renegade siege with his gentle touches and soft commands. I feared him more than I feared Master A. I wanted him gone. Immediately. But a large part of me wanted to continue being petted because it'd been so long since anyone had. I wanted him to free me.

However, I never got what I wanted.

Master A inched closer, glowering at Mr. Prest's hand on my thigh. "Do you like his touch better than mine, Pim?" His voice was a hazardous rumble. "I'd advise you say you prefer me over this stranger."

He stared.

I stared.

No reply.

He didn't deserve to know, even if I did want to speak. I would *never* prefer him. I wanted to bury his ashes and get every dog in the neighbourhood to piss on his grave. In that respect, yes, I vastly preferred Mr. Prest's touch, even if he stole rather than requested.

Master A's temper swirled as silence lingered. "There's been enough sharing for one night. Time to remember who your real master is. What do you think of that, my sweet Pim?"

Real master.

That meant kicks and whips and chains.

I bowed my head, keeping my face covered.

You told me to obey him.

Anger churned in my chest because I knew no matter what happened in their business agreement, I would be in a world of pain the moment the door closed on Mr. Prest.

Wobbling a little from too many shots of bourbon, Master A stomped from the lounge toward the front foyer.

My heart clicked 'start' on a stopwatch, mourning the swiftly ticking seconds before I was hurt again.

One,

two,
three,
four.
Please, don't let me endure anymore.

Master A bellowed, "Leave, Mr. Prest. Our business is over. Pim and I need to have a little chat." Glaring over his shoulder, he waited none too subtly to kick Mr. Prest out, all while his gaze hammered knives into my chest.

Mr. Prest's fingers tightened on my leg, digging perfectly trimmed nails into my skirt. He held the pressure for a second too long, holding his breath.

I daren't look up. Even though I knew he wanted me to.

He'd yanked more answers from me without speaking than Master A had managed in two years. We had an unspoken understanding between us. A chemistry recognising our connecting similarities. What made us notice each other? Why did I sense as if I could know him…

I hate that you can see my secrets.
But in return, I see some of yours.

His talk of business and weapons weren't who he was at heart. Such talk was cobwebs and prisms, keeping the truth hidden.

How I knew that, I didn't know. How he could read me, I didn't understand.

And it terrified me as much as it intrigued me.

"Return to your master, silent one. I hope to see you again."

You can't go.
I…

He released me as he stood. With half a smile, he moved sleek and sedately toward the exit where Master A paced with his arms crossed. I'd never seen him so angry with another man for touching me.

"Come here, Pim." Master A snapped his fingers, tugging the invisible cord around my throat.

Instantly, I stood on creaking bones, keeping my chin

down in taught respect. Only utmost servitude would save me tonight.

Already my blood popped and fizzed with terror. My body wept achy tears at the thought of what would happen. The only thing granting courage to inch across the floor was the intoxicating scent of Mr. Prest and the warm heaviness of his blazer.

I belonged to a beast. But if that was true and Master A was an animal, then Mr. Prest was the game warden. He was the master with the locks and keys and power. He had the jurisdiction to whip such animals into submission, to starve them for bad behaviour, and force them to behave against their base desires.

I didn't know which was worse.

The animal or the ringleader.

"Get Mr. Prest's jacket off your worthless fucking body, Pim!" Master A snapped as I padded closer, making me flinch.

My fingers rushed to obey, pulling at the immaculate lapels and slipping the expensive material down my arms.

I mourned the loss of heat and comfort immediately.

Mr. Prest held up his hand. "No, I said she can keep it." His eyes turned evil as he looked at Master A. "And I do mean that. When I return in a few days, I expect to see she's still in possession of it. Got that?"

Master A swallowed his rage, unsuccessfully hiding the anger on his face. "Fine."

"Good."

Turning his dangerous gaze on me, Mr. Prest murmured, "Until we meet again, silent one. Don't ruin my gift." With a last lingering look, he permitted himself to be ushered from the white mansion.

The way Master A kicked him out offered no respect or politeness.

The way Mr. Prest stalked outside extended no gratefulness or acceptance.

Battle lines had been drawn, and I had an awful feeling it'd been because of me.

I hadn't instigated it.

I wasn't a spoilt girlfriend flirting with her lover's acquaintances to cause problems. I was just a girl begging for a quiet existence, wishing to vanish so she never had to see another male again.

Rage from both of them plaited together, buffeting my body as the door slowly swung closed. Rage that would earn me broken parts, and salvaged parts, and parts I wished would just give up living and perish.

Breathing through an oncoming panic attack, I kept my eyes on the final sliver of the driveway.

The last thing I saw, before everything dissolved into a fit of agony, was the terrifying stranger and his powerful back as he walked away.

Pimlico

THE MOMENT MR. Prest left, I drifted toward the corridor and staircase.

I'd played my part. I'd been the pawn in Master A's business transaction.

I was done.

"Oh, Piiiimmm." Master A's taunt rang out behind me. "Where do you think you're going?"

My back straightened even as adrenaline shot down my legs. Every instinct screamed for me to run. Run and hide and get as far away as possible.

But I wouldn't run.

I *never* ran.

Because running was a weakness, and I was many things, but I refused to be that.

Cocking my chin, I gave him a look and continued my trajectory toward the corridor. The sound of his shoes on tiles sent carving knives flaying my spine.

"You know not to turn your back on me, Pimlico."

Just keep going.

A few more feet.

My left hand splayed out to touch the doorframe as I left the lounge and took a shaky breath. One step, two, three. My bare toes touched the first stair; my racing heart made me shudder as I clutched the polished banister.

"Come back here." Master A picked up his pace, appearing a few metres behind me. He cracked his knuckles, tilting his head in a well-known threat. "You didn't think you'd get off so easily, did you? You know you fucked up tonight."

His teeth shone savagely white. "You sat at my fucking table, you bitch. You ate my food. You enticed my guest. You were rude to me, and you know what that means."

Every step he took toward me, my cells bellowed louder to bolt.

It was so hard to ignore. So hard, I had to clutch the banister to keep myself in place; my poor knuckles popped with pressure.

But I didn't increase my speed.

No matter he stood like a gun ready to fire, just waiting for me to fly away, I climbed the steps slowly, regally, with my head held high and silence draped like a glittering gown around me.

I'd let myself down once tonight with my panic attack. The undermining terror that I couldn't control struck my fragile power at the worst possible time. To think the stranger had seen me that way. Heard me breathless and blue.

Oh, God.

The embarrassment was new. I'd had no reason to value what another thought of me for so long...until him.

But it didn't matter. He'd left. I'd never see him again. After what Master A would do to me tonight...who knew if I'd ever see anyone again.

Seven steps, eight, nine.

Twenty-seven more to go and I'd be in my room, my jail. If I could get there, perhaps Master A would remember that I was *his* not Mr. Prest's. Another man could touch me, use me at the discretion of my owner, but they would never take me away.

Only I could do that by taking my life or his.

My spine crawled with imaginary cockroaches, scurrying faster and faster.

Master A ascended the stairs soundlessly behind me. My ears strained, waiting for him to charge and pounce. But he never increased his speed, content to stalk me up the stairs, happy to see what I would do.

He wasn't in a rush to chastise me. We both knew no other alternative existed for tonight.

He felt as if I'd disobeyed him.

I didn't agree.

The pain would be the same.

"Are you ready for another anniversary present, my dear?" His chuckle was rancid with malicious intent. "I think you're the one who owes *me* a present after I let you sit on my couch. Don't want you believing you're worth more than you are."

The landing was so close. My speed increased just a little.

He growled as my feet grazed the top step. "Running won't change what I'm about to do to you, Pim."

His oath shoved me forward like a phantom hand between my shoulder blades. It was no longer a battle between slow and quick, strong or weak, brave or meek. I was a warrior who faced combat head-on. But I was also a defeated soldier who wanted to sprint from enemy lines.

Go!

Instinct made me do it. The animalistic need to hide gave no room to argue. I couldn't stop my legs from breaking into a scurry, just like I couldn't stop my heart from tearing through my kick-bruised chest.

I shouldn't.

I'd be punished.

I should fight my terror and drop to my knees. Like always.

But I couldn't. Not this time.

I bolted.

"Pim!" He chased me. Just like I knew he would.

My brittle legs hurtled my skinny body from the corridor into my room. There were no doors to slam, no locks to secure. Even my ensuite had no barricade—no privacy offered at any time.

I supposed I was lucky to have my own space, but it was just another element to Master A's board game of pain. No matter where I ran, no matter where I hid, he found me. Because he was god in this house, and I was merely his whore.

My mouth parted with a silent scream as he appeared in the doorway, panting with angry-sharp eyes. "I thought we'd taught the lesson of no running a few weeks into your stay?" Storming toward me, he growled, "Did that fucking prick somehow undo all my teachings the second he touched you? Did he? *Answer me!*"

Every cell cowered, my blood dried up, my heart stopped beating.

Melting to the tiled floor, I went one step further in begging. I didn't bow with my chin tucked and shoulders rolled. I threw myself entirely on the ground with my arms outstretched as I'd seen monks do in deep prayer, pleading for mercy but knowing I wouldn't get any.

"That won't save you this time, bitch." My breath caught as he stomped on my left hand, twisting his foot so my skin pinched and did its best to spiral-fold.

I screamed in my head.

Pain.

Pain.

Pain!

My silent scream was so loud it made my eardrums bleed.

"You liked him touching you, didn't you!? Don't fucking deny it. I know the truth." He trampled harder on my hand, putting his entire weight on the tiny, breakable bones. "You think I didn't notice? That I wouldn't see the way you looked at him? Fuck, Pimlico you're *mine!*"

I screamed again, drowning myself in the gonging sound of agony, but the room remained silent while he stomped again and again, doing his best to shatter delicate fingers.

"Just because you won't talk doesn't mean I don't fucking know when you're lying to me!"

Turn it off!

Now!

Fighting a rush of overwhelming nausea, I forced every nerve ending to withdraw deep inside. I did what my body had taught me. A mantra filled my head while the pain receptors in my hand switched off.

After all, that was what pain was. A siren to tell me all was not well and that action had to be taken to avoid worse damage. No shit, not all was well. I got that message loud and clear. I didn't need to hear it over and over.

On or off.

Click.

Off.

It didn't mean I could ignore the throbbing, bellowing agony ricocheting up my arm. It merely allowed me to compartmentalise and stay alert so I could pre-empt what came next.

His shoe lifted from my hand only to pull back and jab sharply into my ribs.

I fought the urge to curl around the new flare. It didn't matter that he'd kicked me only hours ago. It didn't matter that my previous bruises would become new bruises, which would bleed beneath my skin.

All I could do was remain straight and prone for his abuse. I would blanket myself in whatever numbness I could and accept two things: either I'd survive this, in which case I could nurse my wounds in private and finally give in to building sobs, or he'd kill me and then none of it would matter anyway.

Kill me, get it over with.

"Why won't you motherfucking speak?!" He kicked me again, going for my hip, painting me with livid colours. "Talk, goddammit." His sharp shoe stabbed my upper thigh, then my knee, calf, and ankle. "Say one word and I'll stop."

No.

Never.

This battle was not new. I'd endured it many times before.

However, he was more vicious tonight, all because of Mr. Prest.

Damn him.

Curse him.

Never come back.

Don't you ever come back.

Turning his attention from my left side, he angled himself on my right, kicking my ankle, calf, thigh, and rib. At least my bruises would match. A Morse code dotting my flesh. Would it blare a plea for help? Or would it repeat the knowledge that I was his to do what he wanted?

"You won't speak to me, but you spoke to him."

What?

"You spoke to that fucking asshole who thinks he's better than me."

No!

"You think you can lie to me? Even your silence drips with the fucking truth."

What truth?

There is no truth!

He kicked me with every remaining energy, landing squarely on my lower back and earning a deep-seated groan I couldn't control.

"Ah, sweet victory. You *do* make a noise." Crouching beside me, he wrenched my head, forcing me to look at him. "You wanted him, didn't you, Pim? You wanted his cock over mine. You wanted that sick fuck because he let you sit at the table and eat like a human. Because he permitted you on the couch like a *woman*."

Shaking me, he spat in my face. "You aren't a woman. You're mine to be what I *tell* you to be. If I say you're a fucking flamingo, you stand on one leg. If I tell you you're a dog, you get on all fours and wait to be mounted. Do you get that? *Do you!?*"

I flinched, disgusted as warm, oozing saliva flowed over my chin.

I am a woman.

And I'm not yours.

No matter how long you own me, I'll never be yours.

"Those gifts weren't his to give." Yanking me to my feet, he used my hair as a leash, guiding me from my room to his.

I stumbled beside him, breathing hard, tears streaming that I didn't remember crying, all while holding my mangled hand. Every step felt as if I'd shatter into a billion pieces. I *wanted* to shatter. Perhaps then the agony would stop.

My hand was broken. I didn't need a doctor to tell me that.

He tossed me into his room, stormed to his bedside table, and yanked out the rope. I parried backward as he grabbed my wrist, throwing me on the bed.

The moment I lay down, he tore off Mr. Prest's blazer, wrenched down my skirt, ripped off the rest of my ruined polo, and smiled with victory. "I wanted to have fun tonight. Not every day is as special as a two year anniversary."

He shoved his face in mine. "But you had to fucking ruin it, didn't you?! You had to get wet for that cocksucker as he swindled me out of millions. You had the *audacity* to let him touch you and *like* it."

Pulling back, he swiped shaking hands through his hair. His shaking matched mine but for entirely different reasons. I fought terror and the last dregs of strength I possessed. He was drunk on brutality and ready to deliver.

Coiling the rope around his hand, he snickered. "You know what I just realised, sweet little Pim?" His arm lashed backward, bringing the rope hissing forward. "I realised that it's been too many months since I made you scream."

The first sting hit me square on the chest, granting a livid welt instantly.

I clamped my lips together and stared at the ceiling. I would've given anything to roll onto my side and squeeze into a ball. I'd been with him for long enough to know what he planned.

And it wasn't good.

He whipped me again and again, the tiny fibres of the rope slicing through tender skin like a fileting blade. Pinpricks of blood welled on my breasts and lower belly.

"Remember that night...when I broke your arm? You made the sweetest sound." He grabbed his cock through the denim, before quickly undoing his belt and shoving his jeans to the floor. He didn't wear underwear, and his ugly penis sprang from a thicket of blond hair. "When I heard you scream? *Fuck*, it turned me on."

Tearing off his t-shirt, he climbed on the mattress, naked with just the rope in his hands.

I tore my eyes away.

From now on, I wouldn't look at him. He would do his best to make me bellow. He would force me to watch. Order me to listen to every depraved thing he said. But he couldn't make me stay.

As his sweaty grip lashed my body to the bed and coarse rope bit into my wrists and ankles, I said goodbye to Pimlico and became Tasmin instead.

I sank and sank.

I returned to a happier time.

Shedding my slavery, my mind skipped into innocence.

Where nothing and no one could touch me.

ELDER

WHO THE FUCK is she?

The question drove me mad.

She was in my mind with her judging silence; in my thoughts with her knowing stare.

She was just a girl. A beaten, skinny, insolent little girl.

So why did I recall her as something so much more than what she was? Why had she made such an impression on me?

No one had left such an imprint since I'd lived on the streets full of coldness and cruelty. She reminded me of that time. A time I tried so fucking hard to forget.

"Sir, the contract is drafted."

My head snapped up from my laptop. I glowered at Selix. He was one of the very few to know me before wealth found me—well, before I stole wealth and made it mine.

I ran a hand up my bare arm, tracing the Japanese words inked around my wrist. The proverb taunted me, reminding me of the promise I'd made to my mother when I'd been a better man. "Good. Arrange the final meeting so we can get the fuck out of this port."

"Very well." He retreated from my office, carrying the thick manila folder full of schematics and fine print. I didn't relax until the soft *hish* of the closed door met my ears.

The moment I was alone, I planted my elbows on my desk

and scrubbed my face.

I was too fucking busy for this nonsense.

She's just a girl.

Shit, don't call her that.

She's a slave.

Over the past two days, my mind had slowly transformed her from possession to human.

I didn't want that.

I wanted her to remain faceless…worthless, so I could forget about her and move on. I had too many assholes asking for my services to be side-tracked.

Besides, if I needed a woman, I could have two or ten delivered within the hour. I didn't need her. Not that I often gave in to bodily cravings. Bad things happened when I gave in to my desires.

Look at my current kingdom.

Somehow, I'd turned petty crime into full-blown racketeering. I'd evolved pick-pocketing into an illegal dynasty, and no law or rule could stop me. I operated on international waters. I was free from country propaganda and constitutions. In effect, I was a pirate with his own agenda.

Thinking of the open ocean, my eyes drifted toward the horizon. A physical craving clutched me to shed the anchor and go. To sail far away from this filthy fucking town.

Soon.

One more day.

Then I could leave this godforsaken place and travel to my next business appointment on the other side of the globe.

Alrik was true to his word. His funds had cleared, and my bank account was millions of dollars wealthier.

Not that measly money meant anything these days. I could survive with nothing—I'd proven that—even if what I'd done to survive didn't fit the approval of many.

Before I had money…life was easy. I knew who I was. I knew *what* I was. But then, fate decided to give me gold instead of dirt, raising me from nobody to somebody.

I was meant to smite those below me, to manipulate and control. So why the fuck did I feel like I'd just crushed a gutter rat beneath my shoe when I'd been nothing but courteous and kind?

Damn that woman.

Standing, I shoved aside my chair and stalked to the floor-to-ceiling windows revealing a sparkling harbour with catamarans, speed boats, and brightly painted dinghies. We'd pulled into port almost a week ago, and it was time to leave. I didn't do well locked in one place.

"Fuck." The curse fell quietly as a woman with dark brown curls laughed on the jetty in the distance. She looked nothing like the skinny slave I'd met, but her hair colour churned things inside I no longer recognised.

I'd earned what I wanted from the meeting with Alrik.

I should be happy.

But I couldn't rid myself of this disgusting aftertaste as if I'd done something I wasn't proud of.

My hands curled into fists. Hadn't I given her the very fucking jacket off my back? Hadn't I spoken cordially and ensured she ate?

Yes!

So why can't I forget her?

She should've been grateful for my attention. I treated her a hell of a lot better than her master ever did.

What happened to her in the two days since I'd been there? Had she been molested again? Beat again?

Not that it mattered.

I'd seen people have their teeth kicked in and bones broken on the street. I'd seen men with fingers cut off while standing in a five-star restaurant where mob bosses had no fear of retaliation.

I lived in violence.

I *was* violence.

So the thought of a girl getting smacked around—it shouldn't fucking bother me.

But it does…

Someone knocked on my office door.

Wrenching my head up, I growled, "Enter."

One of the servants tiptoed in, carrying a tray with unknown lunch beneath a silver dome. She didn't say a word but walked with confidence, placing the food on my desk with a polite smile before retreating.

She moved with freedom and happiness.

Pimlico moved with servitude and depression.

I want her.

My body stiffened with the obsessive need to abduct Alrik's slave. Swiping fingers through my hair, I tried to tame the thick black strands, forcing such ideas to flee.

Pimlico had a lot to share—an entire story to tell. She'd been intrigued by me, too. I'd felt it. Her interest hadn't been because she wanted my wealth but something deeper. Something, I couldn't figure out. Something, I would never know because she wasn't mine and I had laws in place that I had to follow.

I'd seen her once. Touched her once.

Once would have to be enough.

Because a man like me could never have a second chance.

It was my most unbreakable law.

Tomorrow, I would go back and complete our bargain.

I should be excited about another contract well struck.

However, I couldn't give a flying fuck about that.

What I did give a fuck about was the slave and her silent secrets begging me to reach out and steal.

Do I have the willpower to do this?

Pacing in my office, I scowled at the expensive décor with its library shelves and handmade furniture. I'd lived with my unusual appetites all my life. I wouldn't let one broken girl destroy my strict guidelines.

I would see her again.

I wouldn't talk to her.

I wouldn't look at her.

And I definitely wouldn't demand to fucking share her.

Pimlico

TWO DAYS PASSED.

After the beating, when Mr. Prest left, Master A used me mercilessly. By day, he made me wish I'd been braver and killed myself the moment he'd bought me. By night, he made me curl like a dog on the end of his bed where he could kick me in his dreams then take me when he woke.

By morning, I was sleep deprived and trembling from residual agony.

He didn't call the doctor to set my hand, and after making him breakfast, I ransacked the medical cupboard in the downstairs bathroom, doing my best to patch myself up. I found a bandage and painkillers—not nearly good enough to fix what he'd done—but it was better than nothing.

Why did I bother?

I had no idea.

He would merely hurt me again and *again*. It was pointless to give my body a hundredth attempt to survive when my soul had already packed its bags and leapt overboard.

However, as I strapped my broken fingers and smeared arnica over my arms and legs from his kicks, my mind wandered to Mr. Prest.

He'd caused my pain.

He was the reason Master A turned so vile.

I had no intention of ever forgetting it.

I wanted nothing to do with his blazer, his scent of incense and spice, or any thoughts of his black eyes and fierce features.

He was nothing to me. Just like I was nothing to my master.

The only saving grace was I hadn't seen Darryl, Monty, or Tony since the night they were thrown out. I didn't think it was because Master A needed a rest from his so-called friends, but because he was jealous over the attention bestowed upon me.

"Oh, Pimlicooo? Come out, come out, wherever you are."

I shuddered as my nemesis appeared in the kitchen.

"Ah, there you are."

Yes, here I am. Doing your laundry and dishes and every task you require.

Coming up behind me, he wrapped awful arms around my painful body. "I missed you."

Go to hell.

Pressing a bruise on my collarbone, he murmured, "Have you been a good girl while I've been in my study?"

An hour or so ago, he'd retreated to his office, firing off emails and doing who knew what. I'd enjoyed a few moments away from his foul eyes and critical curses. While he was occupied, I'd done my best to find the sleeping tablets he sometimes used. I couldn't handle another beating so soon, and planned to crush a few into his food so I could have the night off.

However, the bottle had been empty.

My plotting to avoid more agony foiled.

If I had to hit him over the head with the frying pan...I would.

I would hit and hit and *hit* until his skull cracked like a rotten egg and I could finally stride from the front door as a free woman.

Free...

My chin raised as I glowered into the distance. My bare toes dug into the cold tiles as my naked body crawled beneath his touch. Ever since Mr. Prest's departure, I'd been naked—all clothes had vanished once again.

One moment, Master A squeezed me, the next, he threw me toward the sink, walloping my cheek with his fist. "I asked if you were a good girl, Pim. *Answer* me."

I glanced through glassy tears, holding my smarting cheek. *You'll never learn.*

No matter what you do…I'll never *answer you.*

His hands fisted as we entered yet another staring contest that normally ended with me bowing at his feet for mercy.

All day, he'd been in a diabolical mood. It began with him waking me by forcing my face into his crotch, making me gag on his morning wood.

Breakfast was endured standing on the table like a naked figurine so he could throw utensils at me while eating his cereal.

Lunchtime had earned my body pushed into the white leather of his couch and held down while he whipped me from behind.

And now, it was night.

The worst time.

For years, I'd retained some dignity. I'd kept my silence. I cursed him with glares and swore with a sharply tilted jaw. And no matter what he did, I never *ever* let him break me. But in doing so, I became so tangled with thoughts of murder and escape that I could fill an entire encyclopaedia.

I was ready to kill him or be killed.

I couldn't live like this any longer.

I wanted out.

Now!

Shaking out the fist he'd just shoved in my face, he snarled, "Get upstairs, Pim. It's past your bedtime, and I have just the thing to help you fall asleep."

* * * * *

Three days since Mr. Prest disappeared.

Lunchtime.

I'd been fed this afternoon, which was the first in twenty-seven hours. Not that I'd been counting or anything. It consisted of lasagne leftovers served in my dog bowl.

It was one of my small victories. I'd won last night.

I'd pre-empted his plans to take me, and with a few well-placed stares, I switched his mood from volatile to sane. He still hurt me but not as much as he'd prepared. And today, he'd agreed I was a good girl.

Idiot.

However, now that I'd done the dishes and knelt at the foot of the couch while he watched some god-awful action movie, he snapped his fingers for me to crawl to him.

My stomach flip-flopped as nausea rushed up my throat.

I knew what he wanted—the same thing he always did when he watched a movie before dinner.

A blowjob.

The first couple he'd forced me to give, I'd tempted death by biting. Not hard but enough to voice my displeasure in the loudest actionable way possible.

He'd hit me around the head so fiercely, I'd blacked out, only to come to as he used me without my permission.

I licked my lips, running my tongue over cracked flesh and sore gums. To me, I did my best to prepare my body for such an unsavoury task. To him, it came across as sultry and wanting to suck.

Master A groaned as he arched his hips off the couch, undoing his zipper, and pulling out his cock. "You've become so talented at this, my sweet Pim." Grabbing the remote control beside him, he turned off the sounds of explosions and gunfire, replacing the movie with soft strands of violin and piano.

Instantly, I shivered with repulsion.

Classical music.

Intrinsically entwined with my abuse. I didn't know if Master A was smart enough to shackle my mind with music while making my body do heinous things. But my mother would've been intrigued by his methods. She would've had a field day figuring out why I wanted to burst into the tears the moment a quavering note from the softest instrument echoed around me.

Reclining, Master A snatched my nape, guiding my face to his lap. "I'm so glad you're behaving again. Seems our little talk did you a world of good."

I despise you to the bowels of the cosmos.

My soul recoiled. I fought the tug as much as I dared.

But ultimately, I let him guide me to where he wanted, keeping my eyes squeezed as his cock nudged against my lower lip.

Bing bong.

We both froze.

The doorbell hovered in the space with demand.

Master A breathed hard, his chest working with anticipation of my mouth. "Who the fuck is that?"

How the hell would I know?

Rearing back, I thanked whoever it was. They couldn't stop this from happening, but at least they'd given me a small reprieve—enough to swallow back my lunch and mentally shut out the classical music, so I might be able to do my task while blank and numb.

Shoving me away, he didn't care I sprawled on my hands and knees as he clambered off the couch, quickly tucking himself into his jeans and wrenching up his fly. "If that's fucking Darryl, I told him tomorrow."

I hope all your friends rot.

Master A looked over his shoulder, pointing at the wall. "Kneel. Behave."

The doorbell rang again as he vanished from the lounge.

Fuck you.

I stuck out my tongue. It was juvenile and ridiculous, but it made my heart lighter in a teeny-tiny way.

With the small second alone, I glanced at the windows to

my left. The sun had dipped below the sea, extinguishing itself in a bonfire of pinks and oranges. The view from the white monstrosity never held beauty, no matter if the sun set or rose. It was merely a vista of my prison.

I hated it.

I hated many things these days.

Tearing my eyes away from falling dusk, I crawled toward the spot he'd told me to wait.

Cradling my bandaged hand, I glanced up as Master A stalked back into the lounge. His face had lost its lust from before, replaced with stark annoyance. He threw something soft and white at my naked body.

"I fucking forgot he was coming today."

My heart bucked like a bronco until I promised I'd wrap it in a noose to perform the gallows' jig if it didn't stop.

Who?

Who's coming?

Ducking, he shoved a finger in my face. "Get dressed. *Now.* Keep your eyes down, obedience high, and if I fucking catch you looking at him, the past few nights will be considered preschool before heading to boot camp." Tipping my chin with his biting finger, he kissed me hard and sloppy. "Got it? You're mine. Not his. *Mine.* Now, cover yourself and don't dare move."

Not waiting for me to obey, he stormed toward the foyer, leaving me to stroke the white sweater dress he'd given me.

Clothes.

The last time he'd given me clothes...

Oh, my God, he's come back.

Elder bloody Prest.

The man who'd provoked my master. The man whose fun almost cost me my life. The last few days, he'd probably counted his millions and forgotten all about me while I suffered broken bones and agony.

Now, he was back for more.

My skin broke out in fire and frost, battling for supremacy.

I didn't know why Master A wanted me covered for this guest when he allowed others to stare, but I didn't hesitate in slipping my hands into the long sleeves and pulling the stretchy material over my head.

My shoulder blades screamed. My elbows popped. Every inch of me bellowed as I stood on my knees and shimmied into the dress. It came to my calves—not enough to hide the bruises on my lower legs, but enough to cover everything else.

He's here.

I couldn't soothe my heart, no matter how soft I petted or whispered for it to calm down. It no longer listened to me after I'd threatened to hang it.

Mr. Prest was just a man. A man I didn't like. A man who brought more pain into my world simply by visiting.

But still just a man.

I'd survived living with one for this long…I could survive another.

Heavy footfalls sounded in the foyer as I sank back onto my knees and ran my good hand through my hair, deliberately shielding my face from seeing too much. He'd returned, but it didn't mean I would look. If Master A wanted me to be invisible, listen to their business conversation, but not pay any attention to Mr. Prest, I would do every instruction.

I guess the command to obey Mr. Prest is revoked.

Resting my sore hand on my lap, I sighed into the clingy material of the given gown. Once again, claustrophobia clawed, whispering of panic attacks and weakness.

I clenched my teeth.

You're stronger than that. You're better than all of them.

Breathing hard through my nose, I dared believe my lies and forced my blood to calm.

The hard flooring chilled my knees as low murmurs came closer. My ears pricked as the gentle click of men's dress shoes filled the stark space. My chin begged to rise, to give me a postcard-perfect view of Mr. Prest as his scent and presence surrounded me.

I forbid it.

Instead, I locked my gaze on the grout line between tiles, following the softer grey from the lounge rug to the dining room table.

"I trust you received payment okay?" Master A asked.

Mr. Prest's legs came into my vision.

I dropped my head further.

He's not here.

He's not real.

Don't look or listen or linger.

My heart chugged with steam and coal, but I won the war. My eyes remained steadfast on the floor.

Mr. Prest came forward a few steps, planting his long, powerful legs where I wished he wouldn't.

Legs weren't so bad.

I could handle his legs...ankles really.

That was fine.

But anything else, I didn't want to see.

"I did. I sent you the schematics and in-depth blueprints in return." Rustling sounded as Mr. Prest pulled something from the leather binder in his hands. "Here."

How do you know it's a binder?

Shit, my eyes had steadily crept upward.

Up his broad thighs, past the slight bulge in his trousers, up the svelte lines of his chest, to the sharp ridges of his throat.

Drop your head!

My command made my shoulders roll as I bowed deeper into the floor. I couldn't meet his eyes. That was where the danger lay.

If I slipped and looked up, I doubted I'd live to tomorrow if Master A deemed I had some sort of sick fascination (or was it attraction?) toward this monster I couldn't stand.

No, it isn't attraction.

It couldn't be.

After losing my virginity to sexual slavery, I'd been cured of finding anyone pleasing to the eye or connected to my soul.

I doubted I'd ever find anyone like that.

My fate was different to my friends who would live long lives and give birth to kids with boys they'd fallen in love with.

I wanted to be alone.

Safe.

Far away from men.

The two villains talked in low murmurs about delivery dates and inspections.

I didn't bother straining to hear. I didn't care.

My skin prickled as Mr. Prest's voice mingled with Master A's. The awareness of both of them watching me wrapped a plastic bag around my heart, suffocating me slowly. I didn't dare move; I could barely breathe. Mr. Prest somehow stole every sense keeping them zeroed in on him.

The battle to keep my eyes down and head ducked became harder and harder to win. Every shuffle of his feet and rustle of his clothing whispered for me to indulge in just a peek.

One peek.

I can't.

Taking a deep breath, I did what I never thought I'd do and focused on the classical music rather than my abhorrent fascination with our visitor.

I willingly let stringed instruments distract me, even though they only brought nightmares.

That was what Master A was: a nightmare. And one of these days, I'd wake up and this would be all over.

Wake up, Pim...wake up.

After ten minutes or so, Master A snapped his fingers, ceasing their conversation. "Get Mr. Prest a drink, Pim."

Get up?

Move?

Run the risk of stealing a glance I wasn't allowed to steal?

My spine rolled in disobedience.

When I didn't leap into action, Master A lowered his voice. "Did you not hear me?" Nudging my knee with his toe, he grunted, "Get!"

My body snarled with aches and pains as I scrambled to my feet, skidding into the kitchen. Miraculously, I kept my chin tucked and eyes down. However, even without eyesight, I saw Mr. Prest. *Felt* him watching me. *Heard* him thinking about me.

His shadow lurked in my peripheral as I scurried around the countertop.

Not once had Mr. Prest addressed me. Not once had he tried to engage me in pleasantries—not like the first time when he'd shortened my name with familiarity.

He hadn't been threatened by Master A not to speak or look, so why hadn't he been as strangely kind as he was in the beginning?

I didn't want to admit it, but the cold shoulder hurt more than a kick from my bastard owner.

Something was to be said about cruelty. Give nothing but barbarity and that was all that was expected. Give tenderness mixed with persecution and the fall from hope hurt far, far worse.

Was that Mr. Prest's agenda from the start?

Keeping my face covered by my hair as much as possible, I headed into the walk-in pantry where a small cellar was located in the floor.

Pressing a silver button by the shelf housing condiments, the trap door opened and the current bottle of bourbon Master A had selected shot to the top on an automatic delivery system.

Grabbing the expensive liquor, I trembled as I carried the blasted liquor back to splash generous amounts into crystal goblets.

My pour wasn't neat; a few droplets landed on the bench.

My back turned rigid. I waited for reprimand.

I'd dropped a bottle once.

I'd only been with Master A for a month, and my rebellion hadn't fully stopped. I didn't remember if I dropped it by accident or on purpose.

But I did remember the punishment very well. It involved shards of the broken bottle and generous pouring of spoilt liquor on the open cut he'd adorned me with.

I'd cried soundless tears.

But I hadn't given him what he wanted most—my voice.

Not that it mattered. He'd cured me of my butterfingers with one incident.

Ignoring the scar on my forearm from the horrendous memory, I quickly wiped up the small spillage and stoppered the bottle.

Replacing it back in the cellar, I set the glasses on the coffee table where both men had retired in the lounge and returned to my post by the wall, dropping to my knees with an ill-concealed wince.

Mr. Prest murmured something like gratitude, his eyes tracking me even as the soft clink of toasting goblets sounded over the music.

But he said nothing else. No barb about my wardrobe or fishing hook to taunt me to speak.

His body language shut me off, focusing on Master A.

For the next thirty minutes, I zoned out.

Listening to men—rather than granting forced blowjobs—was a much happier alternative. However, after the past few sleepless nights, I struggled to fight the heavy cloud of drowsiness. I battled drooping eyelids, pinching my inner wrist with demands not to fall unconscious.

I'd done that once: slithered from my bow into a full fetal position on the floor.

Darryl had been the one to punish me that night. Master A had goaded him, saying how undisciplined I was and needed a harsh lesson.

I hadn't been able to move for a week.

The low hum of voices suddenly stopped.

I panicked.

Had I dropped off and they'd noticed? Had I been requested to serve and had a micro nap instead?

My heart did its best to flee. Only, Mr. Prest ensured it stayed in my ribcage with a soft curse. My shoulders rolled even more as he finally chose his moment to undermine my conflict not to watch him.

"At least your dress fits you better than that ugly skirt." His voice acted as scissors, slicing up the dress he'd complimented, licking over my skin with sharp threats.

Inching along the couch, his shadow came closer as the automatic lights clicked on now the sun had well and truly gone to bed.

Don't look.

Do. Not. Look.

He perched on the end of the settee like a black crow of intrigue.

"Let's get back to signing the final contract, shall we?" Master A muttered, nursing his drink.

"In a moment." Mr. Prest waved him away impatiently.

Even with my hair obscuring my vision and my steadfast obedience at keeping my gaze locked on the floor, I couldn't stop myself straining to feel and hear and stare.

I hate you for what befell me.

So why was I still drawn to him?

Magic?

Fate?

What?

Sensing I was listening, Mr. Prest inched closer. Leaning over the end of the couch with his fingers linked around his goblet, his eyes resolutely locked on me. "Still silent, I see." He chuckled, his body violin-string tight with inquisition rather than giving his attention to Master A.

Don't do that.

Don't you see what you cost me?

Look at him, not me.

Tipping forward, he placed his untouched alcohol on the coffee table before training his gaze on my head.

My scalp prickled beneath his stare, heating in degrees the longer we stayed trapped in whatever game he played.

"Mr. Prest..." Paper crinkling and a pen tapping on glass

signalled Master A's none-too-subtle attempt at interruption.

It didn't work.

Mr. Prest merely stared harder, as if he could crack open my skull and drag out my thoughts without having to go through my mute mouth. Shifting slightly, he reached into his pocket.

Don't be a penny.

Not again.

The soft ping of battered copper bounced on the tile by my knee, spinning with a dull bronze glitter before falling face up. "A penny for your thoughts, silent one. Perhaps, today you'll speak."

Stop doing this to me!

Damn him and his pennies.

I didn't want to be paid for words I'd never utter. How about he gave me a penny for every kick I'd endured, every broken bone, every rape, every tear?

I'd be a damn millionaire with the means to run far away from here.

Master A stood.

My teeth clamped onto my bottom lip as I folded into myself.

I didn't do anything!

Hurt him, not me!

But instead of swatting me around the head or kicking me into pieces, Master A wedged himself between Mr. Prest and me. The distance from my position by the wall and the end of the couch wasn't much, and Master A's trousers granted a whiff of the frangipani laundry detergent he insisted I wash his clothes with.

He smelled so different from Mr. Prest, who reeked of power and ruthlessness. I didn't know what flavour those two traits had, but Mr. Prest swam in them, permeating every space he entered.

"Stop giving my slave money." Plucking the penny from the floor, Master A clutched it tight in his fist. "In this business arrangement, *I'm* the one who pays *you*. Which I have, as you well fucking know. I transferred the full funds as per our agreement. I've signed the additional contract for final acceptance. Our meeting is over."

I sucked in a breath as Master A blocked me from seeing. With his back to me, I permitted my gaze to climb, just a little.

The standoff lasted a few heavy seconds.

Instead of rising to leave, Mr. Prest reclined comfortably on the settee. The squeak of expensive leather acted as a chorus bar on the appalling music still raining. "I'm not leaving. Not yet."

What? Does he have a death wish?

Just go!

I caught movement between Master A's legs as Mr. Prest raised his arm, pointing at me. "What happened to her?"

"What the fuck do you mean, what happened to her?" Master A crossed his arms, not returning the penny or stepping away. "She's none of your concern."

I froze as Mr. Prest's accusing finger dropped to my broken, badly bandaged hand. "How did she do that?"

An odd bubble of laughter tickled my insides.

Who cares?

Why did he insist on nettling my owner? He didn't care about me. It was all an act to rile Master A and somehow get better terms for whatever deal they'd struck.

"She did it to herself." Master A planted his legs wider in a threat. "Don't worry yourself over a small accident. Worry yourself over delivering my yacht on fucking time."

"Oh, I don't worry about things like that." Mr. Prest stood too, squaring off with him. "I have utmost belief that your purchase will be the best quality, highest specifications, and delivered perfectly on time."

Master A had no retort.

"So, seeing as I guarantee to uphold my end of the bargain, how about you indulge me in a simple question?" Looking around Master A, Mr. Prest caught my gaze. "Tell me."

Shit!

I'd looked up, forgetting myself.

The moment we made eye contact, my breath evaporated, and every vein attached to my heart popped free like a hose, spraying heated blood in scattered rivers in my chest.

"Tell me how she hurt her hand." His jaw hardened, his eyes like onyx gemstones, far more priceless than any penny he could give. "Lie to me about why she's black and fucking blue."

His rage grew until his face darkened and forehead furrowed into furious lines.

He intoxicated me.

His fury was a hot blanket, reminding me briefly what it was like to be looked at with worth rather than bankruptcy.

My chin tilted higher, my mouth parted as we stared and *stared.*

He licked his lips as something unspoken and unrecognised arched from his body to mine. I had no choice but to let its corrupting electricity spark through my veins before shattering from my chest back to him.

The longer we watched, the thicker the connection grew until every cell hummed for something bigger than me, something stronger, scarier, safer than I'd ever been given.

Look away...

Look away!

I'd stared too long. I'd jeopardised my pain for too little.

My neck argued as I forced my eyes to drop.

It was as hard as pulling out a fingernail, but I did it.

Just in time, as Master A swivelled on the spot, glowering at me meek and behaving behind him. "Her hand? It's nothing. Like I said, she did it to herself."

I would never do such a thing...

"How?" Mr. Prest's bark was sharp and snappy.

Stupid man. You'll never get the truth. Leave before you make me slip again.

Staring at him had somehow overridden my hatred for

what I'd endured, removed my blame off his shoulders, and begged him to stay.

He was the only one with unique power over Master A. What could I do to make him free me rather than destroy me?

Master A sneered. "She fell down the stairs."

Seriously?

God, what a cliché.

I didn't move, waiting for Mr. Prest's follow-up question. How did she fall? What did you do? Why should I believe your lies?

Only, there were none.

Slowly, he grunted in understanding, and that was it.

Moving around the couch, Mr. Prest balled his hands. "In that case, our deal is complete."

What? No!

How dare he prickle with questions he already knew the answers to?

Damn you. Curse you!

Leave! And never come back!

I trembled on the floor. Filling with rage so thick and violent, I bit my tongue.

Master A laughed, instantly relaxing, sensing victory while I wallowed in defeat. "Excellent." Striding forward, he held out his hand. "You'll get in touch in eight months once delivery can be made?"

"That's right." Mr. Prest accepted the handshake, his eyes carrying the weight of Hades and heaven as he looked at me, lingering on my dress-hidden body.

I managed to keep my gaze downcast even as my mind filled with curses and slurs at his awful sport. He'd made me think he felt whatever it was that sprouted between us. He made me believe I was worth someone's piqued attention.

Stupid, Pim.

Stupid, stupid, stupid!

He felt nothing.

Nothing!

My vision turned glassy as furious tears came unbidden. I wanted this entire thing forgotten. Master A was right. I *had* wanted Mr. Prest more than I wanted my owner—not sexually, not emotionally, hell, I didn't know *how* I wanted him.

But I had.

And now, I was cured. I knew my place. I would never be allowed to stray from it.

Sighing with all the disappointment and despair I had left, I hugged myself, resting my forehead on my knees.

I didn't care anymore.

I just wanted to be alone.

Mr. Prest's regal, deep voice tore through my depression. "Does she still have my jacket?"

Yes.

And you can't have it back.

Because I'm going to burn it while thinking of you.

Master A nodded. "She does. She'll fetch it if you want."

I huddled deeper into my crouch.

Don't make me, you bastard. That's mine to do whatever the hell I want with.

"No. It was a gift." Running a hand over his chin, Mr. Prest added quietly, "However, before this deal is one hundred percent concluded, I have an extra term to add."

Master A didn't tense, believing it was something he would willingly agree to. He thought he'd won. "Oh?"

I knew better.

My spine stiffened as I stopped breathing...waiting.

Mr. Prest chuckled under his breath, dragging out the anticipation. "This clause should be easy for you. Something you will have no problem with seeing as you offered such a thing when I was last here."

No.

I dared look up, my head rising while the rest of my body sank deeper into the icy tiles.

Don't.

"I did?" Master A asked.

Stop.

Mr. Prest made eye contact with me, knowing full well I knew what he was about to request. I had no say in this. I would have to obey, and by obeying, I would kill myself.

Why did that terrify me so?

I'd spent the past few days thinking about his death, my death, everyone's death.

I should be glad knowing that after tonight, Master A would kill me himself. I just had to hope it was quick rather than drawn out and agonising.

Perhaps, Mr. Prest will do it?

Once he'd taken from me, I could ask one thing. I could speak for the first time in forever and beg for death so I could win at the final punishment.

Mr. Prest tore his depthless gaze from mine, locking onto his business partner. He smiled, keeping his lips tight over his teeth, unable to hide his predatory conquest from showing.

His hand outstretched, pointing directly at me. "Her."

Master A spun around, catching my head raised and vision glued on Mr. Prest. *"What?"*

Immediately, I dropped my chin, squeezing my eyes as if I could convince him I wasn't staring.

Mr. Prest went from standing to a fast prowl to my side. He bypassed Master A with an elegance and swiftness like an eagle swooping on the doomed rabbit before anyone blinked.

I jolted as his cool hand landed on my scalp, his fingertips splaying over my forehead.

"I want her."

He tugged ugly strands of hair, combing me, petting me, preparing me for whatever he had planned.

I shivered for an entirely different reason.

Master A choked. "No fucking way."

Mr. Prest's touch returned to my scalp. I swallowed a moan as he once again stroked me. The way he fondled me wasn't like a man with a woman. More like a hunter with its prey; a ruler with its defeated quarry.

"You offered to share her. You said I could do whatever I wanted." Gathering more of my hair, he tugged a little, forcing my body to rise from the floor and sit up straight for the first time in months. My ribcage decorated the tight dress like a xylophone as my nipples hardened beneath the fabric.

He held me there like a statue. "I want to take you up on the offer."

Master A's temper swirled hotter, thicker, crazier with every second. "That part of the deal is no longer on offer—"

"It is if you want it to continue." Mr. Prest's voice resembled an axe, hacking through the air. "I want her all to myself. And I want her for an entire night."

An entire night?

Air vanished in the room. I entered some vortex where panic ruled with cymbals and hurricanes.

I'm...Oh, I can't breathe.

My unbroken hand soared to my throat, clutching at the tight muscles as they prevented me from sucking oxygen. Another panic attack swooped from nowhere as my eyes bugged with disbelief.

He can't be serious.

I expected one hour. A request to fuck me then leave.

Not an entire night.

Black spots danced as I fell deeper and deeper into hysteria.

Mr. Prest didn't offer any condolences, merely held me by my hair. His attention was on Master A, waiting for approval.

What will he do to me?

As my fingernails scrabbled at my aching throat, I did my best to settle my drum set bashing heart. It didn't matter. It would never happen. Master A would never let him claim me for a full night.

No one had done that.

No one.

I was borrowed for brief interludes. Not rented for negotiated periods.

He won't let it happen.
I'm okay…I'll be okay.
I had no explanation for the swirling attack I suffered. I'd endured so much worse than Mr. Prest. Yes, he was the devil dressed in angel wings, but he had a refined venom that other monsters lacked.

He was *terrifying*.

"No fucking deal. I'll find someone else to build what I want."

"No one else has the contacts, and you know it."

Master A snarled, "You're not fucking my slave."

"She's a slave for that reason." Mr. Prest's voice never rose, staying royally calm and melodic. "And I will have her…if you want what I have to give."

My body spasmed as I sucked in a noisy breath, hating the way my skin heated at being fought over. I never thought I'd be so wanted, so desired—even though it was for terrible reasons, I was priceless for a fleeting second.

"I've paid you a fucking fortune!"

"And I want something more."

"No way."

Mr. Prest's fingers clamped around my nape, hoisting me unceremoniously to my feet. I couldn't fight the pressure of his strong grip, shackled entirely to his mercy.

Standing didn't help my impending panic attack. I wobbled in place as Mr. Prest forced me to look at him. My watering eyes wrenched up, drinking in his face as if he held the future not the end.

His hair glossed so blue-black and thick, it looked like tar pits—ready to snuff out my life. His gaze flashed with ebony rage. "Yes. And I'll tell you why." His voice dropped to a hiss. "I know you're the one who beat her. I know her hand didn't break from falling down the goddamn stairs. And I know you punished her for things I did last time I was here. I want her. You treat her like shit. The least you can do is give her to me so I can do the same."

My knees buckled.

My girlish whimsy of actually being treated cordially pulverised.

He wanted...not to sleep with me...but to *hurt* me?

That was how he got his kicks? By beating already beaten women?

My anger pushed back my panic attack, giving me a pillar to hold onto while dragging air into unwilling lungs.

How *dare* he!

How damn dare he barter for my body, knowing full well he'd ruin it more than it already was.

Fuck you!

Master A straightened his shoulders, still fighting an already lost battle. "Are you forgetting what she is? She isn't human. She's a possession. *My* possession. *I* paid for her. She's mine to do what I want with—including loaning her to those I approve and denying her to those I don't."

"I suggest you change your mind about denying me. Just because she's yours doesn't mean I won't take her if you won't give her to me."

Dragging me forward, he encroached on Master A. "I'm a thief, Alrik, before I'm a deliverer of war. I could steal her, and you'd never know. But I won't out of respect for our agreement." He narrowed his eyes. "Deal or no deal. Either way, I'm not leaving without tasting her."

Tasting me?

Master A knew he was beat. His gaze fell on me, turbulent and possessive. "You're not leaving the premises with her."

"Fine. I'll stay the night here."

"Where?"

"Does she have a room?"

Master A sighed. "Yes."

"Private?"

He shrugged. "There's no door but yes, private enough."

"Put the door on, give me the key so we won't be disturbed, and you have your agreement."

I wanted to shout and demand they see me as a human. A woman. Not a transaction to be beaten for the night.

They wanted to hurt me.

That was all I was to them.

They both deserved to die.

Keeping my lips pressed tight, I curled my arms around myself, protecting my brittle chest and broken hand.

I'd be having sex tonight.

I'd be hurt tonight.

By Master A or Mr. Prest.

It no longer made any shred of difference.

ELDER

"FUCKING FINE." Alrik glared with all the hate he could conjure.

He had an obsession with his slave. Unhealthy. Dangerous. An obsession that deleted rationality.

And I'd just directed that possessive idiocy onto myself by demanding the one thing I swore I wouldn't.

You weren't strong enough.

I'd come here promising myself I wouldn't fucking do this.

I'd vowed over and over again that I wouldn't look at her, talk to her, even notice her. For the first part of the meeting, I'd succeeded.

But then my mind wandered to the quiet bruised mouse in the corner. Her silence tugged me, forcing my attention to wander back to her every time I yanked it away.

Now, I'd done something I already regretted.

What the fuck am I doing?

This would not end well. I was supposed to get the final paper copies signed, Selix to post to my lawyer, and set sail in a few hours.

I wasn't supposed to be spending the night with a girl who almost hyperventilated herself into a coma because I'd claimed her for a few hours. I couldn't trust myself. I'd already gone too far by touching her.

A man like me had rules for a fucking reason.

My fingers pressed together. I forced myself to forget about the silky strands of her hair against my skin. Her skull had been so small beneath my touch, imprisoned by claws that'd murdered men for my gain and stolen from those who'd wronged me.

Scrubbing his face with both hands, Alrik muttered, "Give me twenty minutes to find the door. It's up to you to reattach it. I won't fucking help."

"I can manage." I swallowed my temper. "And don't bother searching. I don't want you to claim you can't find it and for us to battle again." Looking at Pim, I smiled thinly. "Tell me where it is and Pimlico will help."

The slave girl stiffened, her shoulders stark and sharp.

Once again, her silence was full of sound. If I closed my eyes and listened with every sense rather than just my ears, I might be able to pick up the general curse words she no doubt hurled and the pleas for compassion she tried to hide even from herself.

Pleas didn't work on me.

Never had.

Never would.

Alrik huffed, pulling a few keys on a silver ring from his back pocket. "You don't give up, do you? You want a night with her? Fine. Get it fucking over with." Tossing the jangle of metal at me, he snarled, "She knows where the door is. It's in safe keeping with a whole bunch of stuff she's lost the privilege to use."

Closing the distance between himself and Pimlico—still swaying in my grip—he grabbed her cheeks, pinching hard.

Her lips formed an innocent bow as he glared into her eyes. "Now, sweet little Pim. Mr. Prest is gonna have his fun with you. Just like all our other friends, got it? I don't want this to happen, and neither do you. So think of me, and don't you dare fucking enjoy it."

Her body jerked as she fought the instinct to bolt and

obedience to stay.

I looked away in disgust.

Why the fuck had I argued for one night with this girl? She'd been abused far too much to want me. It didn't matter I would treat her better than the assholes who'd ruined her. In her mind, I was just the same: someone to tolerate, fantasise about their death, and turn off her soul while they thrust between her legs.

Nothing was sexy about stealing from her.

Nothing was right about what I was about to do.

So fucking stop it and just go.

I ignored the thought because that was impossible.

I had to get her behind closed doors. I had to remove her from my thoughts if I was to find peace again.

Already, I felt the corruption inside me clawing for more. One taste, one touch, one kiss, one fuck.

One was all I was permitted.

And if I wanted to use my allotment tonight, that could happen. Because I had no plans on ever setting eyes on her again.

Alrik pecked her forehead like a father would his daughter heading to something she feared. "Behave but don't make me jealous. Otherwise…remember my previous promise about the past few nights being easy."

My gut clenched.

He was so fucking deluded; he didn't even try to hide that her multi-coloured bruises were from his fists. Some, however, were from other wounds…a shoe, perhaps?

My gaze dropped to my own ludicrously expensive footwear. What colour would her skin paint if I used such craftsmanship in the same way? Would her bruises be pretty or uglier? Would I be kinder or more brutal?

So many things to find out.

If I let myself be a monster like him.

Which I wouldn't.

I think.

I'd hurt many people before but never for selfish pleasure. Would punching her feel different from punching a man trying to hurt me? Would sleeping with her be any better than paying a high-class escort who generally enjoyed her job when treated right?

So many questions that I needed answers to so I could move the fuck on with my life. And once I'd gained those answers, I'd end it for her.

Death would be the kindest gift I could give.

However, could I take her final fight, knowing I'd kill her in return? Was I that cold-hearted? Or was I a selfish fucking bastard who would use her without the stomach to murder her afterward?

I guess time will tell.

Alrik clapped his hands. "Go get the door, Pim. Don't make me ask twice."

The girl immediately shot from my hold, dashing from the lounge and into the corridor where I'd given her my jacket and seen her mistreated tits for the first time.

"I suggest you follow her." Alrik smirked. "She's small, but she moves fast. You don't want to lose her. Lots of rooms in this place to get lost."

My eyes narrowed, hearing the threat but not taking the bait.

Without a backward glance, I strode after the slave I'd bartered to spend the night with. I'd been interested in this girl since the second I noticed her. I only grew more curious the longer I followed.

Heading down the corridor, she turned left before entering an internal garage, darting around a white Porsche, and moving toward the back of the space.

There she waited with her eyes downcast, her body facing a locked cage where three doors, knickknacks, cardboard boxes, and other paraphernalia rested in the gloom.

"That's the door?" I asked, passing her the keys to undo the padlock. My question hung unbelonging, dangling unanswered.

I didn't get a reply.

Not that I expected one.

Hesitantly, she took the offered keychain, careful not to touch me.

Turning her back, she tried a few before finding the right one and cranking open the gate. Her eerie silence was even more pronounced in the lifeless garage.

No sound came from her bare feet, no rush of breath, no rustle of clothing. It was as if I stood there by myself.

If I couldn't reach out and touch her—to make sure she was flesh and bone—I would've juggled with the idea of her being a ghost.

My mother would fucking love her.

Not because of her beaten, broken aura but because it was so rare for someone to be utterly silent.

My cock hardened as the girl strode toward the three doors resting like retired guards by the wall. I didn't know what the other two were from, but she stood beside a white lacquered thing with axe marks and scrapes along both sides— most likely from her barricading from the inside and her master doing his best to get to her.

Images of what that experience must've been like swarmed me. Had she huddled and screamed as Alrik fought his way to her? Or had she waited on the bed already dead from terror?

Fuck this.

I stalked forward.

My hand came up.

The urge to soothe her catapulted my fingers to her cheek. My skin erupted from her delicate heat. I'd already had my single touch when I'd petted her hair. I wasn't permitted a second.

But it didn't stop me.

One moment, she stood close, arching her chin at the door.

The next, she was across the cage, flying into a stack of

boxes that tumbled in a clatter of butcher knives, butter knives, and sharp forks.

Her eyes turned luminous in the gloom, locking on mine with rage.

Shit.

I'd forgotten myself by feeling sorry for this beaten wraith, but she hadn't forgotten her overwhelming hatred of men.

I didn't look away. But I didn't explain myself, either.

I'd borrowed her for the night. If I wanted to touch her, I could. The fact that she'd leapt away meant I could report her to her master and have her punished.

Or you could punish her instead.

The distance between us grew thicker as we breathed.

I waited...wanting to know just how deep her education in pleasure flowed.

Tearing her gaze from mine, she swallowed hard. Piece by piece, she hid her loathing, replacing it with reluctant acceptance.

Inching closer, her toes nudged aside sharp blades as she made her way to me and fell to her knees on the cold concrete.

Half of me jolted with insane lust. Most of me shied away with repulsion as her straggly hair covered her face but not before I saw the twisted disgust and echoing despair.

"Get up," I murmured. Even though my voice was low, the cavern of the garage amplified it, layering it with bite.

Instantly, she swooped up. The crackle of her joints and misused cartilage in her bones sounded like tiny gunfire.

"Don't kneel. Not in here."

Her chin bowed as she swayed in place. Awkwardness fell between us. I wasn't used to this. I hadn't bought a slave before. I was used to people doing what I wanted without me telling them. I was too fucking busy to micromanage.

Having this girl linger for a command—any command—showed me I wasn't as much of a devil as I thought. I didn't want to give her a task that she had no choice but to obey. I wanted her to use her free will and choose me, regardless of other options given.

Sighing heavily, I broke the tension by raising an eyebrow at the scattered utensils by her feet. I didn't care about the mess. I only cared about this crazy girl and the livid rage in her gaze.

She did fear me. It stank the cage we stood in.

But she hated me more.

Did she think I would do to her what Alrik had done?

She was right to think that.

I still wasn't sure why I'd requested the night with her.

Her eyes landed on the large butcher's knife by her foot.

My lips curled, following her thoughts. "Have you ever tried?"

Her shoulders stiffened.

"Have you ever tried to kill him?"

An audible gasp fell from her lips. Her face tilted to look, but she kept her eyes down.

Ducking, I picked up the knife, holding it by the blade rather than the hilt. Pressing the wooden handle into her stomach, I whispered, "Touch it. Go on. Have it for all I care. Hide it and do whatever you want with it." My other hand wrapped around her neck. "Use it on him but don't you dare fucking use it on me."

Her unbroken hand didn't claim the weapon. I snatched her fingers, wrapped them around the hilt, and let go. The moment the weight transferred from me to her, I turned and grabbed the damaged door. Not saying another word, I carried it from the cage.

Pimlico sucked in a deep breath, trembling where I'd left her. Lust showed on her features—not for me or sex but for the knife. A few footsteps guided her forward before whatever discipline she'd endured overrode her desire.

A single tear rolled down her cheek as she turned to pick up the scattered knives and forks, tucking the one I'd given her into the box. When the space was tidy, she padded toward me, fumbling with the padlock.

Goddammit.

Of course, she wouldn't take the knife. Who would after years of abuse, knowing full well what would happen if she was caught? Was it kinder to ignore the fact she was too weak to take it or accept that she was strong enough not to steal it? No doubt logistics had filled her head. She had no way of hiding it. No way of carrying it unseen into her bedroom. We were probably on camera in every place we went.

She was right to leave it.

But my voice sharpened in a command anyway. "Wait." Placing the door against the cage, I strolled back and plucked the knife from the box. Shoving it down my back waistband, I ensured my blazer covered the shape before grabbing the door again. "Now, you can lock up."

Her eyes bugged, but she turned around and secured the padlock.

I wanted to hear her thoughts. What was she thinking? Was she worried I planned to use the knife on her? Was she hopeful I'd use the knife on Alrik?

Her silence was wielded far too well, leaving me grasping angrily for answers.

Turning, I carried the door while Pimlico trailed after me. The soft jingling of keys twisted my lips.

The keys sounded like a bell.

A bell around the neck of an innocent sheep heading to slaughter.

I just didn't know if I was the heartless executioner or rescuing shepherd.

Pimlico

WE WERE ALONE.

My bedroom had a door.

For the first time in over a year.

My bathroom still didn't have one, and the shower glittered from where I knelt on the floor at the end of my bed, but at least, the corridor was hidden and peace fell, if only briefly, in my room.

Mr. Prest had pointed at the white rug with a raised eyebrow once I'd shown him which abode was mine. He'd glanced around the nondescript space with furious disappointment.

I didn't know why he was angry. The décor was so bland and stark, no one could take offense from garish decoration.

The moment I took my kneeling position on the floor, Mr. Prest turned his back on me and set about fixing the door. He couldn't do a perfect job without the tools required to secure the hinges, but the wood blocked us from visitors, and he scooted the sideboard in front of it, giving us an element of privacy.

Privacy.

Well...not really.

My eyes slipped to the corners of the room where I was sure cameras lurked.

I'd never been able to find them—even though I'd looked and knew they were there—I'd never spotted a flash of a lens. I should tell Mr. Prest—warn him, inform him that everything we did was on show.

But how could I when I refused to communicate?

The terror that Master A had made me live with for so long slithered over my body. I'd stupidly given in to a small second of relaxation when Mr. Prest secured the door. I'd finally turned insane, believing this stranger and a flimsy barrier would somehow keep me safe.

Stupid, Pim. You're no more protected here than you were running free-range around the mansion.

I'm probably in more danger.

I was in more peril because I knew Master A. I could picture him pacing downstairs, punching a wall or two, glaring at the ceiling as if he could penetrate the floor and see into my room. He would not take my being used privately well.

He'd been banished.

He'll do something…and soon.

I gulped as Mr. Prest turned to face me.

Did he taste how dangerous this liaison was? How flimsy and volatile and terrifying? The moment he'd negotiated a night with me, he'd taken a match to a fuse and lit it, smoking and hissing, chewing up speed until a bomb exploded.

Why, oh why, didn't you take the knife when you had the chance?

For the hundredth time since standing in the garage, holding the keys to so many things that'd been taken away, I cursed myself. Yes, I had nowhere to hide the knife. Yes, Master A would know the moment I took it, where I put it, and most likely use it on me as a lesson that nothing was mine to covet.

But at least when he barged in (once his temper overflowed from watching us), I might have something to defend myself with.

I would be punished for *everything*—not just the small hiccup in the garage.

I should be horrified, fearful, tearful.

Only, I'd been waiting for a day to be free for so long. If I stood on the eve of it, then so be it. Tonight, I would either walk free or die free.

Both were as appealing as the other.

My attention switched to Mr. Prest. I'd hated him for what happened to me but the longer we were together, the more my plotting evolved.

He'd asked for a night with me because he felt what I did.

He wanted to explore whatever this crackling awareness was between us.

Before, I'd planned to ignore him, shut down, and avoid what he would do to me. But what if I could manipulate him into *helping* me? Yes, he had a multi-millionaire dollar contract with Master A that I doubted I could ruin...but it was worth the chance.

I was worth the chance.

Besides, I couldn't stop my curiosity toward the man who'd risked everything.

Mr. Prest wiped his hands on his trousers from touching the dusty door. My attention lingered as he removed the stolen knife and placed it on the sideboard blocking the entrance.

He thought he had me to himself.

He thought he was safe.

He's wrong.

Taking a deep breath, Mr. Prest ran his palm over his jaw. His head cocked, eyes trailing over my white dress and the position I huddled in. Humble and submissive. The perfect well-trained toy.

The longer Mr. Prest stared, the more the room charged with the same electricity from before. I shivered, cursing the goosebumps decorating my arms.

I wasn't used to someone using the same tool I did.

I was silent, but Master A was not. He filled my void with nonsense and threats, constantly telling me what would happen if I didn't obey. His regular chatter allowed me safe haven to be quiet. He enforced my vow to remain mute.

But Mr. Prest was not my master.

And he understood the power of sound all too well.

Like an assassin, he moved toward my bed to sit on the hard mattress.

My bed was the only place I had sheets to cover myself with. But like everything, Master A ensured I didn't have enough to fully warm for a good night's rest. Not that I slept unmolested in my own space often—only at my time of the month or if Master A was sick.

I found it surprising that he'd suffered the flu twice, including three colds and two stomach fevers (that he blamed on me), but I hadn't been ill once.

Even in my malnourished state.

Hoisting himself up the bed, leaning against the white headboard where I'd stuffed my notes to No One, Mr. Prest patted the space beside him. "Come."

The training I'd been given excelled past a diploma in obedience. I might not be at university like my friends, but it didn't mean I hadn't earned a doctorate in complying.

However, it wasn't docility that made me obey...it was cunning.

I needed to learn this man so I could trick him, win him, and find a way to use him.

You'll give me what I want.

You'll see.

Keeping my eyes down, I climbed up (being careful with my broken hand) and once again kneeled with my chin downcast. I was never permitted to lie down or stretch. My body was used to being wound and bound, contorted into whatever pleasure bastards wanted.

Jealousy filled me as my gaze landed on his outstretched legs, long and lithe, crossed at the ankles with nonchalant confidence.

He hadn't kicked off his shoes and the black leather soaked up meagre light. They weren't glossy or ostentatious, matching his all-midnight wardrobe—deepening the grottos of his ebony eyes and matching jet hair.

Shifting a little, he held out his palm where a pile of tarnished pennies rested.

What the hell is with this guy and coins?

Tipping his hand, a cascade of copper tumbled onto the sheet by my knee.

He didn't speak as the jingling money settled in the creases, resting against my skin as if I were a magnet.

"I won't ask you again because I see now your thoughts are worth more than mere pennies." Picking up a coin that'd bounced back toward him, he flicked it with his thumb, making it spin in the air. "So I'll ask without giving a reward. And you'll answer because you want to."

I'll never want to speak; to you or anyone.

"Tell me what I want to know. You're here with me, away from that bastard—safe for the time being...so speak."

No way.

My hackles went up, tasting the trap, already feeling the cold pincers of a snare around my neck.

"You want to talk to me."

No, I don't.

"Yes, you do, girl."

Girl, ugh.

Why didn't he use my name? Even though it wasn't my given one.

Was I so nondescript not to earn a proper address? Did he prefer I wasn't given an owning noun but rather remained an adjective or verb?

I didn't move.

No shoulder shrug or head flick. My body was on gag orders as well as my mouth.

Mr. Prest's voice hovered in the space far longer than usual. The words wisped like smoke from a blown out candle, still visible but slowly fading the more time passed.

When the final syllable was extinguished, he murmured,

"You don't like that, do you?"

Like what?

"That I didn't use your name."

My eyes widened until the delicate skin around them tightened with shock. *What the hell?*

He smirked. "What is your name?"

You know my name.

"Let me rephrase that...what is your *true* name."

I turned to stone. *You'll never know.*

"Where do you come from?"

None of your business.

I stared harder; his eyes narrowed in frustration. "How old are you?"

Too old. Too young.

The novelty of being asked questions threatened to fissure my nightmarish world. They were dangerous but also the most inane and common. If I'd been on more dates, boys would've asked me the exact same things.

And back then, I would've answered.

But not here.

Not now.

Chuckling under his breath, he leaned forward. His legs bent to support his raised torso; the mattress rocked a little beneath his weight.

"You know, I've been around many people who don't talk." He danced another penny over his knuckles with effortless grace. "It didn't bother me then, and it doesn't bother me now." Snatching the coin in his fist, he growled, "I'll get my answers from you, *Pim.*"

You can try.

His smile turned cold. "Before we're through, I'll know more than some superficial bullshit. I'll know who you are—" He shot forward, stabbing a finger in my chest. "—in there."

I flinched beneath his hold. He'd found a previous bruise, amplifying the punishment. Not that that was hard with most of me covered in some injury or other.

His eyes locked on mine.

I wanted to scream. *'You think you'll understand me? I'll know you better. How about a trade?'*

He could have my secrets if he smuggled me out of here. There was something about this man. Something unknown and intrinsic and needed. So, *so* needed.

I was naïve to his monster, but that didn't mean a thing as I stared into endless eyes daring to go to war with him.

The longer we stared, the deeper whatever linked us became. That damn electricity was back, flowing with no limits, hissing in my blood.

Never looking away, his finger became two, then three, then four until his entire hand pressed against my sternum.

I didn't move. I *couldn't* move as he leaned closer, his nostrils flaring as his grip dropped to cup my breast.

Tears welled. Partly due to the invasion of being touched so tenderly but mostly due to the weight of his gaze pushing me deep, deep into the mattress. My heart didn't stand a chance—it gave up trying to beat and just flopped over and played possum instead.

"Do you like that?"

His whisper jerked me from his spell.

No.

Not at all.

Biting his bottom lip, he looked younger and more reckless at the same time. I'd never met anyone like him. No boys in my past or men in my present. He was alien and fascinating and entirely too frightening.

Mr. Prest skated his eyes to where he held me. His thumb grazed my nipple. The damn thing budded for him.

Pearl flashes of his teeth sent more pinwheels over my skin as he bit his lip harder. I never thought a man biting his lip would be hot.

But by God, it was.

Somehow, he made me forget that I wasn't there of my own accord—that we weren't on a date and there wasn't a mad owner about to burst through the door the moment Mr. Prest tried to sleep with me.

The memory froze my spine, stopping it from turning supple with desire. The flow of connection from his flesh to mine ceased as suddenly as if I'd executed him.

Pulling back, I kept my chin high. His hand slid from my breast, falling heavily into his lap. Silence was an enemy rather than a friend as our breathing fell into a slow, tattered rhythm.

"You're different to what I thought you'd be." His voice licked where his touch had been.

And you're different to who I thought you were.

He ran his tongue over his lip where his teeth had nipped. "Do you know why I asked for one night with you?"

I curled my good hand around my broken one, meaning to protect it but squeezing a tad too hard. *No.*

He looked at the ceiling, reclining against the bed head again. "Neither do I." Tossing another penny, he caught it like a cat would a mouse, swatting it with his fist. "But we have all night to find out."

No, we don't.

We have until Master A loses his mind and comes for you.

I watched him beneath my lashes. He sprawled on my bed as if he owned everything in the room and not just me. The same exotic aftershave he wore plaited with the cool air and his very attitude was confident and powerful, chasing away terror of Master A appearing any moment.

Abandoning the penny, he shot me a look.

I dropped my vision, angry that I'd been caught looking.

With a slight grin, he opened his blazer and pulled out a slim cell-phone from the breast pocket. "Almost forgot."

Unlocking the device, he dialled a number, his eyes glued on me as whoever he called picked up. "Selix, I won't need the car tonight."

The tinny reply sounded, but I couldn't make out the words.

"Yes, I'm sure. I'm staying the night. We'll leave at first

light."

Leave? Where is he going?

I wanted him to go. Now. Before I could forsake myself further. But I wanted him to take me with him.

Just break me out.

You can leave me on the streets for all I care.

Just…get me out of here.

"Okay, fine. Stay outside. I don't expect you to, but if you want to sleep in the car, so be it. I'll be out at dawn." Cutting the call, he tossed the phone to the bottom of the bed.

My eyes tracked it.

A phone.

Within touching distance.

A few seconds ticked past as I gawked.

"I take it you're not allowed access to such things." Mr. Prest laughed softly. "It's not going to bite."

No, but it could call my mother, my friends…the police.

Once again, his unnerving ability to read my body language gave me away. "Ah, you're thinking about calling your family." Using the toe of one foot, he tossed off his shoe, followed by the other, kicking them both off the bed and revealing black socked feet. "By all means, try. I'll give you one chance to ring whoever you want. The password is 88098."

I jolted.

You mean…you wouldn't stop me?

Who the hell was this man? And what was his agenda?

Linking his arms behind his head, he whispered, "I won't tell." Closing his eyes, in some strange way giving me privacy, he rested his skull in cradling hands.

For an endless minute, I glowered at the phone. All it would take was a simple crawl and scoop and dial. I could talk to my mother after so long. I could finally inform someone what happened to me, beg them to come, and have this horror end.

"Of course, in order to use it, you'll have to speak." Mr. Prest's voice put roadblocks in my way. "Your call, Pimlico.

Speak and earn your freedom. Don't and the phone remains unused."

My lungs expanded with anger. That was his game all along. *Damn* him. He'd almost won. Yet...if he let me call, and I spoke to my mother...who truly won? Me or him?

Both of us.

My body decided before my mind. My good hand speared out, snatched the device, and curled around it like a tiger would her cub.

Mr. Prest never opened his eyes, but his smirk became a smile. "I look forward to hearing your voice."

Ignoring his taunt, I swiped on the screen and input his password. The code glowed in my head, never to be forgotten. The moment the call menu came up, I stabbed my old home number, making three mistakes because of severely shaking hands.

I had a phone.

I was seconds away from talking to the mother who'd landed me in this mess.

My throat closed at the image of Mr. Prest seizing his mobile and laughing. Or that Master A would choose this exact moment to burst in. Panic swirled. What I would say to the woman who I'd blamed for so long?

I waited and waited for the line to connect.

Mother...

Help.

Ring-ring, ring-ring.

With each bell, my spine rolled further until I crouched on the bed with my elbows digging into the mattress. I couldn't control my trembling, nor the shattered gasp as an automated message answered instead of the woman who'd given me this half-life.

"I'm sorry, the number you have dialled has been disconnected. No forwarding contact has been given. Please refer to other means or call your local directory for more information."

No.

No.

No!

The phone fell from my hand, thudding softly as my forehead pressed hard on the bed.

She'd not only forgotten about me, she'd moved on with her existence. She'd had experiences without me, built an empire without me by her side.

I was nothing.

Why didn't you call the police?

You had one chance!

The stabbing question ransacked me as Mr. Prest grabbed his phone and ended the communication.

My one opportunity to ring for help and I'd been an idiotic little girl desperate to speak to her mother.

I wanted to slap myself.

For a fleeting second, Mr. Prest stroked my shoulder before he settled back against the headboard. "Well, shit. I guess I won't hear you talk, after all."

ELDER

WELL THAT FUCKING backfired.

I hadn't planned to give her the option to speak to her past, it just sort of happened. One moment, my phone was something so common, a tool I used every hour, of every day. The next, it was the holy fucking elixir for this delicate creature who trembled as if it could turn into a portal and carry her far away.

My hands curled into tight fists. "Who did you call?"

Her head bowed deeper into the mattress. The hard as a bloody rock mattress. Not only was she beaten—shadows marking her face and every inch of her body—but her one place of comfort would grant yet more torture.

My mind ran riot with who she called. Her father? Brother? Boyfriend? Who the fuck hadn't been there for her when she finally had the opportunity to ask for help?

Don't be such a fucking hypocrite.

I had no right to despise her past loved ones for not saving her when I was about to do exactly what all the men in her present had done. I should give her another chance—let her ring the police.

Be better than those who imprisoned her.

That thought ought to stop me.

But it wouldn't.

Not after I'd touched her breast and my skin had detonated like the weapons I dealt in. I knew myself, and I knew my limits. I could walk away from other temptations before it grew too strong to be ignored. But I doubted I could walk away from her without taking what I needed.

"Sit up...,gir—Pim." I fixed my mistake. When I'd called her 'girl' before, her ripple of indignation had given me a clue. She hated being owned but wanted to belong to a name.

An interesting contradiction, layering her with yet more secrets I needed to steal.

I held my breath, waiting to see if her despair would override my command.

It didn't.

Slowly, her spine unfurled like a fucking tempting flower, raising her shoulders, bending her neck, followed by her rageful, sorrowful face.

I hadn't lied about being around other silent ones in order to gain talents elsewhere. I'd been initiated into such a sanction.

From the day I arrived to the day I left in disgrace, the masters never spoke, expecting us to know exactly what they wanted. I'd learned another language, becoming more than bilingual but multilingual, understanding the nuances of eyebrows, reading hints from muscle shadows. I called on those skills the longer I was in her presence.

Clearing my throat, I glanced around the room. It hadn't slipped my attention that she'd stared at the corners as I fastened the door. This entire fucking house was rigged up to its window panes in security feeds and cameras.

I might have bartered for an uninterrupted night, but I wouldn't get it. Alrik wouldn't stay true to his word. And the thought of being naked and balls deep in his slave—vulnerable and surprised—wasn't something I planned to let happen.

The moment Pimlico rested upright on her knees, I said, "Forget the phone. No one else exists but us."

Her eyes flickered but she stopped her inner thoughts

from shading her completely.

"In this room, there is no past or future, just the present. All you need to do is behave, and I'll treat you better than the others."

Her jaw tightened.

"Don't believe me?"

The twitch of her chin gave her reply.

"You don't have to believe me. I'll prove it." Shifting onto my knees, I mimicked her position. Unlike her, my joints didn't pop with reluctance. My body was honed, trained, and treated like a priceless tool because that was what it was.

Yet you want to risk your health by fucking this girl.

Well, that and I wanted something more.

I wanted into her damn mind…and if I had to hurt her to achieve that.

I would.

Pimlico

I FROZE AS Mr. Prest balanced on his kneecaps before me.

His suit rustled as he reached out and placed large hands on my shoulders. His eyes dropped to my breasts as if the obstruction of the white dress didn't hide what lay beneath.

I tensed, waiting for him to touch me there again. However, his fingers tightened on my skeletal upper arms, adding pressure until I teetered unwillingly.

I fought him, doing my best to ignore his push.

What the hell is he doing?

"First thing I want from you is..." He shoved me, smiling as I sprawled sideways with my hands splayed to catch my fall and legs locked together. "...stop sitting like that."

Like what?

Like a woman who doesn't have a choice?

Almost as if he heard my snark, he once again put pressure on my shoulders, forcing me onto my back. "Relax."

No chance.

I squirmed upright, wincing at the pain and the throbbing bones in my hand.

I didn't trust him not to punch me in the stomach or take advantage of my body when spread out.

He didn't let me clamber up, pinning me to the mattress

with his fingers around my throat.

Let me go.

I stopped breathing.

My muscles locked.

The provocation of touching me there hurtled me into a whirlpool of horror.

He's touching my neck.

My lips parted for breath, fighting so damn hard not to sink.

He's not Master A.

Ignore the trigger.

Ignore it!

Our eyes met—mine wide, his narrowed as his body hovered close.

Don't.

I didn't know what I asked him not to do. But he stiffened with his mouth only millimetres from my lips. "Keep fighting me, Pimlico, and we'll have a fucking problem."

His voice trapped me in a net, keeping me from floundering in the despicable dark.

How could he tell I was fighting him?

How could he hear my silent retorts?

I had nowhere to hide with him.

I *hated* it.

Suddenly, he sat back, removing his hold on my neck and swiping a hand through his hair.

I sucked in a lungful of relief.

"Something you should know about me, *girl.*" He bared his teeth at the abhorrent word. "I'm not your master. Like I said before, I see more than he does. I know more than he knows. And I hear every refusal you think."

Remaining on his knees, towering over me, he murmured, "I know you fear I'll hurt you like him and take advantage of you."

Won't you, though? That's what this is all about.

I looked at the wall, cutting him off.

Mr. Prest grabbed my wrist, tracing his thumb around the bony joint. "Look at me."

I didn't.

His voice dropped to a hiss. "*Look* at me."

We made eye contact.

Something charged and grew and collided. The electricity became worse, humming with power.

Shit.

Drop your eyes.

Do it!

But I couldn't.

Like cement, his gaze kept me imprisoned, unable to break its hold.

His lips spread over perfect white teeth. "Ah, finally...a response." Smiling coldly, he said, "I guessed right, didn't I?"

No.

"I did. You don't have to refute it." Shifting, he reclined alongside me, his body not touching mine but his heat scalding me all the same. His fingers never dropped from my wrist, stroking with tiny whirls of his thumb. "How about we start this again?"

He brought my hand to his nose, inhaling my knuckles. "You can sit however you like, but whatever you do, I'll do. And whatever I do, *you* do." His thumb pressed hard into the delicate flesh between the bird-brittle bones of my wrist. "Deal?"

No deal.

His fingers pinched harder.

He held me in such a non-sexual place but my skin burned beneath his touch. I stopped breathing as more electricity sprang hot and so difficult to ignore.

"Do you want me to keep squeezing?" His eyes hooded as my fingertips turned white with blood loss. "Because I will if you don't agree."

If I were half as obedient as I thought I was, I would nod and let him manipulate me into whatever he chose. But something about the way he held me made me think of things I'd never been given.

I'd never enjoyed sex or kisses or caresses.

I doubted—after the life I'd lived—I would ever find enjoyment in such activities. I knew that to the depths of my soul. But the way this foreign man held me made desperation and hunger for things I didn't understand toil inside. Things not related to sex and domination but equality and friendship.

God, I wanted a friend.

No One had kept me company, but my scribbles weren't enough.

Nothing was enough anymore.

He chuckled under his breath, his thumb pressing on the mismatch of bones where arteries and veins flowed. His pressure increased as he inched one, two, three centimetres up my arm, making me shiver.

"You're going to tell me what I want to know."

My body jerked as his fingers coiled around my elbow, sending another flood of goosebumps.

"You're going to speak to me."

Speak?

My hazy eyes tracked to the ceiling, searching for where Master A would be spying. Did his cameras have listening capabilities, too? Did he see me lying beside Mr. Prest and believe I spoke in a way I'd never spoken to him?

My heart opened a trapdoor and dove into an abyss.

If he believed I conversed with a man he despised, he wouldn't just kill me. He'd tear me into excruciating tiny pieces.

Listening devices or not, I couldn't afford to let any image hint that I answered questions.

I shot upright, not caring my broken hand burrowed into the mattress. Not caring that my forehead cracked against Mr. Prest's, granting agony and black popping stars. All I cared about was getting away from whatever he wanted because the thought of talking wasn't awful in that fleeting tempting second.

But nice.

Groaning, he reared back, holding his forehead the same way I held mine. "Goddammit."

Ouch!

I rode the wave of pain, slowly blocking it out.

However, Mr. Prest beat me. Rubbing his skin, he shook his head. "I knew you'd be hazardous to my health, but I didn't think you'd try to knock me unconscious."

I blinked, eradicating the final shower of stars.

Serves you right.

"I didn't deserve that." His black eyes narrowed. "I didn't hurt you."

Yes, you did.

Taking a deep breath, he repositioned himself into our original position of knees. His slacks tightened around powerful thighs, straining against the seams. The bulge between his legs seemed larger than Master A, which sent a horrifying cloud through me.

Shedding whatever had just happened, he crooked his finger. "Get up. Seeing as you prefer sitting this way, do what I do."

What was he trying to achieve? How could I pre-empt his next mind game when he didn't know himself what he'd make me do?

I felt like a puppy following its leader as I copied his deep breath, sat on my knees, and recentred myself as much as possible. However, I couldn't stop the jittery feeling he'd conjured inside. I wanted nothing to do with the throbbing interest that was as alien to me as regular meals and going outside.

"Remember, Pim. New rules. What you do, I do. And what I do, you do." With elegant fingers, he spread the expensive material of his blazer to the sides, revealing the black t-shirt clad torso beneath. Slowly, he shrugged out of it, tossing it off the bed as if it held no value, all while watching me as if I was a priceless seductress.

What does he see in me to justify putting his life on the line?

I ought to wrench my eyes away. To stop looking. But he *wanted* me to look.

I can't deny I want to look.

It didn't matter that I found him an oddity and confusing. It didn't matter that he cornered my mind by forcing me to stay present. Master A just took. He gave me the grace to turn off my thoughts and abandon my body to do whatever he wanted.

Mr. Prest did not.

Along with rebellion, he brought life and awareness and even though that awareness made me focus on my smarting forehead from his hard skull and the unwanted tingle in my belly, I couldn't switch off because the night was both long and short.

Soon, it would be over.

Thank God, it will be over.

He'll leave.

He'd...leave.

My shoulders slumped a little before I remembered I *wanted* him to leave. I hated him because of the consequences he lumped me with when he'd walked out the door.

Master A would most likely kill me—that was all I had to look forward to. A clean death rather than endless punishment.

Unless my plan works and Mr. Prest steals me.

What did Mr. Prest have to look forward to? An empire he ruled, a kingdom I could only imagine, in a palace I could only dream.

Tearing my eyes away, I did my best to silence unwanted thoughts and fall back into my lifeless position.

"You can look," he whispered. "I have full intention of looking at you." His shoulders bunched as he reached over his head and grabbed the back of his t-shirt. With a dark glare, he wrenched the fabric off, undressing a torso I'd only seen in my fantasies.

For a man with mixed authenticities, his body wasn't confused as to what made him excel in this world. Long, lithe arms with perfectly proportioned biceps and tight forearms. Broad but not too broad chest with pectorals and obliques and a washboard stomach that seemed too strong for his skin.

But none of that mattered as my eyes drifted toward the sweeping masterpiece.

I sucked in an awed breath.

His ribcage was visible. His flesh open, revealing a dragon hidden beneath the bones.

That can't be.

But it was.

My fingers itched to prove it, to insert my hand into the chamber of his chest and stroke the hissing reptile within.

Somewhere inside me, I knew it wasn't real, just excellent trickery. Whoever had done the ink had made it look so three dimensional, so realistic, I swore I looked into his body and witnessed his heart beating all while the slithering dragon exhaled smoke, protecting its master like the gatekeeper to his soul.

Mr. Prest didn't move. Sitting on his heels, he allowed my inspection as I swayed forward, fooled into thinking if I turned left or right, I'd see his spleen, liver, and kidneys. The tattoo was so lifelike, so deep in detail, I squirmed at the thought of real bones pressing against me rather than encased in human flesh.

"It's not real." He ran his palm over his side that looked cavernous and gaping. His fingers whispered over his muscles with no blood from an exposed ribcage or being bitten by the hissing dragon in his cavity. "See?"

Dropping his hand, he cocked his chin at my frozen form. "What I do, you must too." His eyebrow rose, finishing his sentence. *Remove yours.*

I stiffened.

Being naked in front of him didn't scare me. Nakedness was just another dress code. Master A had cured me of private places or secret spots on my body.

But that was before I saw his beauty, both natural and

adorned.

All I had to offer were muddy bruises and sun-deprived skin.

Mr. Prest lowered his jaw, his eyes darkening. *"Obey."*

The word rippled from his mouth to my ears. Making me angry and itchy and dazed.

He wants to look?

Fine.

The longer I spent in his company, the more I sensed hesitation on his part. He wasn't like others who would've spun me around and taken me over the bed the moment the door was in place.

He wasn't here to take me quickly.

He wasn't here to take something physical.

What does he want?

And what will happen if he gets it?

Sitting upward on my knees, I cocked my chin at the corner of the room, searching once again for the portal where Master A watched. Gritting my teeth, expecting the door to soar open with shrapnel and cannon fire, I grabbed the hem of the white dress and jerked it over my head.

The air-conditioned breeze licked around my flesh. I prickled with awareness as Mr. Prest sucked in a breath, his vision tracing paths from my lips to nipples to core.

The way he watched me frothed my stomach.

I wasn't beautiful like him.

But for some reason, he saw something in me that I'd lost so long ago.

Leaning forward, he snatched the dress from my hands and threw it on the floor. "Fuck, it's worse than I thought. So much bloody worse."

Worse?

Any confidence he'd granted ripped into tear-filled bubbles.

Worse!?

How dare he say such a thing!

With nothing to hide myself with, I wrapped my arms around my body, doing my best to shield my nakedness that he called the worst he'd ever seen.

Anger swatted at my dismay. This wasn't what I chose. I didn't want to be this skinny and broken. How dare he destroy me so callously?

I almost wanted Master A to appear. At least, no matter how ugly and beaten I was, he always wanted me.

Mr. Prest shifted, his large hands cupping the bulge between his legs. "I'd planned on finding pleasure from you tonight." He wasn't subtle as his cupping turned to grasping—the outline of his cock a thick rod in his trousers. "I'd planned on fucking you because, despite your awful fashion sense and wild hair, you turned me on."

Turned me on.

Not *turn* me on.

I should be grateful his attraction was past tense. It meant whatever these mad few minutes had been, it was over before Master A stormed in.

He glanced at what he stroked. "Does that scare you?"

That you wanted me?

No.

I'd been pretty, once upon a time, but it didn't mean my dark brown hair and mossy eyes were what all boys found attractive. However, in this environment, I could safely say all men wanted me. Because all the men I came into contact with were heathenous hounds, not seeing me for me but for what I represented: the freedom to fuck and hurt with no repercussions.

Until him, of course.

My head swam as confusion made me dizzy.

"Unfortunately, now I've seen what he tried to hide beneath those awful clothes." His upper lip curled with revulsion. "And it fucking changes everything."

I couldn't look up—couldn't bear to stare at a man who hired me and then fired me the moment I stripped.

I was a slave.

I had nothing of my own.

My self-confidence was a battered, flimsy thing and he'd just taken the tiny scrap I had left and stomped all over it.

Sucking in a huge gust of air, Mr. Prest scrubbed his face. "Drop your arms, let me see."

I obeyed immediately.

He wanted to terrorise himself further by looking upon my grotesqueness?

Be my guest.

A few seconds ticked past as his eyes roamed over me. Finally, he whispered, "You're more black than white and more blue than healthy pink, but you're not shy about revealing it."

Shy?

It wasn't about shyness.

It was about knowing my place and doing what I was told. *I did what you requested!*

This man had no notion of the rules and laws I lived in. He didn't have experience dealing with bought creatures.

That soothed my rage a little, knowing I might be the worse he'd ever seen, but he wasn't the worst I'd ever encountered.

"What happened to you?" His voice dropped to arctic levels.

My nipples stiffened at the chill while his scorching eyes heated me.

Did he expect me to tell him when the answers were all around him?

Stupid man.

"Silence won't save you from me, Pimlico." Mr. Prest pushed off his knees, reclining on the bed again. His head rested against the headboard, his motions smooth and unhurried. Never taking his attention off me, he straightened his legs and with nimble fingers unbuckled his trousers.

I swallowed hard.

The soft clink of the metal buckle sounded loud as he

tossed the ends of his belt to opposite sides and popped the button before the harsh rasp of a zipper being undone filled the room. "You think I won't touch you just because I've seen your injuries?"

My heart took control, bellowing my lungs like a blacksmith forging steel.

"You think I'm a nice guy who will treat you with more respect than the men who marked you?" He pulled the waistband of black boxer-briefs from his tattooed stomach, inserting his right hand into their depths. His jaw clenched as his hips arched a little, granting some slack for his fingers to wrap around himself.

The way his face etched with deep concentration and his teeth imprisoned his lip was the hottest thing I'd seen since I'd been murdered and sold.

"I'm not." His tongue swiped where his teeth had bitten. "I'm not someone you can fuck around. When I ask for something, I expect to get it. Immediately."

A sudden wash of fear and rebellion crashed over me as his hand shifted in his trousers.

"You have a choice. Give me what I want or I'll *take* what I want." He smiled harshly, his eyes flicking around the room as if expecting company at any moment. "Your pick."

I blinked.

I didn't understand this new game. He'd already told me my bruises changed everything—that he no longer wanted me. He could've taken me the moment he'd stolen me, so why threaten me with sex when he would rather be in a different bed with a different girl?

My chin pressed against my sternum, doing my best to delete such puzzlement.

"Look at me." His voice turned gruff as his hand moved, whispering with sin.

Pinching my thighs to retain some sort of dignity, I did as he requested. This time, I couldn't stop my fascination as I drank all of him. From the way his lips glittered, to his stomach rising and falling and his dragon twisting beneath the optical illusion of rib bones.

"Remember, what I do, *you* do."

My mouth parted in shock.

He…he wants me to touch myself?

I'd *never* touched myself.

First, because a strict mother, who barged into my room at all hours with no care for my privacy, raised me, and second, because I lived with a master who made me despise all nether regions.

Why would I want to touch myself?

Why molest that part of me when it was molested far too often already?

He bit his lip again, this time sucking the wet flesh into his mouth as his arm bunched. "Do you want me to treat you like a whore? You'd rather obey demeaning demands than answer a few simple questions?" His voice gruffed to a growl. "You'll learn to make better choices soon enough."

Our eyes locked before a panic attack latched onto my lungs like a parasite. *I can't believe I felt safer with this man—that I thought he was different.*

His face clenched with frustration as I dropped my eyes, letting him have authority.

"Tell me where you came from. Tell me who stole you and how Alrik ended up with you. Give me that and I'll wrap you in your bed sheet and protect you for the remaining hours we have together. Don't answer and you'll wish you had."

I trembled, hating the way my back rolled on its own accord, making me smaller, tighter—invisible.

Time stretched onward.

Finally, he sighed heavily. "Is talking worth that much to you?" He jerked his hand from his trousers. "In that case…let's see how much your voice is worth when everything else is on the line."

ELDER

I WAS MANY things, but an abuser, rapist, and fucking bastard were not part of my abundant faults and flaws.

Yes, I'd entered Alrik's house ready to take what belonged to him.

Yes, I'd had impure intentions of using her for my pleasure.

I'd even convinced myself she wasn't my problem—just a sweetener to our business deal.

But then she'd taken off her dress.

And I just couldn't fucking do it.

How could I get hard over a girl who had so much strength in her heart but so much abuse painted on her skin? Her silence wasn't the defiance I believed. Her muteness wasn't courage or guts. It was the only damn thing she had left.

And I want to steal that over anything her body can give me.

I'd threatened her with sex. I'd stuck my hand down my pants, forcing her to believe I'd fuck her anyway. Instead of terror and disgust, she watched me with cold resignation. She'd lived in a world of pain and forced sex for so long, it was *boring* to her. Something expected and extracted while she remained hidden in her silent fortress, giving up her body in order to keep her mind.

Fuck, that earned my respect.

But it also pissed me off.

Broaching the moat of her thoughts wouldn't be a simple attack but a full-on siege.

Ignoring my open trousers and naked chest, I shot upright, once again mirroring her on her knees. The tightness of my boxer-briefs hurt my cock. I despised that, despite my repulsion of her bruises, I couldn't ignore my lust.

Or was it abhorrence?

No...

I knew what it was, and it tainted everything—every breath and glance.

Shame.

She filled me with fucking shame.

Her eyes followed me, hiding whatever she thought. The only way to crack her was to confuse her. Turn her in circles, blindfold and enrage her. Then perhaps, she'd break her voiceless oath and give me what I wanted.

"I requested one night with you because I believed you were like me."

She froze.

Had she met someone who used honesty for his benefit all while hiding his past? Did she care that I tasted her thoughts of suicide and understood what that felt like? That I'd once been as hurt as her but won over those who'd ruined me?

She didn't deserve to know because she refused to share a single thing in return.

Pim bowed tighter in her kneeling position. Ugly hair hung around her face, casting shadows over her eyes, preventing me from seeing her secrets.

Not permitted.

Life hadn't always been so black and white. I'd justified my means even while committing a crime—just like I was doing now.

It made me a shitty human being, but so what?

When I was starving and living on the streets, no one gave me a jacket to keep away the snow or bought me a meal to ensure I survived another day.

I was an inconvenience. An eyesore.

She's not an eyesore.

Even malnourished and far too skinny, she had a certain beauty about her. Her green eyes were the largest I'd ever seen. Her dark hair hung limp and lifeless, but the colour still spoke of a richness that hadn't entirely dulled. However, that hair prevented my ability to read her.

"Do you have a rubber-band?" Leaning forward, I scooped her dark strands and tugged them to her nape.

She shivered—her skin breaking into goosebumps. I waited for a twitched eyebrow or slight twist of her lips. I wanted to know what she thought about me touching her this way.

But no response.

Not that it mattered.

By the end of the night, I would know all I needed to.

I'll win, Pimlico.

I always do.

Keeping eye contact, my fingers separated parts of her hair. She sucked in a breath as I wrapped a smaller section around the larger pony and tucked it under.

"There, nowhere else to hide." Sitting back, I stared at her, finally able to see the angles of her cheekbones, the starkness of her jaw, and the sallowed hue of her mistreated skin.

"You can't stop me from getting my answers," I murmured. "So I'd give up if I were you."

Her chin cocked with sharpness.

"How are you still alive?" I chuckled. "When you're so damn belligerent?"

Her eyes narrowed.

"You think you behave and do what's expected of you, but I've been watching." I dropped my voice. "I see you glare at him. I see your hatred. I *feel* it."

Her gaze darted to the corners of the room, her shoulders rolling.

I followed her concern. "You expect an unwelcome visitor soon, don't you?"

She stiffened.

"You're right. He won't permit my presence for long." I glanced at the door. "I don't know how much time we have, so I guess I'll have to work fast."

Her body seized; her bruised stomach fluttered.

"I don't mean I need to fuck you fast."

Her eyes whipped to mine.

"If I do enjoy you that way, it will be *after* I've learned your secrets. Not before."

A ghost of a smile lit her lips.

I laughed softly. "Do you think keeping your secrets will protect you from me?"

Her huff pleased me as I dragged a hand through my hair and slowly relaxed into this strange inquisition. "Secrets have a way of coming out with the right people asking, Pimlico."

In a way, I was glad she didn't speak. My own history was safe. She wouldn't find out the reasons I was drawn to her. She wouldn't know that I couldn't walk away yet because I saw my past in her eyes.

She was a minor hiccup in my world. My interest in her had nothing to do with her damaged beauty or immense courage. Nothing at all to do with the silhouette of what lay hidden between her legs or her tight pink nipples.

Don't be fucking ridiculous.

I had self-control.

I'll prove it.

Pointing at her bandage, I whispered, "I was the reason for that."

She didn't move, but her violence-artwork skin turned white.

Not letting her drown in whatever thoughts she swam in, I gently took her broken hand. "I know I caused this by touching you that night. And I know that, once I leave, you'll be subjected to more." My fingers stroked hers. "But don't think

I'll suffer guilt knowing that. The world is a fucked-up place, and we all have our demons to bear. You won't get compassion from me, but you will get respect."

Letting her hand go, I pushed her shoulder. "Lie down."

She swayed in impudence, but I increased my pressure, giving her no choice. Tumbling backward, her legs stayed locked together, hiding what I wanted to see. Her small breasts bounced making my mouth water.

Fuck, why was I taking it slow with her?

She was mine to do anything I wanted. Torturing myself wasn't my idea of a good time.

Her eyes imprisoned mine, wide but unafraid.

She fascinated me, even though she wasn't sexy with her skin and bones, I found her resilience such a fucking turn-on.

I wanted her. I wanted to let myself loose and do what I'd dreamed about last night.

But I wouldn't...not yet.

I had much more important things to claim. Plus, as much as my life was full of sin (and I asked for no apology for what I was), I refused to be like Alrik. She had enough assholes in her life. While she belonged to me, she'd learn that a bastard could still be a gentleman.

Lying on my side, I propped myself up on my elbow and ran a fingertip up her naked side. Her hard nipples turned to pinpricks while her discoloured stomach panted for oxygen. I didn't say a word as I trailed my touch over one rib, then two, creeping closer to her breast.

With each inch, she shut down a little more. I sensed her pulling away, her mind leaving, whatever mechanisms she had in place to endure such torture tugging her into its safe haven.

I stopped.

She didn't breathe.

"Relax."

She shot tighter than a cello string.

"I see you don't like that word."

Her head turned, granting me turbulent but mutinous eyes.

"Or maybe, you don't *trust* that word." I couldn't fucking blame her. Holding my hand up, I deliberately placed it on the bed in the small gap between our bodies. "Okay, have it your way. No more touching. But you *do* owe me, Pim, and I never forget a debt."

Her forehead furrowed.

I didn't know in denial or confusion, but I enlightened her anyway. "The rule I gave you: what I do, you must do. And what you do, *I* must do." I lowered my head, skimming my nose over her cheekbone. "Are you forgetting I touched myself?"

The mattress rocked as she inched her hips away. It wasn't much—barely noticeable—but I noticed.

And I wasn't fucking happy about it.

If she thought she could avoid touching between her legs, she didn't know my expectations for utmost obedience.

"Do you always oppose the man in your bed or just me?" My hand lashed up, looping around her throat. "You just made me break the no touching rule so soon. Don't make me break the other rules keeping me in line tonight."

Her eyes locked onto mine, pooling with panicked uncertainty.

"Ah, that's intrigued you." Loosening my fingers, I didn't threaten to throttle her, merely held softly, trapping her mind in her body rather than flying free. "I have many laws that run my life." I bared my teeth. "Want to know a few?"

I waited for her to nod, to blink—to do something that could be a signal for yes.

But she was too good.

Or too terrified.

She'd gone iceberg white, her eyes as complex as snowflakes.

"You don't like your neck being touched?" I removed more of my weight but didn't withdraw my fingers. "Does he strangle you...is that why you're looking at me as if I've grown horns?"

She didn't respond in any way, but her pulse gushed like a riptide beneath my thumb. "Don't focus on where I'm holding you. Focus on *why* I'm holding you." My thumb caressed the side of her neck, tangling with the escaped hair I'd secured. "Focus on my questions."

Shadows formed below her eyes as she struggled to override whatever torture she associated with her throat.

Keeping her mind active with other things, I asked, "How long have you been silent? I'm rather impressed. You avoided my question and ignored your body's will to reply—even with the small slip showing your dread."

Her lips pursed, drawing every fucking attention directly to her mouth. Somehow, she transformed from frozen fear to strong stubbornness. Her skin coloured with fight again, burning beneath my touch.

Heat swelled between us. Poisoning desire and consuming intoxication sucker-punched me in the chest.

I wasn't the only one who felt it.

The zinging awareness grew heavier as we both tried to ignore its presence.

Whatever inhuman part of me she intrigued turned drunk and crowded with complicated things.

I hadn't come here for a connection. I hadn't claimed her to feel. I'd borrowed her to steal her secrets.

That was all.

And that's exactly what I plan to do.

"I'll tell you what." I licked my lips. "You answer one of my questions, and I'll answer one of yours."

She swallowed, her neck working beneath my imprisoning fingers.

"You don't believe I can hear your questions?" Trailing my touch to her sternum, I pushed on a yellowed bruise. "I can. Just like I can tell you things about your master. Things I have no doubt you've wanted to know for a while. Do you know why he's letting me use you, even when it angers him? Why he lets me claim his prized possession? It's because you might be his favourite toy for now, but what I'm building for him is worth more than a girl, more than money, more than a life. It's a ticket to power, and for men like Alrik—that's the only thing he craves."

She jolted, unable to hide her shock. Wriggling away like a freshly caught fish, she shot up the bed. Locking her legs together, her arms lashed around her knees as her back slammed against the headboard.

You really shouldn't have done that, Pim.

I pushed off my elbow, sitting upright. "That wasn't very smart." Grabbing her ankle, I squeezed the black-shadowed bones of her foot. "I didn't say you could move. I won't hurt you, so don't fucking run."

Her jaw clenched, dragging me into deeper fascination with her.

I'd exercised my self-control a lot tonight.

She'd just pushed me to the edge.

Pressing my thumb against the metacarpal leading to her big toe where badly healed bones showed injury, I said, "Just like he broke your hand, he broke your foot."

She sucked in a breath as my touch lingered on her toes then crept up her ankle to her calf. "Why? Is it to keep you in line? Are you rebellious and deserving of such cruelty? Or is he just a sick fuck who plays with you?"

A rageful spark ignited in her gaze. For once, I couldn't figure out if she was pissed I'd implied she deserved such punishment or relieved I saw exactly what Alrik was.

"I'll put your mind at rest. I know it's not you. It's him. You don't deserve a single bruise he's given you."

That damn connection spiralled thicker as she stopped breathing. Her eyes tore into mine and whatever enchantment she'd fucking weaved on me grew hotter, tighter, stronger.

It couldn't be permitted to continue.

I only had one night. I only *wanted* one night.

I wouldn't hurt her, but I *would* steal from her, and then…I'd leave.

Because I was fucking selfish and didn't have the willpower to fight the addiction quickly building for her.

My thumb stroked her gently as my constant battle for control won over my scattered thoughts. "I have many questions for you, Pimlico. Questions I didn't really care about until now. However, by trying to dissuade my interest by refusing to obey me, it's done the opposite." I grinned. "It's only made me more determined."

Bracing myself on my knees, I yanked her lower leg. I wasn't gentle or kind. She swooped from reclining to spread, and the moment she was on her back, I locked my fingers around her throat again.

The panic I'd witnessed in the stairwell when I'd given her my jacket unravelled. Her breathing picked up, unable to avoid the trigger whenever I touched her neck.

If I was a nicer man, I would remove my hand and touch her elsewhere.

But I'd already established I had my faults.

She would have to live with them.

I waited for her to erupt into an attack—to fight me off— but once again she inhaled and exhaled, taming her snarling pulse, locking everything from view.

Fuck, she's so much more than I thought. More warrior, more wounded, more woman.

But none of that mattered.

I would still earn my answers.

"Three questions." Shifting my body to lie back beside her, I whispered, "You get three questions. If you answer them, I'll let you go. I won't expect anything more."

Her gaze widened as my hand slipped from her throat to resume my position on her sternum. "However, if you *don't* answer them, then I'll expect everything. I'll fuck you, just because I can. I'll treat you like a slave because that's all you'll ever be if you don't let me into your mind."

I locked eyes with her. My control snarled, begging to snap. But I had just enough discipline to ignore it. "First question, how long is it since you ate?"

Her face went slack with surprise.

I chuckled low in my chest. "Not something you expected me to ask?"

Come on, shake your head.

Answer me.

The longer she was silent, the more my obsession increased.

I will break you, Pim.

Poking her stark ribcage, I said, "I want to know because I'll ensure Alrik is starved the same way, once our deal is complete."

Her muscles tensed, her eyes flying to the ceiling, searching for cameras. I didn't need to be quiet about what I intended to do. We had a contract. That contract would keep peace until delivery of his yacht.

After that, he would try to kill me—like the fuckwits who bought my services always did. And he would fail—like the fuckwits always did. But at least I would've upheld my side of the business and my reputation remained intact.

However, I wouldn't kill Alrik so fast. I'd pay him back, like for like, let him live Pimlico's life before ending his.

What would she say if I admitted my plan? Would she rejoice or cower? I had a feeling if she had the power to make her master hurt, she would be the one to do the dirty work. She wouldn't be satisfied with an outsider extracting tolls she herself had paid.

Our mutual silence filled with thoughts of revenge and the slightest thawing in her gaze welcomed me to ask another question.

She might not know it, but she'd just lost.

She'd let me in.

Stupid, stupid girl.

"How long is it since you've been free?"

Whatever openness she'd given me shut down with the clang of a steel gate. Her eyes closed as she swallowed.

"Months or years?"

She didn't flinch.

Studying her body, counting the breaks and kicks and bruises, I answered for her. "Just like a tree gives up its age when its trunk is revealed, your body answers without words."

Her forehead furrowed, keeping her eyes shut.

"I'll guess a few years."

Anger heated my blood—not because of her pain, but her refusal to reply. Such questions might've made a normal man care. Might've given them second thoughts about being here and doing his best to shoplift a girl's secrets.

But I wasn't most men. I did care…somewhere inside me. But I'd been through my own trauma, and it'd tainted my view of others.

I didn't have a saviour when I'd needed one.

I had no intention of being a saviour to someone else.

Who cared about such generic questions? I'd earn her answers through other means. She owed me a debt. It was time to pay it.

The thought of watching her finger herself thickened my cock.

Alrik was right about one thing. Being at sea made it hard to find a fuckable companion—unless I supplemented my on-board staff or flew in an escort with my helicopter. However, both those options didn't hold allure.

Not like this creature.

I didn't have long before I returned to the ocean. I'd wasted enough time already.

"Enough questions. Time to repay me, Pimlico."

Her eyes shot wide as my hand splayed on her lower belly, trailing up her ribcage, following the slight curve of her breast to the vivid collarbone sticking out with hunger.

I didn't stop touching her—up her throat, to her cheeks where I dug my thumb into one side and my fingers into the other, yanking her face to mine.

She stopped breathing.

I squeezed hard, forcing her to pay attention and listen to every instruction.

"Open your legs."

Her teeth clenched beneath my hold.

My hand tightened. "Do it."

For a moment, utmost detestation glowed then, ever so slowly, her legs switched from glued together to slightly spread. Not nearly wide enough for a hand or tongue but enough to glimpse what lay between them.

My cock turned to stone.

Shaking my head, ridding the pressuring lust and focusing on my control and never-fading shame, I growled, "I'm going to let you go, but you're going to do everything I tell you. Got it?"

Even now, I still expected a nod.

However, Pimlico merely stared at me offering no acknowledgement or refusal. My eyes dropped to her lips, following the cracked pink skin and fighting the sudden diabolical desire to kiss her.

I wanted so fucking much to kiss her. To force her lips to move even if they wouldn't speak.

But shit, that was way too personal.

I was allowed to sample one of everything. One gasp, one night, one orgasm.

But a kiss...I wouldn't fucking do it.

Trusting years of training by Alrik to force her to obey, I let her face go. The loose ponytail I'd formed with her hair fanned on the bed as she rolled completely onto her back and opened her legs a little farther.

"Good girl," I murmured, tracing the bruises on her flesh, almost like roses in different stages of bloom. Some spread and mostly colourless with fading beauty and others as bright and tight as new buds.

Pressing a practically violent green one, I said, "Do you remember what each was caused by? Or do you prefer to forget?"

She stared at the ceiling as I followed the petals of another as it faded into ochres and browns. "The more I study you, the more you remind me of a mouse."

The sharp intake of breath and sudden flinch was the most reaction I'd earned so far.

I latched onto the word that'd unravelled her silence. "You don't like being called a mouse or was it something else I said?"

Her chin tilted. She shut down again.

Too late.

I'd unlocked something. I didn't know what, but I'd find out.

"I think I'll call you that from now on...little mouse. You're a silent mouse tormented in a cage. However, no matter how small and vulnerable a mouse is, they have the power to wreak havoc if they accept who they truly are."

"They also have incredibly sharp teeth." Drifting my finger over her mouth, I inserted the tip past her lips to the warm wetness beyond. "Tell me, Pimlico, do you have sharp teeth?"

She didn't open or let me run my finger beneath her canines. But her heart picked up, siphoning through the visible vein in her neck.

My silent one had become a silent mouse, and it suited her so fucking much.

Her face snapped away as if a memory was too hard to handle.

Nudging her chin with my knuckles, I guided her back to me forcibly. "You don't know me, but you do need to know that if you're in bed with me, you focus on me and only fucking me."

She glowered.

I ran my hand down her right arm and looped my fingers with hers. "I trust you're right-handed?" Glancing at her broken one, I smirked. "Because if you're not, this isn't going to go so well."

Her eyebrow twitched but I didn't catch her retort. Either way, she would do what I wanted. She would touch herself. I didn't care if it took her all night.

Unthreading my fingers from hers, I wrapped them around her wrist, guiding her hand to her pussy.

She stiffened as I placed her palm over herself, hiding what I wanted to see. "Your turn."

Propping my head into my palm, I stared down at her. "Go ahead. Touch yourself as you would when you're alone. Let me see what you do, hear what you moan, watch you fuck your fingers."

She jerked, her hand flying from her pussy to clutch the bedding beneath her.

Temper masked my thoughts. "Don't disobey a direct order, silent mouse. You have to do what I do, remember?" Taking her hand again, I guided it back into position.

Letting her go, I latched onto her knee, yanking her legs farther apart.

The moment I had a full view of her, I swallowed my groan. I'd seen many women in my travels; I'd sampled some and avoided others, but never seen one as pretty as Pimlico.

Could a woman be called pretty down there? Addictive and bare, yes, but pretty? I didn't fucking know, but Pim was. Everything about her was delicate and petite, tucked away as if terrified of yet more abuse but still womanly enough to hold a hint of sex.

Biting my lip, I curled my fist to stop myself from touching her. If I felt her…that would be it. There would be no tease or appetiser, just a fucking banquet as I took her over and over again.

"Touch. Go on. I order you not to be shy."

How could a sex slave be shy? Every part of her was owned by someone else. I didn't understand the sudden terror on her features.

"Wait…" I paused. "You have come before, right?"

She froze.

Ah, fuck.

"You've…never come?"

What was I supposed to do with that?

She squeezed her eyes, trembling as if preparing for a beating. Would Alrik hurt her for such a thing?

Would I?

I ran a hand over my face. "You've never orgasmed with another person? How about on your own in private?"

Her entire body shot pink with embarrassment.

Her answer was loud and fucking clear.

Shit, how old is she?

How old was she when she was fucked for the first time? Surely, at some point, a release would've found her? Or at the very least, curiosity would've forced her to find it on her own if not with another?

My first orgasm was when I was twelve while I slept behind a dumpster. It'd been the only good thing in a sea of awful. After that, I'd become rather addicted to the brief but blistering bliss I could administer.

If Pim had never been given such a tool, how had she survived this long? How had she not wasted away and willed herself into a coffin whenever Alrik summoned her?

Goddammit, tonight just became far more complicated than I'd planned.

At least, she hadn't moved her hand this time.

I shifted my body closer, wedging my dragon-tattooed chest against her nakedness and placing a trouser-clad leg over her thigh, holding her down. With our eyes tangled, I once again looped my fingers with hers directly over her pussy. "You have to do what I do. But for now, we'll do it together."

Putting pressure on her middle finger, I forced her to stroke her clit. The warmth from her skin seeped into me, regardless that I wasn't the one touching her.

My cock hardened to the point of pain. Seeking salvation, I rocked against her hip.

Her eyes flared.

I rocked again, hating that her sharp hipbone dug so bloody right against my erection. "I'll show you how. But to do so, I'm going to have to use you in other ways. Otherwise, I'll go out of my fucking mind."

She shied away even as I forced her hand south, finding her entrance.

"No, you're not running. Not this time."

Breathing hard, I ordered my rapidly fading control to stay strong. This would test my limits. *She* would test my limits.

"Get ready to touch yourself, silent mouse. I'm going to enjoy this."

Pimlico

HOLY SHIT, WHAT is he doing?

I stiffened as his hand forced mine, pressing my middle finger, giving me no option but to obey. My knuckles grew hot as his large palm smothered me.

I couldn't look away as his teeth clamped his bottom lip. He made it impossible to prevent every cell burning with the erotic way he thrust against my hip. He hadn't removed his trousers, but that didn't stop the steel heat of his erection branding me.

Too much was happening.

Too many stimuli.

I didn't know what to focus on: his body sandwiched along mine, his hand ordering me to feel myself, or his cock taking pleasure from me in the strangest of ways.

He made me claustrophobic and prickly.

I want to run!

But then, everything else faded as the tip of my finger entered me.

Stop!

I deplored it.

I loathed it.

I...hated, hated, *hated* it.

My finger was so slim and small compared to what

normally brutalised me. My nail was sharp as it slid inside me with the aid of Mr. Prest's domination. My body stretched to accommodate the skinny digit and the strangest sensation of feeling myself made me shiver with wrongness.

I'd never touched anything so weird in all my life.

I wanted it over.

Now!

"Does it feel strange?" Mr. Prest angled my hand, pushing deeper.

My face contorted as the pad of my finger found an odd ridge inside me—something not quite as flexible or as warm as the rest.

Was it a scar from the mistreatment I'd endured? An injury that would never fully heal? Whatever it was vanished in importance as he forced me to sink further.

His deep voice rumbled from his chest to mine. "Do you like it?"

Like it?

No, I don't like it.

I suffered guilt and shame and confusion.

He chuckled softly. "You'll grow to like it…just wait and see."

I doubt it.

He laughed again, his wrist shifting to capture my first finger and dip inside me, too. This time, the pressure and stretching was greater. However, two of my fingers were still far narrower than Master A's cock.

I turned rigid as Mr. Prest's hot breath fluttered my hair, his erection jamming against my hip. "You need to come, Pim. I need to give you that so I've paid in some small measure for the things I'll take from you."

No way.

No chance.

Mentally, physically, spiritually, there was no way I could do it.

Come?

Ha!

I didn't buy into such elusive make-believe. No way could I switch off my self-preservation, give into someone so completely, and trust that they wouldn't hurt me at the pinnacle of my surrender.

He was a damn comedian if he believed I could do such a thing.

Let me go!

I squirmed, glaring into his black gaze.

Leave me the hell alone!

"Close your eyes."

Fuck you.

He cocked an eyebrow when I disobeyed him, keeping my gaze wide.

"You want to watch?" He added more pressure, pulling my arm downward so my fingers disappeared entirely inside me. "I can get a mirror if you'd like? Talk you through it. Show you what your naughty hand is doing."

I desperately wanted to shake my head—in case he thought my silence was a request for such revolting things. But he just chuckled at my discomfort and pulled my fingers free. "Let's see if you hate this as much."

Slowly, ever so slowly, he glided my touch upward until it brushed the one part of me that'd shed its protecting numbness and flared with foreign feeling.

My clit.

The moment my fingers slipped over the hard bud, I jolted.

His smile was hell itself. "Ah, there you are, little mouse. Slowly coming alive."

Once again, the name 'mouse' tightened my muscles, revoking everything that I'd lived through. Any other name I could tolerate. Any other rodent noun or whore's address— even a dreaded verb would be better.

But *mouse?*

How could he use that?

How *dare* he use something that meant so much to me?

Gritting my teeth, I shoved aside the memories doing their best to rise. I hadn't let myself think about him in years. It was too damn hard. My mother wasn't often in my thoughts, but at least she was still alive and blissfully unaware what had become of her daughter.

My father, on the other hand, was dead.

He was in heaven watching me from above, mourning my circumstances and seeing every foul activity I was made to do.

Horror and self-pity sat so heavy, I couldn't breathe. I fought to sit up, to remove my hand from Mr. Prest's hold and unlock my leg from beneath his.

I needed space.

I needed to block certain memories before they drove me mad.

But he didn't let me go. His thigh merely tightened, his fingers forcing mine to swirl around my clit. "You hate that even more than when I call you *girl*." His mouth moved, but his voice was soundless as a breath, almost apologetic while coaxing my secrets. "Tell me why."

How when I refuse to speak?

Why when I don't know you?

Never because you don't deserve to know.

I hated how handsome he was reclining beside me, stealing my freedom with the artistry of his exposed torso and tattoo. His raven hair matched the opaque lines of the cavernous cavity where his organs ought to be, his lips so damn intoxicating.

But beauty did not hide a beast, and I wouldn't be fooled.

I was done with this.

"Close your eyes, Pim. It's much easier to let go when you're—"

I bucked, breaking his sentence, determined to remove his control.

I refused to do what he ordered—not when I didn't trust him.

Wait, you don't trust Master A, but you obey.

That was true, but I knew what would happen if I didn't. I was smart enough to choose the least painful journey. With Mr. Prest, I didn't know what he would do in retaliation.

And it was worth risking agony in order to find out.

He might not have the balls to hit me. He might let me get away with it, and I could avoid sleeping with him, which in turn would please Master A because he didn't want to share me.

It was a convoluted plan...but still a plan.

My shoulders rose from the bed as I struggled harder than I'd struggled in years.

His face darkened while surprise highlighted his eyes. "Keep fighting and your night will be ten times worse, silent mouse."

I jerked, but in my unwound state, I didn't focus on the nickname. However, I gasped as his teeth clamped over my collarbone with no finesse. I flinched as his tongue lapped over the bite of his incisors.

I couldn't control my shiver.

"You dare disobey me?"

Yes, I dare!

I'm so over all of this!

The snout of his dragon hissed where his ribcage cracked open as he held my wriggling form. But it didn't stop me. It didn't scare me. The only thing that could was knowing no matter what Mr. Prest did it would *never* be as bad as what Master A would do.

I had to use this man to help free me or prove to Master A I was loyal and submissive. If he saw me fighting...he might be kinder to me. If Mr. Prest saw my strength, he might break me out.

Two scenarios from one brave, reckless move.

He froze, following my gaze to his tattoo and where our bodies kissed. His face etched with temper, unable to hide his frustration. For his confidence at figuring my silent replies, he would never understand why 'mouse' was the one name he could *never* call me without me hating him for eternity.

The impenetrable mask he wore (hiding everything that made him real), slipped for a second. He lost the uncouth businessman he projected and became someone riveting and unknown instead.

He studied me just as hard as I studied him.

I saw a man with control issues.

A man so used to the world bowing at his expensive feet.

But I also saw a man who knew what it was like to be me. To be the one without a choice, without a life…without hope.

Then, as if remembering that I was nothing more than a whore who existed for his discretion, his mask refastened into place.

His touch turned harsh.

"You don't get to direct this evening's fun, Pimlico. That's my job."

My breath caught as he forced my fingers to swirl harder on my clit, gathering yet more tingling electricity.

"I'll find out sooner rather than later. You *will* answer me. But for now, I refuse to waste any more time."

His cock wedged on my hip, throbbing beneath his trousers. "I want to be inside you, but for your sake, I'm going to wait until you're dripping wet." His nose skimmed mine. "Isn't that fair of me? *Nice* of me?"

Grabbing my broken hand with his free one, he slammed it above my head, restraining me. Pinned to the mattress by his fist, body, and hips, I was completely helpless, hopeless, and utterly at his mercy.

I gulped as his throat worked hard, his hair falling over one eye as he pressed his forehead against my temple. "You're going to feel something good, Pim. It's all in your head." His fingers manhandled mine to drift from clit to entrance and back again. The stroking felt different this time, less strange but just as appalling.

I clamped my lips together as a betraying moan built in my chest. Not in pleasure but in a plea.

He could hurt me, force me, demand me, but I wouldn't

come.

I can't.

How could I do something that I'd never done before? How could I fix something that'd been broken from the start?

I would never enjoy this.

Ever.

I would never want this.

Ever.

And if he'd become just like Alrik and only wanted to fuck me...so be it.

I had a way to protect myself.

I would leave while he ravaged my body.

And I would never think of him again because he'd destroy any feelings I might've developed.

Run...

Taking a deep gulp, I tightened and relaxed all at once. I vibrated and tingled all at the same time as my sex clenched on its own accord and my sovereignty over my limbs vanished.

I became floppy—exactly like a doll these bastards favoured.

My muscles puddled into the bed, my legs fell open, and my mind...that was the best part.

I escaped.

I disappeared inside me, swirling faster and faster until I was too deep to be reached, too far to be beaten, too protected to be ruined any more than I already was.

I didn't care his dragon blew smoke in anger.

I didn't hear his tormented groan.

I didn't feel my fingers inside me.

I

was

gone.

ELDER

SHE WAS STILL here.

Her hot body still lived beneath our joint fingers. Her breathing still tickled my chest. Her presence still made me hard.

But everything that made her Pimlico disappeared.

Her fight, her righteous anger, her confusion and strength and courage.

All vanished.

So that's how she's protected herself.

She might not know pleasure. She might only understand pain. But she'd figured out how to garrison her mind. Fuck, if that didn't intrigue me more. If I were any more interested in this woman, I wouldn't be able to walk away when the moment came.

Even now, we'd run out of time. I was shocked Alrik hadn't barged in while I'd touched her. (Not that I'd touched her, merely guided her in self-exploration).

The fact he hadn't arrived yet set my teeth on edge and wariness living in my blood.

But now, I'd fucked up and lost the girl and her secrets. The only thing I could do was coax her back to me before it was too late.

Unlocking our joined fingers, I rearranged my cock so it

didn't fucking give me blue balls and sat up. The bed rocked, but Pimlico remained staring blank-gazed at the ceiling.

She didn't flinch when my shadow fell over her or curl into a ball when I reached out and cupped her cheek.

She merely lay there, waiting.

If I wanted to steal from this slave, I'd have to use her conditioning against her.

I couldn't ask questions anymore.

I'd have to demand answers.

It was the way she'd been taught.

The only way she'd respond.

Running both hands through my hair, I shed my need to give her some margin of enjoyment and sat taller.

My lips parted to give her a command to return. To order her to snap out of it.

But something stopped me.

She looked so innocent and so damn tired. Shadows lived permanently beneath her eyes while exhaustion sat on her limbs.

I'd pushed her too far.

The least I could do was grant a moment's rest. My impatience siphoned away as gentler memories of caring for another gave me the ability to be kind.

"Roll onto your side," I whispered, pushing her shoulder.

She shifted obediently, but gave no recognition of listening.

Once she faced away, I slid up the bed to recline against the headboard once again.

My gaze locked on the door as I placed my hand on her naked back. She didn't flinch—not because of trust and acceptance but because she'd left her body behind.

She didn't care what I did to it because she'd blocked me from affecting her mind.

How long had it been since she'd slept safely? How long since she dreamed of happier times?

My palm moved on its own accord, stroking her softly, granting comfort after I'd given nothing but hardship. "Rest,

Pim. I'll watch over you."

I couldn't see her face, but her body remained tense and vacant.

Placing one arm above my head, I looped it through the headboard and prepared to pet her until she gave into me. I frowned as my fingers touched something soft sticking from the slats of the frame.

I tried to figure out what it was, but Pim suddenly jolted, heaving the heaviest sigh I'd ever heard. Her spine unwound, her muscles relaxed, and she sank into my caressing as if finally accepting my gift.

Her willingness to give me that tore away any other thoughts and I settled into my task of protecting her all while touching her with kindness.

The first few minutes, I was acutely aware of her every inhale and exhale. But as time ticked onward and our presence grew used to one another, I found her comforting.

I hadn't been with another person in this way for so long; I'd forgotten how rewarding it was to look after someone.

It's also hard and draining and demoralising.

That was true.

Caring for my mother and doing my best to fix what I'd fucked was the reason I carried so much shame.

Family had expectations.

Pimlico had none.

She would accept what I gave her without dismissing my attempts at generosity. And in return, it made me want to give more.

So much more.

My mind wandered, and my free hand found its way to my pocket and the dollar bill tucked inside the money clip. I didn't mind silence in people, but silence in my surroundings wasn't a good thing.

Memories had a way of finding me when things were too still. Memories that had too strong a hold as I smoothed the dollar bill with my left hand while never ceasing caresses with my right.

She twitched now and again, falling deeper into sleep.

As she slumbered beside me—not knowing the type of man I was, yet trusting I'd do what I'd promised and keep her safe—I folded the money in an age-old shape and let painful recollections and suicidal slaves sleep.

Pimlico

MY MINNIE MOUSE *watch announced it was 12.33 a.m.*
My mother hated me wearing this thing—said I was too old for such childish baubles. But I loved its tatty face and time-worn strap. It was all I had left of him. The man who called me Mouse ever since I could remember.

The memory of his nickname for me resonated with every tick of the hands over Minnie's big ears. The pet name came from my true address and somehow morphed into a Disney character. Tasmin became Min, which became Minnie, which became Mouse. I had so many names, but only my dad called me Mouse while everyone else called me Tas.

He died when I was seven.

Which was why I would never take it off—no matter how juvenile. I would never grow up when it came to my father.

It drove my mother bananas.

According to my watch, I'd been at this party with her for five hours, and wanted to go home. My feet hurt, my tummy rumbled, and I was done being polite to people who didn't deserve it.

But then Mr. Kewet smiled and asked for my company on the balcony; I stupidly went with him, even though I recognised him for a wolf.

I was a psychologist's daughter. I was here to schmooze her clients and endorse her sponsorships. I wouldn't let her down.

The conversation was unremarkable. Mr. Kewet complimented my dress, my hair, my smile. Then his eyes dropped to my Minnie Mouse watch, and his smile turned cruel. He was no longer a wealthy man who carried the totem of worldly age over me but a killer licking his lips at his dinner.

"Why is such a pretty girl like you wearing an ugly thing like that?"

Warning shivers scattered down my spine as he inched closer. The urge to bolt fizzled in my legs but my drilled lessons to remain polite at all costs overruled. "It means a lot to me. It's not just a watch."

"That so." He laughed. "In that case, I'll hold it for you for safe keeping."

My eyebrow rose. "Hold it?" I had no intention of giving this man my father's final present. Cupping my fingers protectively around the red and white wristband, I shook my head. "I don't plan on giving it to you."

"Oh, it's not a matter of giving." One second his hands were by his sides. The next they were on my throat. "It's a matter of taking."

My fingers soared to scratch; my mouth opened to scream. But he didn't strangle me softly—he didn't work up to murder. He committed it with swiftness and strength.

Vice-like hands blocked my windpipe. Tears spilled as my brain gave way to hypoxia and shock. My arms became useless paddles. My legs turned from kicking missiles to pointless sticks. My head roared, and it seemed only a second where I was alive and breathing and then dead and...not.

Even when I came to in a garage below the party, with his vile lips on mine blowing air into my deflated corpse, all I noticed was my wrist was bare.

My watch was gone.

My childhood stripped away.

He'd not only stolen my life but my nickname, father, and happiness, too.

* * * * *

I fell asleep with soft caresses into welcoming arms of memories. Good ones, bad ones...ones that reminded me I'd been a girl once and not this dying slave.

I didn't have heart palpations at the thought of yet another day in hell. I didn't break out in a cold sweat wishing I could retreat into sleep and never wake again.

However, that wasn't how I woke.

The reoccurring nightmare disturbed me first, heralding my fingers to my empty wrist, the common pang of loss lacerating my heart, and homesickness carving a hole in my soul.

But none of that mattered as a sultry purr saved me from my heart stabbing itself over and over with the past, giving me an order I could hold onto.

"Come back, Pimlico. Now."

Sleep swirled away, trading the night I lost my life with a hard mattress and contented relaxation even with a stranger in my bed.

How long had I been away from this existence? How long had Mr. Prest let me rest? And how much longer before Master A bombed his patience and came for me?

I blinked as Mr. Prest swung his legs to the floor, his hands balled beside him. "Stand up. Immediately."

Finally, a command I could obey without a second thought.

I didn't have to return to full awareness—merely the automation of a slave.

Dropping my eyes from his hissing dragon, I sat up and prepared to slip to the carpet.

However, his bark stopped me mid uncurl. "Don't get on the floor. Stand on the bed. Hold the frame if you need to."

Okay...

Unfolding, I planted my feet on the unstable ground and stood.

He grunted as my full body opened to him.

The bare pussy that Master A demanded I shave. The concave stomach of a starving girl. The small breasts of a woman with no spare fat or hips to be feminine. I wasn't attractive. Not curvy or bootylicious like the pop singers I'd danced to a few years ago.

I loved nothing about me when staring in the mirror. Including the discoloured purple, green, and blue decorating me from top to toe. My bandaged hand ached as I spread my fingers for balance as if the minor air displacement would help me soar.

I dared look at him.

No matter his odd way of hurting me and attempts at robbing my mind, I still feared he'd snap and be like all the rest. He'd been so oddly kind, letting me sleep when he could've used me for his pleasure.

I don't understand.

To him, I was nothing more than a possession he was happy playing with. But what if he grew bored? What would he do then?

Then again, maybe I was wrong. Maybe, he truly didn't want to rape me and merely wanted to talk. Perhaps, he'd let me rest because, beneath his shady business and contracts of armoured yachts and warheads, he had some decency left.

He paced my bedroom floor, rearranging his erection unabashedly, but he didn't look at my bare form or mottled injuries. His eyes never wavered from my face, drinking in the way I watched him, biting his lip harder as I went against all my vows and sucked in an audible breath.

We didn't speak.

Just stared.

Me standing like some fallen from grace goddess and him like some devil worshipper doing his best to find the light.

Time stretched on but he didn't stop pacing. His jaw tensed, his throat worked, and his body twitched as he worked through whatever thoughts he chased.

The longer we stared, the more awake I became.

Whatever chemistry existed between us became tainted— different.

My ideas of using him for freedom seemed ridiculous now I wasn't so fuzzy headed and afraid.

He should leave before Master A killed him. *This charade has gone on long enough.*

"Fuck." His head fell back as a low growl escaped his

bitten lips. "I have no idea what I'm doing here."

I shivered with a mixture of disgust and enthrallment.

Did he want me to care? Did he want me to sympathise with his confusion?

I won't.

I was grateful for the small reprieve he'd given but I wouldn't forget what he'd done before. He'd made me retreat to protect myself. He'd proven he didn't understand the word no, even if I never verbally said it.

I huffed, ignoring the urge to cross my arms and cock my chin at the door.

You can leave whenever you want.

"Is it screwed up that I find you stunning? Is it fucked up that I don't care you're not standing naked because you want to…only because I ordered you to." He resumed his pacing. "Shit, this was a bad idea."

His eyes flew to his blazer thrown over the edge of the bed.

Huh, he must've picked it up. It was on the floor when I'd fallen asleep.

His face contorted as if battling the desire to get dressed and leave or stripping naked and finishing what he'd threatened.

If I were any normal girl, I would've fallen to the mattress and covered myself from his lewd stare. To answer his dilemma and force him to choose the first option and leave.

But I wasn't and I hadn't been given instruction to fold, so I remained standing, even when he paced away with his trousers and belt jangling, entering my bathroom to splash cold water on his brow.

With no door hiding him, I continued staring.

Not that he cared.

What had he been thinking about while I slept? Whatever it was had put him on edge.

Had Master A attempted to come in? Did Mr. Prest do something I didn't know about?

So many questions with no voice to ask.

After swishing his face, he wiped back his hair and buckled his belt. His eyes found mine in the mirror, black with secrets. He didn't turn away as he dried the final droplets on his hands using the small towel by the sink.

Entering the bedroom, he sat on the stool that complemented the dressing table I never used. Linking his fingers between his thighs, he leaned forward, planting his feet on the white carpet. "Come here."

Rebellion shook its head, but I fought it down.

These games he played were starting to intrigue me, despite myself. My desire to disappear and avoid him faded, forcing me to remain here with him...for better or for worse.

"Pim, come."

His heavy timbre forced my limbs to move. I leapt off the bed, hiding my wince as my bruised body did its best to cushion such a stupid activity.

He crooked his finger, summoning me closer. "Don't be afraid."

I didn't make a sound as I padded naked and barefoot to stand before him.

My broken hand hung loosely by my side while my right tightened into a fist, forcing myself to let go of my confusion and questions, becoming mute in both thoughts and body.

Mr. Prest looked up.

With him sitting down, it gave me a few inches above him. But I didn't for a second believe he'd given me any control over what would happen next.

His voice was a seductive whisper. "I won't force you to do something you don't like if you promise you won't vanish on me again. Deal?"

No.

Yes.

Who the hell are you?

"You're confused by what we did together, but you didn't mind it as much as you think you should."

Stop putting words in my mouth.

My toes clutched the carpet as I dropped my gaze, hoping he wouldn't be able to read me.

"Seeing as you won't tell me your thoughts, I'll tell you mine." He shifted a little on the stool. "I entered into this deal with Alrik because he has contacts I want. However, in my research, I found he's a sick fuck who's killed four other women he claimed were his lovers and has never been prosecuted. He's also dispatched a few men, but that's none of your concern. When I dove deeper into the autopsy reports, claims of long-term abuse were prevalent yet still not avenged."

His hand flashed out, curling around my hip. "He comes from three generations of money. His great-grandfather was in steel manufacturing, his grandfather gambled the stock market well, and his father died young, leaving all of it to him. He's swindled most of it away, and I did my part in taking a fair chunk off him. However, I knew nothing of you. He kept you hidden. And fuck if that doesn't piss me off. In my line of work, I need to know everything there is about a person. Now, I know more than enough just from spending time with you."

He looked at where he touched me.

My skin crawled and heated, utterly confused if it should find some margin of joy from being touched or throw up at being held.

"I came here tonight wanting to fuck you. But I see now that I've got all I can out of Alrik. I won't screw you over too because as idiotic as it sounds, I feel something. I don't understand it, and it doesn't make a fucking difference, but there *is* something between us."

My nostrils flared.

He felt it, too?

Holding his palm away from my hip, he hovered a few millimetres from connecting. The longer he hovered there, the deeper the tingle from my flesh to his became.

"Feel that?" His eyes captured mine. "Because I do. And it makes me so fucking mad because I can't seem to resist you."

His hand clamped onto my side again, dragging me into the prison of his spread legs. "The moment I saw you and knew what you were, I wanted you. I don't care that you're locked here against your will. I don't care that I should do the right thing and free you." His fingers dug harder. "Know why?"

Because you're just like them.

"Because I've lost everything that made me human a long time ago. I shamed myself. I have no fucking honour. I take and take and take. I *steal*. And when I steal, I find something worth living for. So you see, silent mouse, I'm not here to be the gentleman. I want my answers, and then I'll leave and never look back."

His fingers bit into a swirling orange bruise from Master A's shoe. "I want you out of my mind. Out of my head. Do I make myself clear?"

Wait…you thought about me?

Those three days since we met, I'd been in his mind like he'd been in mine?

My lips twitched to think we'd both thought about each other, not with affection or desire, but with hate for different reasons. He hated the smidgen of power I had over his body. I hated him for the end he represented to my life.

I fought a shiver as he brought me forward with biting pressure, pressing my bare pussy against his tattooed chest. "I'd planned on giving you something in return. So at least I wouldn't have stolen everything; that I would've paid in some small measure. I wanted to give you an orgasm. But I see now…you won't let me."

It's not that I won't…it's that I can't.

The expensive material of his trousers tickled my legs as he tightened his knees, keeping me trapped. "You truly are the worst sort of woman, Pimlico."

What?

I jerked back, fighting his grip.

He chuckled. "Don't be offended. I meant it as a compliment."

You suck at compliments.

"Want to know why you're the worst?"

My forehead furrowed.

No...

Okay, fine.

"You're the worst because you're an addiction. You have so many secrets that all I want to do is rip them out. You have secrets even *you* don't know. It takes all my fucking willpower not to do what he does and hurt you to pry them free."

For all his pompous judgement of Master A's murdering escapades, he was as bad, maybe worse, than the monster I belonged to.

That hurt more than I thought.

Men are all the same.

"That surprises you, I see."

You saw nothing.

"Are you more surprised that I have the urge to beat you, that I fight the desire to fuck you, but I'm going to walk out that door without laying a finger on you? Or are you more surprised that I'm honest and told you how obsessed I've already become with you?"

His touch spread from my hip to my belly button. Never looking away, he pressed his fingertip into the indent in my stomach, pushing hard, somehow activating a thread of pleasure I never knew existed.

I hated sex.

I only knew pain when it came to fucking, and pain did *not* turn me on. Even the one instance where fumbling fingers and sloppy kisses had conjured any sort of desire was overshadowed by the fact that Scott (my first and only two-week boyfriend) had used me just like any man.

He might not have sampled my body but he'd used my mind. Copying my answers on his homework, asking me to help him cheat his exams.

Maybe all of this is my fault, and I just let men use me?

Not just men.

My mother had used me as her perfect daughter.

A killer had used me as a convenient sale.

Why should Mr. Prest be any different?

He interrupted my dark thoughts. "The thing is, you'll never understand me, just as I won't understand you. I don't talk much, either. I prefer silence. I find it grants more than takes away."

I tilted my chin in disagreement.

You're pretty talkative currently.

His eyelids hooded as his arm wrapped around my back, dragging me forward. His nose skimmed my belly. "You're right. For some reason, I talk enough for both of us when I'm around you. Let's just say, I like to talk when in bed. Sex is where the truth comes out, regardless of what we try to hide."

We aren't in bed...

His excuse made no sense.

"Fuck, what am I saying?" Launching from the stool, he paced toward the door. "I need to go."

Go?!

But you can't...not until I figure out how to use you to free me.

The rigid outline of another erection showed in his slacks. He hadn't put on his t-shirt and his tattoo was just as impressive with the dragon's tail flickering with impatience over his liver as it was from the front protecting his heart.

"Ah fuck, I can't. Not until I've—" Yanking a hand through his hair, he exhaled heavily. "Shit, I shouldn't—"

Stopping by the mattress, he shook his head and once again crooked his finger. "Fuck it. Come here. There's something I need to do."

My feet glued to the carpet.

Do what, exactly?

Did it matter? I was running out of chances to make him want me enough to steal me. He'd already admitted he wanted me in ways he shouldn't. I needed gumption to use that addiction against him.

I took a step forward.

234

He smiled, sharp and as dangerous as his dragon. "Good girl. A little closer."

I narrowed my eyes, studying him as his hands opened and closed by his thighs. He looked back and forth between me and his blazer, once again guilt and bewilderment on his face.

Whatever he wanted to do would pain him as well as me.

What is he afraid of?

Curiosity was stronger than my fear.

I tiptoed toward him.

ELDER

WHAT THE FUCK are you doing?

I turned off my mind.

I couldn't control my body or its pounding lust as Pimlico padded closer, but I could switch off the berating questions of my sanity.

I'd promised myself I wouldn't do this. While she slept and the desire to take what I wanted snowballed, I'd chained myself with obedience.

Fucking good my self-control turned out to be.

I'm allowed one of everything.

And I wanted one of this.

So. Fucking. Much.

But this goes against—

I shut off my thoughts.

Even if it was wrong, I'd never have it again. I needed to know what it felt like before I walked out the bloody door and never looked back. After this, I would leave. I wouldn't wait for Alrik to bulldoze through our sanctuary and steal his slave.

He could have her.

She was too much for me.

Too much work, too much temptation, far too much addiction. I was glad Selix had hung around with the car because the sooner I was out of here, the better for everyone.

When Pim reached my side, I pointed at the bed. "Sit down."

Unlike her other fractiousness, she obeyed immediately.

Her thighs hid the place she'd touched so unwilling, her ribcage pressed against her skin as she breathed faster with uncertainty.

She looked so goddamn beautiful even while bordering broken.

Looming over her, I paused.

If I did this, I would be slaughtering more than one law in my world. I would pay for it for months afterward.

But if I didn't do this, I would forever wonder, and I didn't like fucking wondering. It was a waste of time. Time I needed to dedicate to my empire. I'd take this one last thing from her and then…it was over.

Never looking away, I slammed to my knees.

She gasped as we became eye-level and every wildness inside me told me to flip her over and fuck her. Just take what I wanted.

But she would shut down like before.

She'd bury herself deep.

And I didn't want to claim her body.

I wanted her mind.

She was wily and adaptive and this was the only way I could harness a piece of her and make her stay.

I just didn't know how much of myself I would give up in the process.

Pimlico

HIS HANDS CAME up.

I jerked away, but his strong fingers lashed around the back of my head, keeping me pinned. Familiar terror froze me as the button for pain doused my senses. I couldn't stop it. I'd been brutalised too many times to override such an instinctual shutting down.

"I won't hurt you." His breath kissed me first. His promise did nothing to calm my nerves. The way he kneeled before me twined barbwire through my heart, making it bleed. In that one small position, he gave me more power, more respect than I'd ever been given.

It *gutted* me.

But then his lips landed on mine.

And the world slammed to a stop before spinning wildly in the wrong direction.

I didn't know what to do, how to act.

Should I pull back?

Bite him?

Give in to him?

I froze.

Should I flee?

Hide?

Sink down where he couldn't touch me?

I shivered.

I couldn't do anything because his lips were the perfect collar, keeping me leashed tight and trembling.

First, his questions had worn me down, and now, he'd finally taken something physical.

A kiss.

His tongue slipped into my mouth.

My chin arched on its own accord, desperate for passion even when I didn't know what it was. Bubbling, bulldozing heat whipped like horse-galloping chariots in my blood.

Master A rarely kissed me, and if he did, it was wet and wrong. But this...there was nothing wrong about this. Peculiar, definitely. Astounding, absolutely. But wrong, not at all.

My lips sparked for a different type of kiss from a different type of man, but for some reason, Mr. Prest stopped.

His mouth feathered on mine as if testing to see how far he'd pushed me, how far he'd pushed himself. His eyes blazed with the need to stop. But his lips beckoned me to start and never cease.

I wanted him to stop.

I *needed* him to stop.

But a small microscopic part of me denied my lies. My heart shook its head, reaching out for more tenderness, knowing without being told that this was the only time I would receive such a thing.

If I didn't let myself live in this second, while a handsome stranger gave me something I'd forever thought was lost, then I was an idiot.

I *did* want this.

I *needed* this.

I deserve this.

"Do you want me to kiss you? Will you let me take one thing from you?"

Once again, his question was meant to trip me up and force me to reply.

He was good.

He'd befuddled my mind with dreams and kisses and now expected me to nod with permission.

But I'd been silent for too long to slip.

Instead of nodding or pulling away, I remained where I was. Our breaths mingling, our bodies tingling, and the chemistry that'd made us aware of each other from the beginning dragging us faster into its charm.

He half-smiled, huffing in impatience. "You really won't talk, even though you know I'm not like him."

I stared into his eyes, forcibly ignoring the call to answer.

I expected him to end the kiss he'd bestowed, to stand up and stalk away. But his gaze dove deeper, tearing past my unruliness, finding something he accepted.

"Fuck, you're strong." His lips landed on mine again.

His fingers tightened around my face, holding me firm. His hold was both comforting and a shackle.

Most of me wanted to run.

But as his tongue once again teased my mouth, I let go of what I should and shouldn't do. In two years, I'd never allowed myself to think I was broken. I *wasn't* broken. I was still alive. But I knew something Mr. Prest did not.

Master A wouldn't care that his guest hadn't slept with me. He wouldn't care that nothing had truly happened between us. He would kill me anyway.

I'd been his most expensive trophy, but tonight was the night another man tarnished me, and I'd slipped from mantel to box.

To a coffin.

My heart jangled as if trapped in a money jar, desperate to feel something good before more bad could find me. I leaned into the kiss, giving him a soundless reply that yes, I wanted him to kiss me, that yes, I was grateful for what he'd given me, even though I still loathed him for using my father's nickname for me.

The kiss changed from foreign to welcoming; our bodies fell together. His hands slipped from my face to my hair, yanking my head to kiss me harder. My fingers—both usable and broken—looped around his wrists, holding onto him rather than pushing away.

I never thought I'd find something so singular and sweet. But I had.

He'd found me.

He'd given me one night of demands and acceptance, and this was goodbye.

All control drained from my body as my head lolled in his hold. I gave up entirely. Whatever this was, I didn't want it to end.

His lips pressed mine harder, encouraging sparks as our mouths never stilled.

I shifted restlessly, desperately as my attention riveted to his dexterous tongue and masterful manipulation.

He forced me on a strange tide where I no longer listened to the outside world but my inner one.

The one I'd lost touch with since I was murdered and bought. The one that was so much bigger than the universe I lived in.

The slow incineration quickened as our mouths turned hungry and messy. There was no synchronisation anymore.

"Do you feel it, Pim?" He panted between kisses. "Do you feel your body preparing for me?" His voice switched to a growl, his lips brutal on mine. "Shit, I want you."

My back bowed as he jerked me forward into his embrace.

Something happened to me.

I was no longer on the same path.

I'd stepped off it.

No, I'd been dragged off it. By this man.

This sinful angel who'd somehow become my defender and liberator all in one.

I didn't know him.

But I wanted to.

He'd saved my life by giving me a second of happiness. I wanted him to *remain* in my life. But I knew that wasn't possible.

He practically hissed with heat. I couldn't think while he looked at me like that, kissed me like that, stole everything from me like that.

His tongue slid leisurely along my bottom lip, making me crave what he gave so recklessly. I wanted his tongue on me, inside me, consuming me. I wanted things I didn't understand or ever thought I'd contemplate.

His heavy-lidded glower was furious, angry, full of lust, lust, lust. He screamed sex. But not rape. *Sex.* Consensual sex—so far from the realm of everything I knew.

His chest rippled as his hand cupped my cheek again. His belly tightened, making his dragon smoke and sizzle.

"I've finally made you talk, Pim." The glitter in his gaze danced with knowledge. "Your body likes me, even if you don't."

The surge of complicated, unknown emotions battered me just as nastily as Master A's fists. I didn't know why, but in that second, I was devastated—not from the pleasure he'd given, but the low that would hit so damn hard once he left.

I wanted to live in this moment for eternity.

I wanted to find self-worth and happiness in this false togetherness. I wanted companionship but by wanting that, it made me weak because I wanted to lean on him after leaning on myself for so, so long.

I *liked* him.

He kissed me again, stopping my thoughts and forcing me to accept him on a deeper level than I ever intended.

I was no longer a slave or imprisoned or trapped.

I was kissed.

Kissed.

Mr. Prest slowly pulled away, taking his heat, warmth, and protection with him.

That was... I didn't have words.

Exquisite?

Devine?

Terrifying?

I hovered in the final bliss of the best thing I'd been given in so long, plummeting into lethargy so heavy and consuming, I struggled to keep my eyes open. What had he done to me? Why did I feel drugged and obsessed and so, so tired?

He didn't move.

His gaze waged war with things far too deep and dangerous for just a kiss, and I was grateful when he shook his head, carefully masking whatever had happened.

His lips arranged into a self-satisfied smirk. "I take it that was your first?"

My cheeks heated.

I closed my eyes, already coming down from the torrential high he'd shown me.

His knuckles nudged my chin, startling my gaze to open. "How many other firsts have you been denied?"

What…what do you mean?

Standing from his kneeling position, he sat on the bed and ran a hand over his mouth.

Something hot and needy sprang to life inside me. I didn't know what it was, but it was tentative but strong, confused but focused.

Twisting to face me, he pressed his fingertip against my forehead. "Has someone made you wet just by talking to you? Telling you what they're about to do? Giving explicit detail of what they like about your body, what you sound like, taste like, beg like?" He bowed closer, his baritone making me drunk. "Whispering how fucking much they need to be inside you until you shatter the instant touch is given?"

Wow…

The shock and power of his voice almost made me forget my muteness. My head shifted slightly side to side in a very clear and none permitted *no*.

He exhaled heavily. "I take it that's another first. Finally answering a question." His teeth flashed in the low-lights. "Don't worry. I won't tell."

The strange thing was, I believed him. He hated Master A almost as much as I did. He wouldn't run to him and spill whatever we'd just done. It wouldn't benefit him in any way.

I stiffened as his finger dropped from my forehead, along my nose, to my lips. "How about this first?" His head lowered, his mouth landing on mine for another brief kiss. "Has anyone kissed you so fucking hard you're bruised when you come up for air? Has anyone kissed you for fucking hours, tormenting you until you're drenched for his cock?"

God, stop.

I pressed my lips together. A slight tenderness existed from his attentions.

This time, I fought the urge to reply, but he read the way my tongue licked the redness he'd graced me with.

I shivered as he swayed upward, removing the temptation of his kiss.

The talk of firsts and the indescribable way he spoke about them shoved aside my circumstances and made me wish.

Wish for a life to indulge in firsts. Rather than wish for death to end them.

His finger moved again, leaving my mouth to trail along my chin, neck, to my breasts. Cupping one, he murmured, "What about here, Pim? Has anyone sucked so fucking hard on your nipple it swells and stings? Anyone bit until you cried for mercy or clamped toys on you, making you obey all commands?" His touch rolled my nipple, squeezing just a little.

No...

My breathing turned into a gasp as his fingertip followed the soft curve of my breast, to my ribcage, waist, finally tracing my belly button. His intense gaze hinted he wished to touch me between my legs, but he wouldn't.

Caught up in the insane web we'd woven, I trembled as he said, "I wanted to give you another first. I wanted to make you come. I see now it would've been impossible for you because you've never felt true pleasure."

His forehead furrowed. "There are so many firsts to

explore with your pussy, Pim. Have you ever felt a man's tongue inside you? His mouth on your clit? What about his fingers so fucking deep inside you, you forget how to be human and become an animal instead?"

The tightening in my limbs layered me with yet more sultry seduction.

"I want to give you so many firsts." He leaned toward me, his eyes hooded, his mouth only millimetres from mine. "I want to—"

Disaster struck.

The door exploded inward.

Shrapnel clattered as hinges buckled and wood panels splintered.

No!

Tony's grunts ripped through the silence as he destroyed the entryway with a baseball bat—demolishing the one thing protecting us.

Master A stood behind him, barking instructions.

My heart sprinted from the tentative wandering in paradise and slammed back into its prison.

No, no, no!

That was why he'd given us so much time. Why Mr. Prest had the privilege of lying beside me unhurt.

Master A called for backup.

"What the fuck?" Mr. Prest launched himself upright, his body sprung and ready for a fight. "Get the hell out. I'm not done."

I shrivelled as Master A stalked into the room. In his hand, he held a gun.

I'd never seen him with the black revolver, but the way he wielded it—with confidence and precision—said he wasn't a stranger to such things.

His gaze leapt between my nakedness and Mr. Prest's trouser-clad form. "Did you have fun fucking my slave?" He cocked his head condescendingly, glaring at me. "Did you *behave*, Pim?"

I looked down, hiding behind sleep-tangled hair.

Fuck off, you mutant!

The usual proverbial sword and shield I fought with had been stupidly abandoned during Mr. Prest's wicked kiss.

I didn't have the strength to fight anymore. To live in hatred and pain anymore.

Nonsensical questions ran riot as I did my best to sink into mute protection.

How long had Mr. Prest let me rest all while tracing the sweetest strokes on my back? How much time had we wasted that could've been spent kissing before Master A arrived to tear us apart?

It doesn't matter.

It's over.

I was on my own again. Like always.

Mr. Prest sucked in a breath. "Did you not hear me? I. Said. I'm. Not. *Done.*"

"Oh, yes you fucking are." Master A turned brick-red with rage as his hand trembled around the gun. "Get out. I want that yacht, Mr. Prest, but I've paid you more than enough. *Leave!*"

My shoulders slumped as a crystal-clear conclusion hit me. My plans to use Mr. Prest to free me vanished. He would never free me. He had a contract with my owner, and that contract trumped whatever silly kiss we'd just enjoyed.

Don't ask him for more.

It would be your fault if he died.

Tears stung my eyes as Master A stalked forward. He barely looked at me, obsessed at kicking this trespasser from his house.

The fact he'd waited for Tony to act as support reaffirmed what a spineless coward he was. He couldn't stomach facing Mr. Prest on his own.

The muzzle of the gun came up, pointing squarely at his dragon tattoo.

Memories of Mr. Prest telling me the murder count of my cowardly owner sent catastrophic energy into my legs. I knew my fate. I accepted it. But I wouldn't let another bleed for me—even if he wasn't innocent of crime.

Mr. Prest was the only man who'd been nice to me.

I won't watch him die.

Instinct controlled my body. Impulse overrode sanity and submission. I did something I'd never done. And I didn't do it for me.

I did it for him.

Dashing forward, I placed myself in front of the thief who'd kissed me. In front of the gun. In front of whatever would happen to me because of my bold stupidity.

The room shot silent.

I froze solid.

Horror at what I'd just done compounded with lead weights, making me sink, sink, sink with fear.

Tony's mouth gaped as his watery gaze gawked. "Holy shit."

Master A's eyes literally popped from his head. He spluttered in livid disgust, "Get the *fuck* out of the way, Pim. I'll deal with you later."

My shoulders squared, not caring my naked form would offer no protection. There'd been no one to stand up for me. I would die. But at least the sad cycle would be over.

The terror at what I'd live through rolled my spine as I fought the urge to step away and obey. I didn't know why I stood up for a man twice my size with so many more skills at staying alive than me.

But I did.

It was my last attempt at being Tasmin before Pimlico was gone.

Don't shoot him.

Let him go.

Mr. Prest yanked me back and behind him, wrapping his naked arm around me. "She's confused. I ordered her to protect me if you fucking barged in." His fingers dug into my skin. "Don't hurt her for a command I gave."

You're lying.

He's trying to protect you.

"Oh, she'll be hurt all right. Don't you worry about that. All you need to worry about is getting your fucking ass out of my house. Right now!" Master A's finger teased the trigger, pointing directly at Mr. Prest's tattoo. Cocking his head at the mess Tony had made of the door, he yelled, "I want you out!"

"It's not dawn."

"Don't care."

"She's mine until I go."

"Wrong." Master A's hand whitened around the gun. "She's mine, asshole. I won't ask again."

Mr. Prest didn't budge. He just crossed his arms.

I tiptoed from behind him, wanting to be in position to either run or kneel—needing to do something to cease this tense situation.

Master A changed tactics. His blue eyes smiled cruelly as he swung the gun's muzzle from the interloper to me.

I stiffened.

"You have something I want, Mr. Prest. Count yourself fucking lucky because if you didn't, I would've shot you the moment you took my Pimlico. However, wanting something is your issue, too."

I gasped as everything blackened with impending murder.

The sinister hole where a bullet would fire hypnotised me. I couldn't look away.

If this were the most humane way it would end, so be it. I'd had my first proper kiss. I'd been treated well for the first time in years. If this was the epilogue on my awful, awful story, I was fine with that.

My muscles relaxed, ready to accept the tearing, lacerating, excruciating lead.

Please, let it be a clean shot.

"You want this whore." Master A waggled the weapon. "You want her enough to keep her alive. I'll gladly fucking kill her if it makes you obey our deal."

Do it.

Get it over with.

Mr. Prest's face turned monstrous. "You'd kill your own slave rather than give me a few more hours?"

"Absolutely." His reply was instantaneous. "So, what's it gonna be? Her or you. I've been tolerant enough. She needs a fucking shower to rid your filth and then a reminder who she belongs to."

Just shoot me.

I didn't want a reminder. I didn't want anyone touching me ever again.

Mr. Prest glowered. "You're a cunt."

Master A bared his teeth. "What's it gonna be?"

"You won't do it."

"I won't?" His forehead furrowed with rage. "You want me to fucking prove it?"

He'll do it.

Maybe, that was Mr. Prest's plan? To have me shot so he could walk away, knowing I wouldn't suffer anymore? He said he wouldn't care about my treatment—that we all had personal demons to bear.

It was merciful to dispatch me this way.

Master A stomped toward me and fisted my hair, jerking me close. "Let's see how much she bleeds, shall we?"

Mr. Prest took a step, forgetting himself as fury coated his features. "Get your hands off her."

The cool threat of death lodged against my temple as Master A grunted, "My patience is done." He stabbed me harder with the gun.

The tang of metal shot up my nose.

"Say goodbye to the whore. Keep your fucking yacht, I don't—"

"Stop!" Mr. Prest dropped his arms, splaying his hands in surrender. "Don't kill her." His gaze locked on mine, full of livid acrimony and apology. "You've just made the worst mistake of your life, Alrik Åsbjörn."

The gun twisted against my head. The round bruise numbed my skull where a bullet would ricochet and end me.

"Wrong, Elder. *You* did. Give me what I want—what I motherfucking paid for—and I'll forget this ever happened."

Mr. Prest laughed. The sound landed aggressively on the floor, smoking with icy mirth and arctic promises. "Fourth time you used my name." Storming forward, he snapped, "You've just fucked me off, Alrik and that is *not* a good thing to fucking do."

Swiping his blazer and t-shirt from the carpet, he gave me a look. "I thought I could do it. I thought I could watch you die. But I won't. Your life is yours and I won't meddle in it anymore."

He shook his head. "So much for more firsts, Pim. I'm sorry."

Master A's red face flowed like lava as he harpooned the air with the gun. "Out!"

"You'll regret this." Mr. Prest lowered his jaw, watching him from murderous eyes. "I'll make you curse everything that you are." Pointing a finger at me, he snarled, "Don't fucking hurt her. It's my fault—not hers. Let me fix my own mistakes." Throwing me one last unreadable look, he vanished out the door.

Wait, you can't go!

The moment he'd disappeared, Master A smirked. "I guess I won that, huh? Shit, that makes me hard." He kissed my cheek. "Get in the shower. I have something special planned for you." With the threat lingering in the air, he pushed me away and followed his unwanted guest, leaving me alone with Tony.

Tony—the asshole who'd shared me too many times—blew me a heinous kiss. "Do what he says, sweetie. The games will begin as soon as that bastard is gone." He turned to go, then paused. A loud cackle fell from his lips. Bending over, he scooped up the knife Mr. Prest had stolen from the garage.

My heart sank even further into quicksand.

Shit.

Tony whipped around, tapping the blade against the baseball bat he'd beaten the door with. "Hiding contraband now, sweetness?" His chuckle sickened me. "We'll just add that to the tally of your bad behaviour and make sure you learn your lesson."

He saluted me with the knife. "See you soon."

He left.

His steps echoed as he skipped down the stairs, cracking the baseball bat on the banister.

A panic attack swooped in on killing wings, suffocating me instantly.

I can't breathe.

The room squeezed.

Stagnant unhappiness rained.

Tears ran backward down my throat as I forbid them to stream from my eyes.

I was *grateful* Master A had gone.

But I screamed at the hole Mr. Prest left behind. A hole that'd been warm and almost content for a few stolen hours now whistled with gales of cavernous fear.

Did he really just walk out the door?

Without a goodbye?

Without a...

What?

A thank you?

What did you expect? He gave you pleasure. He let you sleep peacefully. He gave you more gifts than anyone, and you expect more from him?

I laughed soundlessly. I was an idiot. A *dead* idiot.

I sucked air as my pulse two-stepped than four-stepped, desperately trying to calm.

You don't have time for this!

Breathe!

The moment Mr. Prest was kicked from the house, Master A would return. And he wouldn't have the gun with him. He'd have much more inventive ways to kill me. Ways that gave him entertainment and pleasure.

If only he'd left the weapon on the bed.

I would've grabbed it, turned the muzzle on myself, wrapped my fingers around the trigger, and said goodbye.

I would've traded any hope of heaven by committing suicide just for the tease of finally being free from this purgatory. I would welcome death with frost feathered wings, hoping I'd paid enough atonement for a better life.

How will I survive this?

As my mind ran riot, and my body continued to suffocate on terror, I compiled a last will and testament in my head.

Not that I had anything to give.

I flew back to the past and my room in London, reliving dinners with my mother at our window bay table and sneaking in trash TV when I was supposed to be doing homework. I went over my meagre childish belongings that, at the time, had felt so important and were now completely inconsequential.

To my mother, I bequeath my rare collection of English stamps. To my friend, Amanda, I leave my DVD collection of Anne of Green Gables—

Stop it, Mouse. Just…stop it.

I winced.

I'd called myself Mouse—just like Mr. Prest. I'd spent too long in my memories, too long with a man who made me remember another way of living.

I collapsed in shock and horror, stumbling to the mattress but landing on my knees instead. My heart pulled out its drum set to crash on castanets and cymbals.

Don't let him hurt me. Not again.

I would've preferred to be shot.

A hundred times over.

I wanted my first kiss to be my final memory. I wanted to go into a never-ending sleep where I found my father and he had my Minnie Mouse watch. I wanted so many things that I would never earn.

But as much as my heart ached, and I wished to hate Mr. Prest for making me live if only for a moment before death, I couldn't despise him. He'd done what he said and got me out of his system. He'd kissed me to rid any hold I had over him.

He'd given me no other promises. In fact, his only oath was that he would use me and then leave me.

He'd upheld that oath.

I wasn't his.

I was Master A's, and the rental agreement was up.

Fighting back abandonment and foolishness far, far painful than any abusive wounds I'd suffered, my world once again went dark as I closed my eyes and prepared to meet my end.

I grabbed the sheet, yanking it to cover myself. However, something crinkly fluttered with the whiteness, landing on the floor beside me.

The shock of something unknown interrupted my panic attack.

What on earth?

Hiccupping, I sat upright. My hands shook as I picked up the dollar bill.

An American dollar bill.

But it wasn't folded like normal money. It wasn't flat or creased in half like other well-transacted currency. This was in the shape of a tiny butterfly complete with wings and delicate feelers.

The light green of the note gave the illusion the wings were made of thread and ink while its body cocooned with the numerical value of paper wealth.

It's so pretty.

But where did it come from?

The answer was obvious.

Him.

But why?

Fingering the linen parchment, I flashed with anger. My panic attack faded, finding strength once again. Was this Mr.

Prest's way of paying me for what we'd done? Was I only worth a dollar to him?

Instead of pretty origami, all I saw was something cheap. Something that made *me* cheap.

Was our kiss that *worthless?*

Tossing it away, the flash of black writing begged me to unfold it.

I didn't relish the notion of destroying the creation—even if it was demeaning—but curiosity itched too hard. I scooped up the little butterfly, then tugged on the folded lines to reveal the note inside.

Scrawled with masculine penmanship the letter read:

I came here to get you out of my thoughts. But you fell asleep, and I'm beginning to doubt I will ever achieve that. For a man like me, that is an issue. Therefore, I'm leaving the moment you wake up.

Goodbye, silent one.

That was it.

No odes of promises to come back or hints that he'd request to share me again. He'd had his one night and been honest enough that I wasn't enough to capture his attention.

His words sharpened until they glittered with stinging barbs, delivering venom into my heart.

Don't hate him.

Don't die with hatred.

If that was the only pleasure I had, at least I knew what it felt like.

I have to tell No One.

I have to write it down so I never forget.

Mr. Prest would become a figment of my imagination, locked forever in my toilet paper novel.

I wouldn't tell anyone about him.

I wouldn't grow to know him or care for him.

Just one more reason why I would remain silent forever, holding my secrets.

Until the end.

ELDER

HOW *DARE* HE fucking throw me out!

Did he think our deal would proceed as planned after such bloody rudeness? Did he honestly think I wouldn't rip him into motherfucking pieces for the lack of respect he'd shown?

I'd hurt him for what he'd done to Pim, but I'd *kill* him for what he'd done to me. No one was permitted such intolerable insolence.

If he'd given me a few more minutes, I would've walked out the damn door on my own accord.

I would've run because of his slave.

That kiss…*shit.*

I should never have done that.

Big mistake.

Huge fucking mistake.

And now, Alrik had committed his own.

Dawn had only just broken, but I wanted out of that white hellhole. Touching her? Tasting her? Fuck me, it was more than I could handle. I had no intention of being alone with her again because I knew my issues and I knew what would happen if I did.

I was glad she belonged to another.

This way, I had no way of going back for seconds.

For an awful moment, I'd wanted him to shoot her. I

pictured the bullet tearing into her brain and the light in her eyes snuffing out. She'd be gone and I'd be granted absolution.

If she was dead, she was free from me and Alrik.

I was so fucking close to letting him pull the trigger.

But even though the right thing to do was put her out of her misery, I didn't have the balls to have her death on my conscience.

I already had enough shame to devour me.

I couldn't handle anymore.

No, I left because she wasn't my problem.

Her life—no matter if it was full of hell or happiness—was not my issue.

She's. Not. Mine.

I had to believe that and accept it if I had any chance of being somewhat sane.

I'd had my fill.

Done.

Over.

"Sir?" Selix leapt from the car as I stalked toward him, slinging my jacket on. The pockets crunched with things I'd pillaged as I did up the middle button. The poor guy (true to his word) had spent the night waiting. He knew I preferred to do business on my own. I could handle my safety if a double cross went down—I didn't need him for that. But I was grateful he was here to get me as far as fucking possible from this place and Pim.

She'll be hurt.

Not my problem.

He might kill her.

Not my problem.

When I'd taken her upstairs, I'd done so with the promise to kill her afterward.

I hadn't kept that promise.

What did it matter if it was me or Alrik who finally did it? Who cared if I was there to watch or back on the ocean where I belonged?

Fuck!

Selix cleared his throat. "Everything okay?"

Nothing's okay.

"I want to leave. Immediately." I jerked hands through my hair. "Is the yacht ready?"

He opened the rear door. "Yes. All prepped and ready for sail."

"Good. I want to leave this shitty country as soon as I can."

"I'll call ahead. Make sure we leave the moment you step on board." He closed the door, encasing me in the black sedan before dashing to the driver's side.

Taking one last look at Pim's prison, I muttered, "Take me to Phantom. Now."

Pimlico

DEAR NO ONE,
I don't know what happened.
All my notes and confessions to you...they've vanished. Did you take them? Please, tell me you took them. I can handle that. Tell me you're sick of me writing to you, and you flushed them down the toilet, or burned them, or tossed them out the window.
Tell me anything as long as it isn't that Master A found you.
Don't tell me that!
They were there before breakfast yesterday. I checked.
I didn't check last night as Mr. Prest kept me company.
But now, I've lost you.
I don't want to lose you!
Oh, no. I hear him coming.
Shit, No One...what if he—

"You damn little *bitch*." Master A shot across the room, snatched up my letter, and shredded it into confetti.

No!

My heart screamed as if he'd murdered a living, breathing friend.

"All this time, you've been writing and hiding it from me!"

Stop!

I cowered, slipping off the bed to bow on the floor. Any

humanity and self-awareness I'd earned thanks to a few hours with Mr. Prest disappeared. I slithered back into my role as slave, pressing my forehead against the carpet.

Don't hurt me.

Just kill me.

I wished for freedom. I begged for happiness. But I wouldn't find either of those here, especially now my notes to No One had vanished and Mr. Prest was gone.

He'd left, knowing what I'd suffer—understanding how severe my punishment would be from him touching me.

It's not fair!

None of this is right.

"You fucking hid these from me!" He held out his hand even as shredded words dripped from his fingers. "Give me the rest. Now!"

Tears slipped over my nose, seeping into the white strands beneath me. I ought to be relieved. Master A hadn't been the one to take them.

He wasn't a good liar. He preferred to gloat too much. That meant the thief was Mr. Prest.

Why?

How could he?

A slap painted my cheek. "Give me the other pages, Pim. Don't make me ask again."

I don't have them, you asshole!

How could Mr. Prest take my last possessions? Not after he stole everything with his kiss...

How had he found them?

While you slept. While you trusted.

That isn't possible.

Is it?

"Silence won't keep your secrets this time." Master A paced, his body hyped on adrenaline. "Don't tell me where they are. I'll tear your room apart and find them myself." Ducking to his haunches, he hissed, "And when I do, the punishment will be the second most painful thing you'll live through."

Wait, second?
What's the first?
What a stupid question!

My nostrils flared as my mind tried to untangle the puzzle.

Confusion kept me befuddled, prone for his fist as it sailed through the air, connecting with an awful *thunk* on the side of my skull.

Oh, God...

The agony. The pressure. The throb.

Wrapping my hands over my head, I toppled sideways, biting my tongue to stop from crying.

"You can avoid that, if you tell me where the rest are. I'll give you one last chance."

I blinked back stars as my eyes shot around my room, doing my best to spot the pages before he could.

If Mr. Prest *had* found them, why did he take them? Maybe he didn't know what the paper was and left them on my dresser or abandoned on the floor? Was that what the dollar butterfly was for? As payment for my darkest, deepest innermost thoughts?

He's a thief.
He took my first kiss.
Just like he took my novel.
But why?

"Answer me!" Master A punched me again.

Stars became sunbursts, obliterating my vision completely.

Every inch of me wanted to crawl, run, sprint away. I couldn't stop my mind racing.

Why did he steal my treasured words?

To read my emotions and laugh? Laugh at my stupidity and slavery?
He said he would forget about me.
Why take something to remember me by?

My hands scrabbled at the carpet as I rode through the current wave of agony. The unfolded dollar butterfly brushed my fingers—just as broken as I'd become.

Snatching it, I used it as a talisman of hope. As long as I

held it, I would survive.

I hoisted myself forward, doing my best to move away from abuse.

Squatting by my head, he chuckled. "Trying to crawl from me, sweet Pim? Stupid girl. You know there's nowhere to go; nowhere to hide. A few hours with that son of a bitch and you're already ruined."

My stomach roiled with nausea as he stood up again.

"But don't worry. I'll make sure you remember who your master is and what happens when you forget."

My lips parted for sour oxygen as he strode from the room, his cold laughter trailing after him.

What will he do?

I don't want to know.

In the few minutes I was alone, I didn't bother trying to sit up. I stayed curled on my side, nursing my dizzy, pounding head, and clutching my single dollar.

He came back.

I managed to suffocate my sob as my gaze fell on what rested in his hands. He'd swapped the black revolver for the thing I hated the most.

The noose.

The noose he used to hang me like a four-pointed star off his ceiling. The noose he used as a leash, a collar, and disciplinary tool.

My most hated enemy.

I scrambled backward as he grabbed my hair, twisting it around his wrist. "You're going to learn, Pim. You don't want to talk? Fine. Don't fucking talk. Write your stupid notes to a diary that doesn't give a shit about you. Even lie to me and hide it. All of that is forgivable because you're mine, sweet little Pimlico, and being mine means I'm possessive of your mind but lenient, too."

His fingers tightened, tearing a few strands from my scalp. "But if you think you can spend the night with a fucking stranger, lay beside him, fantasise about having his fucking cock inside you, and keep what you said to him a secret, think again."

Wrapping the coarse rope around my neck, he tugged hard. "You're going to tell me what happened. You're going to fucking spill, Pim. I've been patient enough. You talked to him, didn't you?" Spittle flew from his mouth as he dragged me from my room and down the corridor. "You want him to be your master and not me. You can't deny it."

Carpet burned my hands and knees as I did my best to keep up but failed.

My teeth clacked together as he wrenched me down the staircase. I lost my footing, bouncing downward as he clutched the noose, choking me as I came to a stop in a jumble of body parts at the bottom. My joints bellowed but I never let go of my dollar butterfly.

"Get the fuck up." Tugging the rope, he forced me to my knees.

I flicked through the almanac of my pain, seeing if there were new entries to fear. My broken hand screamed, but nothing else seemed to be shattered.

"I'm going to teach you—"

Bing bong.

He froze as the doorbell tore through the house.

I panted, unable to stop the torrent of tears now they'd begun.

He came back!

Thank everything that's holy, he came back.

However, while I celebrated with relief, Master A grinned with depravity. "Ah, perfect timing."

Wait, what timing?

Who's at the door?

Panic hissed through my blood as more terror than I'd ever known befell me.

No!

Stop!

My fingers flew to my neck (broken hand and all), clawing

at the tight coarseness.

Get it off!

I can't do this anymore!

Master A jerked the rope hard as if I were an unruly horse tethered with reins. "Stop that!" He headed into the lounge, dragging me behind him—cutting off my air supply as the noose grew tighter and tighter.

My eyes bugged as pressure built in my already throbbing head.

Wrenching me into the middle of the space with tight little jerks, he tied me to the coffee table leg. "Stay."

I couldn't stop my satanic hope as he disappeared to answer the front door.

Please, let it be him.

Every click of his shoes, I begged for it to be Mr. Prest.

Was it wrong that I'd given up hoping for freedom and would settle for a new master instead? Freedom was unattainable, but a new owner might be feasible.

If he returned for me, he could keep me. I wouldn't try to run or kill him.

Just save me and I'm yours.

But I was stupid.

Instincts knew the truth. Master A was happy not furious.

Tony lurked in the kitchen, watching me with nefarious eyes. "You ready for some fun, Pim?"

I clutched my folded dollar as male voices sailed to my ears, echoing with two sets of footfalls.

"I'm glad you're here." Master A appeared, smiling at his friend.

Every last hope and stupid notion of a pain-free end evaporated.

Darryl.

"Hey, mate." Tony slithered toward him, slapping Darryl on the back.

"Gonna have us a party, huh?" Darryl grinned. "Where is the little fiend?"

"Right there." Master A pointed in my direction.

Darryl's gaze fell on me, his fingers tightening around the black duffel he carried. "Hello, Pimlico. Been a bad girl, I hear." His dirty blond hair matched Master A's, making them brothers in sin if not in blood.

"Very bad, I'm afraid," Master A muttered. "The minute that bastard delivers what I paid for, he's dead. If I didn't need his product so much, I would've killed him the second he entered my house."

"What's so good about what he can make, anyway?" Tony wiped his nose with the back of his hand. "It's just a boat."

Master A snarled, "It's not *just* a boat. It's a floating city. No, it's more than that. It's an ark, you idiot. And I need fucking protection."

Darryl smirked. "You finally run out of money, A? Loan-sharks gonna come knocking?"

"None of your damn business." Master A suddenly laughed. "Let's just say, the only sharks I want around me are the ones beneath my fully armoured yacht where I can nuke the shit out of them."

"Good one." Tony guffawed.

Their voices were as nauseating as razors on glass.

I hated this part. The anticipation of what they'd do. The ease of conversation between friends before they hurt me just for fun.

I looked behind them, tensing for Monty to join in. But there were no more visitors.

I should be glad. Today, I only had to entertain three instead of four.

You can do this.

You've done it a hundred times before.

So why did this feel so much worse?

"Right, enough chit-chat. Let's get started." Undoing the rope from around the coffee table leg, Master A hoisted me upright with a yank and a well-placed kick to my thigh. The moment I went from ball to straight, he let the rope dangle between my naked breasts. "I can't believe that bastard. He touched Pim. He touched *my* Pim. He was about to fuck her, the cunt."

That's not true.

And I couldn't unscramble why I was frustrated with that. Why did he threaten me with sex but never follow through? Had I failed in some way? Did he decide I was too high risk to sleep with?

If he was wary of sleeping with a slave girl because of diseases, he didn't have to worry. I'd lost my virginity to this ogre and his friends all underwent tests before Master A let them near me.

"He's gone now. It's time for her to pay." Darryl licked his lips, pacing away with Master A and Tony, their heads bowed together, discussing my punishment.

They loved this part—making me stew, building my terror.

They muttered and cursed too low for comprehension. Occasionally, a loud swear rent through the room, widening my eyes. Finally, when the itch of the coarse rope around my neck became too much to bear, and my fingers turned white protecting my dollar butterfly, Master A slapped Darryl on the back. "Yes, you're right. I didn't want to, but I'm sick of giving her so many chances." His gaze met mine, dark and depthless. "She doesn't want to talk? Let's give her that wish."

What?

What does that mean?

Tony stood back, crossing his arms as Darryl smirked. "Hear that, girl?" Pacing to the couch where he'd placed his black duffel, he unzipped it. "How cool is that?" Tugging something free, he kept it hidden as he moved toward me. "You're the one who decided we're not worthy of your voice. I think it's only fair others aren't privy to it, either."

Master A stuck his face in mine. "You spoke to him last night, didn't you? You whispered to that fucker as he thrust his fingers inside you. You begged for more and pleaded for him to rescue you." His hand shot into my hair, tearing a few more stands in his outrage. "Answer me, Pim. You'll speak to him but not to me!?" A maniacal laugh fell from his lips. "Well, not for long. That Prest bastard is gone. Our contract is signed. And he'll never see you again and for sure never *hear* you again."

Cackling like a mad beast, he snapped his fingers.

Darryl came forward instantly.

I jerked, looking between the two men and the horrendous item in Darryl's hand.

Large shears.

The kind to cut bolts of fabric or slice through pieces of metal.

I gulped.

No...

Squirming, I tried to wriggle away, but Master A punched the side of my head already swollen and tender. I fell to my knees, clutching the carpet as the room yawed and swayed. While my kneecaps hollered and my skull fought against cracking, I was helpless to prevent anything else.

I was hopelessly lost as hands rolled me onto my back.

Knees pinned my hips.

And cold laughter filled my ears as rancid fingers pried open my mouth and pinched my tongue.

Master A's voice whispered around me. "You refuse to talk, my dear sweet Pim? Now, you'll never talk again."

ELDER

DEAR NO ONE,

Is it wrong that I still hate her?

After a year of being someone's toy, I should harbour no ill feelings to those who never hurt me. I should be grateful to my mother for giving me life—even if I hate it.

I was lucky before I was sold. I had smiles and school and safety.

But that's gone now. And I hate that I didn't appreciate what I had before it was stolen.

He took my virginity without any pre-sex whispers with my mother or giggles over silly boyfriends. Not that she would've indulged me in such things. But now, we will never speak again. She doesn't know me anymore. She has no idea what I've lived through. I hate that she isn't there for me. I hate that she hasn't searched and found me.

I hate that I'm no longer her daughter.

I'm his.

I hate that I'm gone to her, but I'm still here.

I'm still here, No One.

Fading, crumbling, decaying.

But still here.

*

DEAR NO ONE,

Today, he broke a bone for the first time. You'd think I would be more afraid, more in pain. But I'm not.

I expected this the moment Mr. Kewet killed me only metres away from my mother. The minute his fingers went around my throat and he stole my watch, I wasn't living anymore—merely a corpse brought back to life to serve.

He might have given me CPR, No One, and saved a few years of heartbeats, but I died that day and didn't get back up.

So what is a broken bone next to death?

It's nothing.

I'm nothing.

I just want it all to stop.

*

"Stop the car."

What the fuck am I doing?

That question was getting bloody old.

My fingers shook as I ripped through toilet paper scribbles, one after another. When I'd pushed my hands through the headboard last night, trying to get comfortable on Pimlico's hard mattress, I'd found something soft sticking from a crack in the wood.

Pimlico had distracted me from that first touch, and I'd kept busy writing a note and folding her the small origami gift. However, once the butterfly was formed, I couldn't stop my fingers trailing back to what they'd found.

I'd tugged.

And a fucking storybook spewed into my hands.

I should've stuffed it back where it belonged. I should've respected her privacy. But as the mute girl slept beside me, her breathing just as silent as everything else about her, I read a few lines.

And I couldn't fucking stop.

I learned about her time in the trafficking hotel and a market-place called the QMB. I learned she'd lost her virginity to that raping bastard, Alrik. I learned about her hatred for her mother, her homesickness for her past, and just how desperate her world had become.

My heart (that'd long ago calcified to the hardship of others) thudded for the pain she'd endured. She'd lived through more than anyone ought to face.

However, it didn't change facts.

I'd bartered for one night with her. That was all I wanted. All I could have.

So when she'd stirred, and guilt infested me for reading her private thoughts, I'd resumed stroking her skinny back. I'd shoved fistfuls of her pages into my blazer pocket because I had no other choice. It wasn't right to take the only possession she had in a world where she had nothing—but that was who I was.

A thief.

With deeper issues I couldn't control.

I stole because I loved it.

But also for another reason.

Her story was mine now.

I justified the robbery by tracing my fingers over the beads of her spine, following contusions and blurs, giving her sweetness after so long of none. I expected her to flinch and wake, but she'd burrowed into the sheets, murmuring unconsciously and giving me so much fucking trust.

I'd found such reward in that. That she sought comfort in my touch even though I'd borrowed her from a master who treated her like shit.

The partition between Selix and me slid down with a soft whir. "Sir? Did you just say turn around?"

My fingers tightened over the soft papyrus where Pim had spilled her darkest confessions. "Yes. *Now.*"

"But...you'll miss—"

"I don't fucking care. Do it."

Every inch of me craved to go home. To feel the sea beneath my feet and put this shitty debacle, including the night I spent with Pim, in my wake. But I also couldn't ignore that she would die because of me.

She might already be dead.

He could've shot her.

It would've been kinder than other things he might do.

I'd accepted her death, believing it was the best thing for everyone. But she'd paid too much. She was owed something better before dying so damn young.

She was worth more than a bloody grave.

So fucking what no one was there for me when I'd been at my lowest? So what no one had helped me?

I could help *her.*

I could do the right thing...for the first time in my godforsaken life.

Her imaginary friend, No One, had cared for her up till now. And if I couldn't protect her better than a fucking fictional entity, what sort of man did that make me?

A coward?

Cold-hearted?

Honest about the fucked-up nature of the world?

You could have her for yourself.

The thought wasn't new. She was a slave, after all. And I was a rich bloody bastard. I could buy her from him. I could keep her locked away to use whenever I wanted with no distractions from my company.

The idea was far too appealing.

She'd be a pet.

An unseen, unknown pet. I wouldn't have to take her for walks or give special treats. As long as she had food and a place to rest, she would have a much better quality of life with me than she ever would with Alrik.

But why would I buy her when I could take her?

I shouldn't.

I should leave before I hurt her more than Alrik ever could. But I'd lied when I'd folded the origami butterfly with my note inside.

I couldn't forget her until I'd taken what I needed from

her. And what I needed wasn't fulfilled yet.

I want to fuck her.

Once.

A single time.

Then, I could either sell her or free her. One thing was for sure, I wouldn't keep her for long. It wasn't possible for a man like me.

But for a short while...

"Yes, I'm sure. Turn around."

"Right away, sir."

Screw keeping business separate from pleasure.

I was a thief.

And I would steal the silent girl and make her talk.

Pimlico

MY HEART RELOCATED into my mouth, bouncing on my tongue like it was a damn trampoline, uncaring that the sharp shears would soon cut off the one piece I *desperately* wanted to keep.

Was it odd that I wanted my tongue over a finger or toe?

Was it wrong that thoughts of bargaining and offering up other parts ran riot in my mind?

Take my pinkie.

No, my index finger.

Wait...take my big toe.

Just don't touch my tongue!

I thrashed beneath Darryl's weight as Master A moved over my head to hold me down. Wedging my skull between his knees, he stared at me, his face upside down.

His lips moved, melding with the agony inside me.

"I promised you what would happen if you didn't talk to me one day, Pim. This is what will happen."

My broken hand flared as I pounded the floor and tried my hardest to squirm away. The dollar in my other palm wasn't enough to bribe my way free.

My struggles turned violent. But there were two men and one of me—men who'd eaten in the past twenty-four hours and had muscles that weren't atrophied from malnutrition.

I didn't stand a chance.

Darryl grinned as he opened and closed the shears with a flourish. The blades scraped together in a sinister hiss. "You ready?"

No, no, no!

His nails cut into my tongue as he held it firm, not letting my saliva lubricate his fingers. The piece of muscle grew dry the longer he kept it from my mouth.

Don't!

The part of me I hadn't used in so long was on death row. My silent curse would become reality.

Even if I wanted, I'd never be able to speak again.

I'd gone into this as silence being my weapon. A choice not to talk.

Now that choice would be forever taken away.

How could I tell the police what'd been done to me if I couldn't speak? How could I beg another to help?

My body quaked as I silently sobbed, tossing my head as much as I could in the confines of Master A's knees.

For a few hours, I'd been in the safety of another man's control. A man who put even Master A in his place. Why, oh why, didn't I talk to him when I had the chance? Why was I so damn stubborn? So afraid?

I deserved this.

I'd been so stupid.

And now, I would never utter another word for the rest of my life.

At least I still had my fingers. I could write. I could tell my tale.

But my tale has vanished!

Years of stolen memories.

Perhaps this, right here, was the point where I gave up. Where I admitted I was broken and done. Maybe once they cut out my tongue, I would die from blood loss, and it would finally be over.

Please, be finally over.

It might not be as painless as the gun, but it would give the desired result.

The fight in my limbs faded. Not from accepting the inevitable, but because I literally had nothing left. I couldn't win. I'd *never* been able to win. All I could do was stop and accept.

Finally accept that Tasmin was dead and Pimlico would be, too.

The moment I ceased thrashing, Darryl laughed. "Finally realised you can't stop this, huh, pretty whore?"

You'll rot in Hell.

My eyes narrowed as he yanked on my tongue, pulling it further from my lips.

He smirked. "How about one word for your master? One little word..."

Master A chuckled. "Yes, go on, Pim. One word and I'll reconsider not cutting out your tongue." He bent and kissed my forehead, his hair tickling my nose. "If I like your voice, I'll let you keep it."

The dilemma sat heavy.

If I did this, he'd finally won. My imprisonment would include willingly screaming or answering his torturing questions. If he broke me down to utter one word, he could do two and three and four.

He would never let me be silent again.

Or I could take my self-imposed silence for real. Like a devout religious follower denouncing all monetary wealth and entering a nunnery, no longer just practicing their faith but *becoming* their faith.

I would be mute no longer by choice but by disability.

Was I vain enough to hate the thought of not being perfect anymore? Or strong enough to accept that it was the price I had to pay to win?

Master A's fingers pinched my cheeks. "Make up your mind, Pimlico. You have ten seconds to decide." He looked at

Darryl. "Cut on one. If she tries to speak, let her have her tongue to do so."

"Got it, A."

My heart started a countdown, marking each second with dynamite as Master A said, "Ten..."

Should I speak?

"Nine..."

What should I say?

"Eight..."

What word will keep me safe?

"Seven..."

Do I truly want him to win this way?

"Six..."

How quickly will I die if I refuse?

"Five..."

Will I drown in my own blood?

"Four..."

Make a decision!

Darryl's fingers tightened, the faint taint of copper filled my mouth as his nail dug deeper, pulling my tongue out as far as possible.

Do it!

One word.

How about: Help. Or mercy. Or please.

"Three."

I saturated my lungs with oxygen, inhaling hard for the first time, knowing I would finally transform air into sound waves through the magic of human engineering.

"Two..."

I shook my head, eyes wild with promise that I'd talk.

The men paused, eyebrows arched, but Darryl didn't release my tongue. "Go on, Pim...one little noise. Show us you'll obey before you get your tongue back."

A noise was easier than a word. He'd torn worse from me before.

I obeyed.

The tattered moan rose with rust and misuse, vibrating strangely in my chest.

Master A smeared terror-soaked sweat from my skin. "Good girl. You finally obeyed." Kissing my forehead, he whispered, "Pity for you...I don't really like the sound of your voice."

Slapping my cheek, he nodded at Darryl. "One."

He cut.

ELDER

THE CAR STOPPED.

I climbed out.

The front door was locked.

I used my skills as a burglar to gain entry within seconds.

The instant I entered, the alarm shredded my eardrums with a shrill alert.

I ignored it, stalking forward through despicable corridors.

The white house mocked me as I erupted from foyer to lounge.

And then suddenly, I no longer saw white.

But red.

Lots and *lots* of red.

I didn't pause to think. I didn't second-guess. I let the instincts I'd spent years trying to dull rage into being; muscle memory took over.

Along with my sordid past, I'd done things that'd evolved me from thief to killer, from killer to assassin, from assassin to heartless stealer of souls. Fighting had always been more than just a hobby. It'd been in my past for generations. And because of my unique personality flaws, I'd become a master at it.

My hand formed a blade, my fingers tight and long, locked together like a machete. I brought the weapon in a swinging arc right onto the juggler of the man sitting on top of Pimlico.

He toppled sideways, unconscious from the single blow.

Pimlico didn't move as blood poured down her front, drenching her nakedness. A pair of large scissors fell from the unconscious man's hand, clattering to the floor.

"What the fuck!?" Alrik shot to his feet, leaving his girl to bleed all over the carpet. Moving away, he gave me the opportunity to get closer to her.

The man who'd hacked down the bedroom door with a baseball bat lunged at me, swinging the same knife I'd taken from the garage. "You freak! You're dead meat."

Normally, I would have fun with such an idiot. I would parry and feint, slowly wearing the assailant down until he begged for the fight to end.

But Pim needed me.

It took one tiny thought.

One second, the man stabbed air, doing his best to gut me. The next, the knife was twisted from his hand into mine and the hilt buried in his stomach.

He screamed as I slashed his insides before yanking out the knife and impaling it in his heart.

His gaze lost focus the moment I tore through the muscle keeping him alive. However, it didn't stop his body pumping blood and unspooling intestines as he collapsed onto the carpet.

Pimlico scrambled back, her eyes as large as twin moons.

The man was dead. He was no longer worth my time.

Her gaze met mine, wild and agonised. Blood rivered from her mouth.

What had they done to her? What fucking monster did such a thing?

You've done worse.

Yes, I had. I wouldn't deny it.

But never to a woman.

Never to an *innocent* woman.

Dropping to my haunches, I pulled her into a sitting position, cradling her against my chest.

I didn't care about the blood.

All I cared about was making sure she'd survive longer than a few minutes so I could do what I should've done at the beginning when this asshole contacted me.

Kill him.

Screw the contract.

Screw the fucking money.

He's dead.

Alrik gaped like a koi carp at his dead friend with his guts coiled on the floor. His other friend remained unconscious beside him. "You bastard!" Shaking his head in denial, he back-stepped into the kitchen.

I let him go.

Most likely he had another gun stashed somewhere. He thought he had power over me with such a useless weapon.

Idiotic asshole.

Wielding a pistol wouldn't save him from me. Bullets didn't stand a chance with the methods of killing I'd been taught.

Discounting him, I pried open Pimlico's mouth.

Blood made everything slippery and slick.

She winced, tears mixing with her bloody mouth as I forced her to show me what they'd done.

From previous experience, I knew what bled so copiously. The tongue.

And because I wasn't stupid, I understood why they'd do such a thing. She refused to talk. I'd made suspicions bellow that she spoke to me instead of him.

Why hadn't she talked to me?

Was this the reason? Because she knew I would leave and did her best to avoid the upcoming brutality?

This was my fault.

I'd done this.

But at least, I'd come back to fucking fix it.

Pimlico struggled in my arms as I traced the damage to her tongue. I expected to find a severed piece of meat, but I hadn't been too late.

A huge slice had cut her a third of the way through the muscle.

It would hurt. It would continue bleeding. But she wouldn't lose the power of speech. And she wouldn't die...hopefully.

"You'll be okay." Picking her up, I laid her on the white couch, taking supreme satisfaction as dark crimson rained over the pristine surfaces. "Stay there. I have to finish a few things."

Alrik had vanished, but banging came from the pantry as he grabbed whatever he could to make him safe.

I let him. I didn't chase him to start the war before he was armed.

I wasn't that type of person.

He wanted a fight.

I'd fight.

However, the asshole who'd cut Pimlico's tongue didn't deserve such respect.

Pim's eyes locked onto mine as I strode toward the unconscious man and grabbed the scissors from beside him. My thumb smeared the still warm blood from the girl I couldn't stop thinking about and fisted the bronze handles.

Pim gasped, holding her mouth, doing her best to contain morbid ruby streams.

I shook my head. "Don't swallow. Just let it flow. I've got you. Just a few more minutes, then we'll leave."

Leave to go where?

My yacht?

A hospital?

I'd decide when it was time. For now, I had other things on my mind.

She didn't relax. How could she with such an injury? But her eyes dropped from mine to the shears in my fist.

She didn't speak, but I heard her question through the arch of her eyebrow and shimmering hate in her gaze.

What are you going to do?

I lowered my jaw, watching her beneath my brow. "I'm going to kill him."

That was the only warning I gave her. Dropping to my knee, I jammed the heavy blades through the throat of the man who'd hurt the woman I'd steal.

The shears were sharp.

His neck was supple.

The two met and did what supple and sharp did.

His throat sliced open, revealing the innards of gristle and esophagus before blood welled and joined the mess of Pimlico's in an avalanche of red.

A gunshot exploded above my head, whistling past and embedding in the large oval window behind me.

The glass shattered, raining outward, letting sea breezes enter the otherwise calm space.

"Get the fuck out of my house and I won't kill you." Alrik shuffled from the kitchen, both hands on his pistol, his fingers shaking on the trigger.

He still thought I'd deliver what he'd paid for.

Even after this.

I laughed. "If you were half the man you think you are, you would've shot me."

He scowled. "I'm a better man *because* I didn't."

"No, you're just a greedy bastard who still thinks our deal will go through."

He blanched. "I paid. You agreed. Of course, it will go through. I need that fucking yacht!"

"Need and deserve are two entirely different things." Moving around the couch, I trailed my fingers briefly over Pimlico's blood-soaked cheek. "Our deal was void the moment you mutilated a young girl."

"She's mine to do with as—"

"As you please." Raising my hand, I painted her red, red life-force on my cheekbone, dousing myself in the pain of the person I was protecting—just like those of my lineage. We'd fought for empresses and queens. We'd given our lives in the service of others and avenged those who'd wronged us.

This was no different.

The many lessons I'd indulged in came back, flowing like magical memories through my veins. I missed my sword, but my hands would do in this case.

"You went too far this time, Alrik."

"You have no authority to tell me what I can and cannot do."

"Yes." I moved closer to him. "I do."

His arms trembled. "Think again."

The flinch of his muscles gave me all the warning I needed. He pulled the trigger and another bullet did its best to break the fabric of air and speed.

I ducked effortlessly then charged forward, ploughing into him with my shoulder, crunching him against the kitchen bench.

All the oxygen in his lungs exploded. The solid thud of his spine hitting marble had a good probability of leaving him disabled.

He dropped to his knees, only to scramble breathlessly back to his feet.

Didn't disable him, after all.

Oh well, no loss.

My brain turned off as I reached forward and plucked the nuisance gun from his grip. I tossed it onto the couch beside Pimlico.

Immediately, she crawled for it, holding her mouth with one hand and doing her best to support the heavy weight of the black pistol with the other.

I wanted to tell her I'd protect her, help her, but my intentions weren't that of a kind man. I'd come to steal not free.

She didn't need to know that. Not until I had her exactly where I wanted her. Not until she was healed.

Alrik swung at my face now he'd been stripped of his weapon.

His fist connected only because I let it.

Pain was used as power in my training, giving animalistic instincts ammunition when bodily harm threatened.

I could kill him fast or slow.

If I had my way, it would be slow.

But Pimlico wouldn't last for the hours I'd like to torture. I didn't have the time to starve him for years with mental and physical abuse. He was getting off fucking easy.

For now, for her sake, it had to be quick.

My hand soared forward; my fingers jammed into his larynx.

He choked.

While he buckled over, doing his best to suck in a breath, I grabbed his shoulders and crunched his face onto my knee.

With killing hands, I seized his chin, ready to snap his spine.

I was disappointed how fast three lives had been snuffed out. This cold dispatching did not satisfy me.

But this wasn't about me.

It's about her.

A feral sound warbled behind me.

I froze, looking over my shoulder.

Pimlico draped over the back of the couch, blood everywhere, both hands holding the gun. She shook her head—the most response I'd ever earned—as her eyes dropped to Alrik scrambling in my hold.

"You want to do it?"

She nodded.

Her shaking was too much. She wouldn't be able to aim.

But I wouldn't deny the only thing she'd ever asked of me.

"Fine." Moving around Alrik's body, I hoisted him up using his jaw and nape, threatening to break his neck. "Stand, you worthless sack of shit."

His feet slipped on the tiles, but he did his best to obey. "You don't have to do this. You want more money? Have it all. You want her, take her. I don't fucking care."

"It isn't about that anymore." I smiled. "It's about karma and paying for what you've done. If it were up to me, you'd suffer for decades—just like you made Pim and countless other girls suffer. But we don't have that luxury, so consider yourself fucking lucky."

Pimlico never took her eyes off him, her finger feathering the trigger. She gagged as more blood flowed, forcing her to vomit red over the back of the couch. Wiping tears away, the gun wobbled as she tensed to shoot.

"Wait," I ordered.

Dragging Alrik toward her, I nodded as I kicked his leg to make him kneel and pressed his sweaty head against the muzzle of the gun. "*Now*, you can kill him."

She sucked in a gasp, scarlet rivulets staining her naked breasts. The look she gave me—so full of thanks and relief and vicious, vicious victory—clutched my gut. She was insidious in her hate; after two years of torture she'd won.

My cock hardened, recognising the conqueror inside her. *That* was why I couldn't forget her. Why I had to steal her.

She was unique.

My equal.

Even though I'd never admit such things.

"Do it, Pimlico. Slaughter him." My voice ruffed with impatience and greed. "Finish it."

Alrik locked his hands in prayer. "Wait! Pim...sweet little Pim. Don't do this. I love you!"

She spat another wad of blood, splattering it all over his face. Her loathing told him exactly what she thought of his so-called love.

Alrik squirmed, his temper once again getting him into trouble. "Why, you little bitch! I'll whip you so fucking—"

My fists clenched to punch the bastard. But hot rage settled over Pim, giving me a split-second warning to get out of the damn way.

Dropping Alrik, I sidestepped to avoid an incorrect aim or ricochet. I jolted as the gun exploded.

The scent of sulphur hit my nose as the boom of a bullet tore around the white lounge.

For a second, Alrik stayed swaying where I'd placed him. Then, he fell.

Dazed and confused, he stumbled as his hands came up to hold a newly formed hole in his belly.

Pim stared. Shock merged with disbelief that she'd finally repaid him with pain.

He screamed, "Fuck, you shot me! You sho—shot me."

She did but it's not enough.

It wasn't a mortal wound.

I had no intention of leaving here with any chance of him being found by paramedics.

Taking a step forward, my fingers ached to finish it.

But once again, Pim surprised me.

She smiled with a gruesome red grin, pulling the trigger for a second time.

Boom!

The shot went into his cheekbone.

Two holes but still alive.

She'd missed his brain and heart.

Alrik screamed harder, no longer stringing concise words together but howling for his life.

Sobs wracked her body as adrenaline quickly switched to stupefaction.

She'd pass out any second—I was shocked she hadn't dropped already—but I didn't want her to black out without seeing him dead.

She needed to see that.

I refused to let him haunt her.

Moving around the couch, I kneeled beside her and took her trembling hands in mine. "Here, I'll help you."

Alrik garbled, "No! Do—don't!" Blood spewed from his cheek as he did his best to hold both wounds.

His pleas didn't register as I guided Pim's rapidly failing

strength and pointed the gun directly at his forehead. "Go ahead, silent mouse."

Her body jerked at my nickname for her, but her finger latched onto the trigger for a third time.

Bang!

Thrice was the charm.

There were no screams, no begs—nothing but throbbing silence and the steady drip, drip, drip of her blood raining on the couch.

Alrik turned from rapist to corpse, doing the world a favour by no longer breathing.

She didn't gloat over her kill.

She didn't cry or question.

And I didn't let her wallow in what she'd done.

I had more important things to worry about—not about police or witnesses or other trivial things. No, much more important than that.

The woman I'd come to claim was dying.

I couldn't permit that until I'd taken what I needed.

Almost as if on cue, Pim dropped the gun by Alrik's cadaver, toppling spent and fading over the settee.

"Shit." I caught her, bundling her into my arms and climbing from the furniture.

Her skin no longer held pigment, looking blue and bloodless as I strode from the room. I gave no heed to the three men turning the lounge into a lake of gore. I only focused on the tiny but formidable woman in my embrace.

"Stay with me, Pim. I've got you."

She didn't respond as I marched through her prison and carried her over the threshold, stealing her from the white mansion into freedom.

Pimlico

IT HURT.

So much.

It was all I could think about. The only thing I could focus on.

I washed in and out of blackness.

My body wanted to sink and sink…to shut out the pain. But my willpower had waited too damn long for this.

He's dead.

I killed him!

I couldn't sleep now.

I'm free!

But, oh my God, the agony.

Mr. Prest's arms around me couldn't compete with the excruciating stinging of my tongue. Fresh air after two years of being locked away went unnoticed. The world and everyone in it were nothing as I lived in a torturous hell of warm oozing blood choking me and more pain than I thought possible.

I couldn't understand what was going on.

I was outside!

Away from the white mansion for the first time since Master A outbid my one million to buy myself.

The crunch of pebbles beneath Mr. Prest's shoes were muffled. The view of Master A's house perched high on the cliff with ultimate sea views was hazy. I wanted to kiss the concrete of the driveway and dance in the soil where bright green bushes slept.

The breeze. The salt. The screech of seabirds. So much chaos after so much silence.

And I was too swaddled in agony to enjoy it.

He's dead.

Darryl, too.

Tony.

All dead.

Mr. Prest did what I'd dreamed of for years.

Even that knowledge was muted and not quite real. I needed my tongue to stop drowning me in blood, so I could focus on this new reality.

I just witnessed a murder. A gruesome, awful murder.

I just *committed* murder. A cold-blooded revengeful kill.

And I rejoiced!

I didn't suffer sadness for the deaths they endured. It was their karma. If anything, they didn't endure enough. However, I couldn't figure out what came next. Would Mr. Prest slay me, too? Why had he returned? What plans did he have for me to pay him back for his rescue?

Should I run, scream, beg?

I couldn't do any of those things with my body quickly dying, but I needed to know, to prepare...*what is my new fate?*

Along with a constant wash of copper, I struggled to breathe. My tongue had swollen to the size of a cruise liner. It didn't listen to my commands to move. It merely sat, partially severed and agonising, distracting me from everything.

Mr. Prest carried me to his car, ignoring the shocked look from a man with dark hair standing motionless, his eyes dancing up and down the driveway as if expecting law enforcement to appear at any moment.

"Sir..."

"No questions." Mr. Prest waited until the man opened the vehicle then jumped inside. He didn't speak again as he manhandled me, sitting down all while keeping me in his arms. My blood decorated his cheekbone where he'd smeared it as war paint, daubing him as the devil I suspected while fresh crimson soaked like oil into his clothing.

I shivered from pain and cold.

Understanding without asking, Mr. Prest slid me across the black leather (no longer white and white and more white) and wrenched off his blazer. Draping it around me, he tucked in my arms, not caring my blood saturated his clothes and car.

How much had I lost?

How much could I afford to lose before I died?

Already, I was light headed and wispy. My tongue continued to swell, blocking ability to swallow.

For so long, I'd begged for death.

And now that I was only heartbeats away from it, I didn't want to go.

I was free.

I was in a world of colour rather than monochrome.

I don't want to die.

If I wasn't so confused and wracked with pain, I might've cared that this rescuer, this dark angel, saw me drooling and glassy eyed. He watched me fade in and out of unconsciousness.

"Drive, Selix."

The muffled sound of a door closing happened a nanosecond before the car tore off with tyres screaming.

"Where to, sir?"

"Phantom. Call ahead. Tell Michaels to be ready."

"Right."

The sliding partition rose as Mr. Prest dragged my woozy form back into his arms. He kept me tight, acting as a seat-belt as the vehicle soared around corners and squealed down roads I'd never seen before.

Breathing hard, he ran a death-dirty hand over his face, smearing blood over his brow and chin.

I huddled in his embrace, trying to turn invisible all while gagging on flowing metallic.

Oh, God, please let the pain stop.

Please, don't let me die.

Not now.

Mr. Prest looked down, catching my out of focus vision.

Close your eyes.

You're safer that way.

It was a stupid trick, pretending he couldn't reach me when I couldn't see him. But my loss of blood and strange vaporous agony gave whimsical fancy solid reasoning.

Curling tighter in his arms, my skin prickled with intensity as Mr. Prest bowed his head, his hot breath skating over my bloody face. For the longest time, he sat there, still and silent, waiting for me to open my eyes.

But I couldn't.

I can't.

I wished I was blind as well as mute. Deaf too, so I would never hear the squelching sound of my tongue being cut or the crunching of bones as he threw Master A against the kitchen bench.

Finally, his patience ran out. Taking my chin, he guided my face upward.

I was weak and queasy and had no choice, but I obeyed because I'd just witnessed what happened to those who angered him. He killed so quickly, so easily—it was nothing to him.

I didn't want to be nothing.

I wanted to remain in his good graces. There, I might find a kind word or gentle stroke. I didn't want more violence. I'd had enough to last me a lifetime.

Mr. Prest cupped my jaw, his fingers slipping in sticky blood. "He deserved to die for what he did."

I agree.

He deserved to die in a hundred ways.

I didn't move. No nod, no twitch. Nothing.

He frowned. "I know you understand. What are you afraid

of? You're safe now."

Afraid?

I'm afraid of you.

I don't know what's worse, you or death. And I don't know how to get answers before it's too late.

My eyelids fluttered as icy blackness stole over me, blanketing everything for a moment. Was that death? Or merely shock?

I was vaguely aware of Mr. Prest growling at his chauffeur, "Drive faster, Selix."

The car lurched at his command, engine snarling.

A few minutes passed.

I danced between awake and unconscious.

His voice dragged me back; his question made me open my eyes.

"Are you grateful? That I saved you?"

Tired, so, so tired.

I stared.

No.

Yes.

Thank you.

He stared back, unable to stop waiting for an answer that would never come. Finally, he huffed. "Well, you shouldn't be."

My heart tap-danced.

The car bounced over a bump, pressing our bodies closer. His fingers dropped from my jaw to lash around my floppy wrist forming a new bridle, a new master, a new life in servitude. "I'm not the hero in this story, Pimlico. I'm another villain. You'd do best to remember that."

Looking down at the mess I'd made and the shackles of his touch, my eyes fell on the dollar bill he'd given me. I'd somehow managed to hold it while my tongue was severed and three lives were taken.

He noticed too, stealing it from my tight grip. The green money now resembled a macabre tie-die with threads of dirty crimson. "You found my origami."

It's mine.

I couldn't take my eyes off the one thing I had left.

I didn't care that it was money. I only cared that it was a gift and I wanted it more than anything.

Sensing I needed it back like a child needed its favourite toy for comfort, he opened his palm.

I snatched it.

"It's yours. I'll fold you another when we're home."

Home.

Where was home?

What was Phantom?

Dark clouds stuffed my head with cotton wool and thunder storms. My eyelids drooped as I skidded into blackness again. However, as my vision stuttered and I clung to lucidity, something flashed white inside the breast pocket of the jacket I wore.

Instantly, the fog lifted.

I know that corner.

My eyes shot to Mr. Prest.

You did *take them.*

My letters to No One.

How dare you!

Tucking bloody hair behind my ear, he smiled. "Yes, I stole them. But now, I've stolen you, so you can have them back."

Did you read them?

Did you laugh at them?

Is that why you returned—because you felt sorry *for me?*

I shuddered, liking and loathing him. Grateful and confused. Shocked and shivering.

His smile was rough. "You have every right to look at me like that. I took something you treasured but I won't apologise." His legs bunched beneath me. "I won't apologise because I've just taken you and that is *not* a good thing."

I sucked in a breath, choking on blood.

Why?

Why is it not good?

He'd rescued me. I was alive because of him. If he wanted me dead, he didn't have to return.

His voice hushed to a whisper as he cupped my cheek. "I will say I'm sorry for one thing."

I trembled as his thumb stroked me sweetly.

"I'm sorry for what I'm about to do. I'm sorry for what I am. You're worth pennies, but I'll make you worth fucking millions. However, what I expect in return will be unpayable."

His face softened just a little, unable hide the ferocity he wielded. The sleekness he harnessed. The threats he promised. "We're leaving this place and you'll never be found. You belong to me."

His lips touched mine, smearing my blood between us. "Oh, and seeing as you're mine now, you might as well call me Elder."

DOLLARS (Dollar Series #2)

Coming September / October 2016

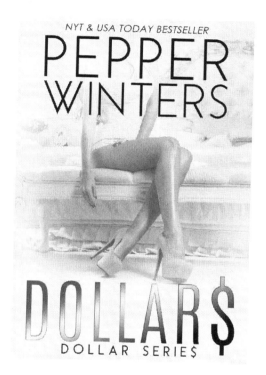

ACKNOWLEDGEMENTS

I suck at these. The hardest part of writing a book for me is this small section at the end. I'm going to blanket thank everyone I've ever spoken to as my brain turns to mush. However, I must give an epic thanks my beta readers: Amy, Vickie, Tamicka, Katrina, Melissa, Yaya, and Celesha. Thank you to Jenny for editing, Katrina for keeping me sane, hubby for keeping me fed, and every author who knows the pain and joy of rewriting a book six times.

I'm also so incredibly grateful to everyone who reads this new series. Since the moment I published Tears of Tess, I've been living a dream and every day that I wake up with words in my head and letters pouring from my fingers, I send huge hugs to everyone who makes that possible.

Have a fabulous rest of 2016 and hope you enjoyed Pennies. xx

PLAYLIST

Monsters by Imagine Dragons
Demon by Imagine Dragons
Skyscraper by Demi Lovato
Defying Gravity by Idina Menzel
Time is running out by Muse
Last Hope by Paramore
Safe and Sound by Taylor Swift
Bring me the horizon by Throne
Madness by Muse

ABOUT THE AUTHOR

Pepper Winters is a multiple New York Times, Wall Street Journal, and USA Today International Bestseller. She loves dark romance, star-crossed lovers, and the forbidden taboo. She strives to write a story that makes the reader crave what they shouldn't, and delivers tales with complex plots and unforgettable characters.

After chasing her dreams to become a full-time writer, Pepper has earned recognition with awards for best Dark Romance, best BDSM Series, and best Dark Hero. She's an #1 iBooks bestseller, along with #1 in Erotic Romance, Romantic Suspense, Contemporary, and Erotica Thriller. She's also honoured to wear the IndieReader Badge for being a Top 10 Indie Bestseller, and signed a two book deal with Hachette. Represented by Trident Media, her books have garnered foreign and audio interest and are currently being translated into numerous languages. They will be in available in bookstores worldwide.

THANK YOU FOR READING!

Made in the USA
Middletown, DE
27 August 2019